Totally Bound Publishing books by Sira Banks

Criminal Desires

Breached

Betrayed

Criminal Desires

BETRAYED

SIRA BANKS

Betrayed
ISBN # 978-1-80250-947-2

Interior text design by Claire Siemaszkiewicz
Totally Bound Publishing

Published in 2024 by Totally Bound Publishing, United Kingdom.

Totally Bound Publishing is an imprint of Totally Entwined Group Limited.

BETRAYED

Dedication

To Becca, Katie and Roxie,
who make every day a wonderful one.

Chapter One

Congratulating the smiling bride, Sharon Richards wished she were somewhere else. Anywhere else.

If it weren't for Simon's hand at the small of her back, she was sure her fight-or-flight instinct would have taken over before long. It was ironic, seeing that the man who gave her the strength to endure this day was also the reason she wanted to flee.

"Sharon, I'm so happy you're here with me today," her mother said, pulling her into a tight embrace, her eyes betraying the pleasure of seeing her when she pulled back a few seconds later.

Her mother was radiant in her rose-colored dress, her vibrant red hair cut shoulder-length. It hadn't been all that long since her mother's eyes had been clouded with sadness over her father's death. Seeing her full of life and energy again warmed Sharon's heart.

"Where else would I be? It's not that often one's mother marries, after all. Well, at least I hope you won't make a hobby out of it," she said, keeping her tone light so her mother knew she wasn't serious.

"I very much hope so, too," Henry, her mother's new husband remarked, joining them. He put an arm around his new wife, a tender smile on his face. He was a quiet man, almost the complete opposite of how her father had been. Maybe that was what had made it possible for her mother to open her heart to him and dare a new start.

"It's good to see you, kiddo," he said to Sharon when he was able to pry his eyes away from his wife, giving Sharon a brief hug. He turned from her to Simon. "I'm Henry Duncan. And you must be Simon."

"Yes, I am. Pleased to meet you, and may I offer my congratulations?"

"Thank you. I know I'm the luckiest man alive today."

"And I'm sure not just today," Simon said.

Traffic had been so awful this morning that Sharon and Simon had barely arrived for the ceremony. There hadn't been time for any introductions before.

The original plan had been for them to arrive a day early so they could enjoy dinner and a quiet evening with her family. A new case in the middle of yesterday had changed their plans. Life as a cop was never predictable and murder refused to stick to a fixed schedule. Sharon's mother had sighed when she called and said she hoped they could make it after all.

On the one hand, Sharon was glad they didn't have to spend last night with her family. On the other, they all would already have gotten to know Simon if they had.

He wasn't the first partner she had introduced to her family, but he was different from her previous boyfriends. While everybody had secrets, his was a little less acceptable in the eyes of society, not that he tried to hide his lifestyle. She did.

There was no easy answer to what he did for a living when the truthful reply was running a BDSM club in NYC. Sharon was painfully aware it wasn't even a question of whether somebody would ask, just when.

Apart from his work not being what her family would expect, that fact would lead to other questions she didn't feel equipped to answer. So far nobody had seemed to wonder why she was wearing a long-sleeved dress on an almost hot autumn day. Knowing about Simon's business would change that, and she didn't care for people to know that her wrists still showed faint marks from a few days ago, when the rope that had bound her had cut into her skin as she'd struggled, halfway delirious from equal measures of pleasure and pain.

"I'm glad you could free some time to accompany Sharon here today," her mother said to Simon now, and she meant it. Contrary to Henry, she'd met Simon once before and had taken an instant liking to him.

Sharon couldn't blame her—he was a good-looking man with impeccable manners, polite and friendly when he wanted to be. He was wearing a dark suit that didn't do much to hide his slender yet muscular body, and one part of her couldn't wait to strip him out of it later.

"It's my pleasure," he said. "And it's been years since I've been to Vermont. I forgot how beautiful the landscape is."

Sharon zoned out while her mother and Simon continued talking. She looked around the restaurant with its adjoining ballroom that Henry and her mother had rented for the day. The owner—Louisa—was her mother's oldest and best friend and she had done a wonderful job of arranging tables so groups of six could sit at each. She had chosen light blue tablecloths and each held a different arrangement of flowers. There also were candles in glasses, waiting for the evening when they would be lit to give the room a soft glow. Right now, sunshine fell through the huge glass windows at one side of the room, bathing the space in an almost ethereal light.

Everything looked fresh, inviting and befitting a second marriage. Her mother might have said yes to marriage but not to church, a white dress and a stilted reception. This was a gathering of family and friends on a joyous but quiet occasion. Forty-two people had been invited and Sharon knew them all, most of them for as long as she could remember. She snapped out of her thoughts when Louisa called out, telling them that the first round of refreshments was waiting.

A few minutes later, with drinks in hand, they all toasted the happy couple and people migrated into new groups, chatting and enjoying themselves.

"Let's get outside, have some fresh air," Sharon suggested. She was glad when Simon didn't ask and took her arm, leading her to the double-wide doors that connected the room to the patio.

Stopping just outside, Sharon closed her eyes, took a deep breath.

"Want to tell me what has you on edge?" Simon asked.

She opened her eyes, met the worried gaze of his dark eyes. "Don't tell me you don't know. Most of the time, you know me better than I know myself."

A small smile curled his lips upward. "I do." He became serious again. "I know you're afraid of your family finding out who I am, but you don't have to tell them anything you don't want them to know."

She sighed, curling her fingers into fists before she could give in to the temptation to rake them through her hair. "I'm not ashamed of you, not at all, but I think some things should remain private. Does *your* family even know what you do?" *Why have I never asked before?*

"My brother, yes, my sister, no. My sister and I are not close. We have a good enough relationship, but she married right out of high school, moved across the country to Portland and we only see each other every other year."

She turned to him, then put her hand on his shoulder, needing to feel him close.

"So what does he think about this, your brother?"

"I think his comment was '*to each their own.*' But to tell you the rest of the story—he came to visit me in New York right after I started the business. He wanted to see the club. I told him he didn't want to know, but he wasn't to be deterred."

Sharon sighed. "I've never wanted to talk to my family about what I like in the bedroom, and I don't want to start now."

Lifting her chin with a finger, he made sure to keep her gaze when he spoke next. "You don't need to worry. Nobody will ask you anything like that."

"But you don't know..."

Leaning in, he kissed her, his lips lingering on hers for a sweet moment, making her long for more. Withdrawing, he cupped her cheek. "Trust me?"

"I do, but..."

"Sharon, there you are."

Turning her head, she spotted her brother making his way over to them, his son in tow. Bracing herself for another round of introductions, she smiled.

* * * *

To Sharon's surprise it was already late in the evening, the room basking in the soft light of numerous candles, with several couples dancing on the improvised dance floor when *the* question came up for the first time.

"So, Martha told me you have a business in the city?" Henry asked Simon while he looked over at his wife and shared a look with her. If Sharon's stomach hadn't been in a tight knot, she would've enjoyed the deep affection between those two.

"I do," Simon answered. "I started working for an oil mining company right after business school, but later I invested what I earned there into my own business."

"It sounds like that was a smart idea," Martha said. "What is it you're doing anyway? I don't think I asked."

Sharon tensed, and Simon, his hand on her hip, stroked her through the fabric of her dress.

"To make a long and boring story short, my business is all about networking and customer service. I provide meeting spaces for people to conclude their respective businesses."

Sharon almost snorted at the description. Martha in turn smiled at Simon. "I was never much interested in business. Maybe that's why I became a teacher. I wanted to deal with people, not concepts and numbers."

"Which is a much more worthwhile cause, if you ask me," Simon said.

"You and Sharon met through your business, didn't you?" Henry asked Simon, but Sharon answered before Simon could.

"Yes, there was a murder on the premises."

"What happened?" Martha looked from her to Simon.

Sharon shook her head. "It's not important. Let's not drag up such a sad story on this happy day. I found out who did it and well, I got to meet Simon."

"Who would've thought that your job could have such nice side effects?" Martha said, looking from her daughter to Simon and back. "That said, how's Jenn doing?"

Sharon was glad for the switch in topics and told her mother all that was new with her friend and partner. A new slow song started soon after and Henry turned to Martha, asking for a dance, prompting Simon to take Sharon's hand.

"Would you care for a dance, too?"

"I didn't know you could dance."

He smirked. "I'm not a professional, but I think it will do."

"In that case, yes, I'd love to."

She let him guide her to the dance floor where they joined the other dancers. He took the lead, and it was good to give in and move with him. It wasn't unlike the games they played in the sanctuary of his club. With him she could completely unwind, didn't need to be strong, to make decisions when she didn't want to.

Closing her eyes, Sharon took a deep breath, releasing some of the tension that had kept her on edge the whole day. Why was this so hard? She wasn't ashamed of him or herself. The last few months had taught her a lot about herself, and she had found a measure of peace and acceptance she hadn't deemed possible.

Simon and she had grown closer during that time, too. They were similar in the way they viewed the world, their humor was compatible and no man had ever respected her and her boundaries the way he did.

They differed in that he liked—needed—control where she needed to let go. They were made for each other.

Still, her job and career demanded her absolute silence when it came to the nature of their relationship. Thanks to the Marlene Davis case that had led her into Simon's club, her colleagues were aware of what Simon did for a living, that he'd been on the list of suspects. If she ever admitted to her relationship with him, they would wonder, at the very least.

"Relax, Sharon," Simon said, tightening his hold on her a bit.

She looked up at him and his worried expression before she scanned the room. Her mom was dancing with Henry, her expression warm and loving. She spotted her brother and his son. While James was doing his best to look happy, he was obviously suffering from the separation from his wife, even though Connie had never been the right woman for him.

There were also others, some friends of her mom, some of Henry. This was a quiet and surreal affair, so different from life in New York where the only peaceful location she knew was Simon's apartment where the building towered over the city.

"I can't," she admitted. "I want to be here, and I want to be as far away as possible at the same time. I love you and I know I'm failing you, but I'm afraid of being found out, being inspected like a butterfly under a microscope."

Simon shook his head. "People will see what they want to see. In this case, they want you to be happy, and I think we could convince them that I'm not about to screw you over. Nobody wants to know what you prefer when it comes to a lover. Nobody will ask. Apart from Jenn, that is."

She laughed. She couldn't help it. He had wanted to break some of the tension and managed to do so without any effort. It was true, Jenn was curious about BDSM subculture, and wasn't afraid to ask whatever came to her mind, which had made dinner with her, her Baptist pastor boyfriend and Simon a special kind of hell.

"It's a pity that the one thing that could help me relax is out of the question here," she said, getting on her toes to kiss him.

Something in his gaze darkened, and it sent an instant shiver down her back. "You're not the only one on edge, and we might not be at home, but I have every intention of doing something about *this*. Soon."

That was a promise...and she couldn't wait for the evening to wind up.

Chapter Two

The bed and breakfast they were staying at for the night was old, and in the darkness, it looked foreboding, reminding Sharon of the scary movies she'd loved to watch as a teen. Knowing the owners, though, she had no doubt they would be safe. The thought made her smile, but she shook her head when Simon asked what was so funny.

There were four guest rooms, all on the second floor, and the walls were paper thin, so she and Simon made their way upstairs as silently as possible. Her mother had offered them a room at her house for the night, but seeing that she and Henry would leave for their honeymoon the next morning, Sharon had wanted to stay somewhere else. This was their wedding night, so the two of them would prefer to be alone. Sharon would feel weird staying in her old room, even though it had been turned into a guest room over a decade ago.

Here, they were a five-minute drive away from her family and could have breakfast with everybody the next morning…and they all could enjoy their privacy for the night. As much as this house allowed, that was.

She turned to Simon, who had closed the door to their room behind her.

"How are you?" he asked.

Instinct wanted her to tell him she was fine, but she wasn't. Stepping farther into the room, she got out of her shoes and sat on the bed, sighing when it released a loud creak.

"I feel like I could crawl out of my skin," she admitted.

She hadn't been so tense in a long time. Her shoulders hurt and her chest was tight as if she hadn't gotten enough air all night.

"I know they didn't mean to, but to me it felt as if they were watching me, judging. Not just Mom and Henry, everybody. And yes, I brought back boyfriends in the past, but I never worried about being found out." She paused to worry at a fingernail where the polish was chipped. There were reasons she didn't make it a habit to put on any. It didn't go with the job and wasn't worth the hassle.

Simon remained silent, and meeting his gaze, she continued. "I know they don't and can't know there's something to hide, still…"

Simon crossed the floor to sit on the bed beside her. Another creak made her sigh. He took her hand, squeezing it. "Do you regret being with me?"

"No. I don't. I never have. This is my problem, and I will try not to make it yours."

"I won't change, Sharon, and my needs won't either."

Their gazes met. She reached out and cupped his cheek, stroking over the stubble goatee he had grown in the last months. "You think mine will?"

"No, I don't. But in my case, I had the freedom and money to build my life around them. I understand that you've got to keep certain aspects of your life under wraps."

How can he read me so well?

"You're too good for me, you know?" she said then gave in to impulse. Leaning closer, she kissed him. She moaned when he deepened the kiss, but he pulled back a few seconds later.

"I think it's time you take a shower now," he said, his voice cool. Without another glance at her, he got up to retrieve his bag.

She bristled at his tone of voice and sprang up as well. "I think I can decide for myself whether and when I want to shower."

He stilled, turned with an eyebrow raised. "I told you I'd do something about this tension, and I will, but you have to decide if this is what you want as well. If yes, then it's my game, my rules." He stepped closer, lifting her chin with his index finger just as he had earlier today. "What do you want?"

She let out a shuddering breath. "I want my mind to quiet down, but how? We don't have the toys to play, we're talking in hushed tones lest we be overheard and the bed creaking can be heard all the way in NYC."

The barest hint of a smile tugged at the corners of his mouth. "You've got a point, but you should know I don't need toys to make you forget."

"You can't have me scream either," she said, almost laughing at the absurdity of the situation. "And you know I'd never agree to a ball gag."

"I wouldn't want to see you with one. Anyway, last chance. You can trust me, or we can go to bed. We'll survive."

That they would. Though she had no idea what he had planned, the decision was an easy one.

"I want whatever you can offer me."

"Then you'll go and have a shower now. Don't take too long."

"Sure."

It didn't take more than one look from him to see the game had already started.

"Yes, Master," she said, straightening.

What would my mother, my brother, my colleagues think if they could see me like this now, referring to my boyfriend as Master?

She discarded the thought. Dominance and submission were their coping method when the jumble of emotions became too much, and this was for no one to judge.

Inside the small bathroom, she took a deep, shuddering breath as she got out of her dress. She loved this town, had enjoyed growing up here, but right now she would give everything for the anonymity of the city. There, almost nobody was even aware of her presence. Here, most people had known her since childhood, even June and Walter, the owners of this bed and breakfast. They were good friends of her mom, and still remembered the day she'd crashed her bike right outside the house. June had come running, had given her a Band-Aid for the wound and an ice cream to distract her from the pain. The scar on her knee was still visible.

Folding her dress, she started the water before getting out of her underwear.

Stepping underneath the spray a minute later, she cursed as she had forgotten to get rid of her makeup and it began burning in her eyes. At least the uncomfortable feeling was distracting her from her thoughts. She let water run over her face until the unwelcome sensation subsided before she reached for the shower gel. Mindful not to use all the hot water, she didn't linger longer than she had to and left the shower not five minutes later.

She considered putting on her nightie, then left it in the bag. She wouldn't wear it for long anyway. Wrapping herself in a towel, she cleaned the remnants of makeup from her face, then walked back into the room.

She found Simon on the bed, lost in thought. He had closed the drapes and lit two big candles, one of them on each nightstand. The ceiling light had been switched off. Upon noticing her, he stood, taking a few steps in her direction. He stopped about halfway, holding up something in his hands. It took her a second to realize it was a blindfold.

"Get rid of the towel and come here," he commanded. He never had to raise his voice to get his point across.

Letting the towel fall to the ground, she walked over to him, not even flinching when he stepped around her to apply the blindfold. He didn't always use one, but often enough that she had gotten used to the sensation of being without that one sense.

Once the blindfold was secured, he ran a finger from the nape of her neck all the way down her back to her ass, and it sent a shiver of anticipation down her skin.

She loved sex with him, making love, yet right now she wished they were at the club where he had an arsenal of toys at his disposal and she could be as vocal as she wanted. There had been a scream of frustration stuck in her throat the whole day.

He stepped closer, so she could feel his warmth behind her. "Listen. I will lead you to the bed now and tie your arms to the bed. Then I will take a shower myself. Understood?"

"Yes, Master."

"Good. When I'm back, we'll discuss what's going to happen tonight. Just know that I expect you to be really quiet. If you can't manage, I won't let you come."

Taking a deep breath, Sharon nodded, knowing he was serious. So far, he had made good on this threat once, and she didn't care for a repeat performance. That night she'd tested him on purpose by disobeying his command to pleasure herself in front of him, and in turn he had kneeled between her legs, licking and teasing her until her legs were shaking and she was close to coming. Instead of providing relief, he had made her get up on her knees and suck him until he came. He'd smiled, then told her to get on the bed before he delivered a lengthy spanking and declared the game over. Utter frustration had made her cry, and after a night where she couldn't find any sleep, she had spent the next day at work, tired, horny and grumpy enough that Jenn had fled the office after barely an hour in.

"Sharon, listen to me." He brought her back from her musings. "I asked if you have any questions yet? Answer me."

"No, Master."

"Good. Then come."

Stepping around her, he took one of her hands, guiding her to the bed. Once she had reached it, she sat.

"Did you notice the headboard earlier?" he asked.

She had. It was wooden, massive and showcased an intricate pattern.

"Yes, I have, Master," she replied.

"Can you find the cord I applied to it?" Simon asked. Reaching out, she found it after a few seconds and ran her fingers over it.

"Velvet?"

"It's a good idea to be smarter this time, isn't it? Velvet is less likely to leave bruises."

He had thought ahead, and warmth spread through her, a genuine smile breaking free.

"Thank you."

She was sure he was sporting that small smile of his when he spoke. "I know you, and I want you to be happy. I also want you to be able to wear short sleeves on days like these."

She reached out, finding the second cord that would restrain her other wrist. The bed groaned when she moved. When Simon spoke, his voice was a mixture of frustration and amusement. "Never mind. Who would have thought that this bed would be the true master tonight?"

Sharon had to quench the urge to giggle. A bit of her tension gave way.

All that had bothered her tonight were things she'd never considered she'd experience in her life. She'd never imagined herself engaging in regular BDSM play. She'd never deemed it possible a creaking bed would throw a wrench into it, either. Life was impossible to plan, and most of the time she liked it that way.

There were the faint sounds of Simon moving, then he lifted one of her arms, securing her wrist with one of the cords, so her arm was halfway suspended in the air. Of course, the bed made another loud noise. "I wouldn't move too much tonight, if I were you," he said. Once he had tied up the other arm, he told her to lie down, then propped up some pillows behind her head.

"I'll take a shower now."

Without another word he left, and she heard the bathroom door close behind him.

She wasn't uncomfortable—yet—though she knew her arms would hurt before long. As the water started in the next room, she tried to relax as much as possible.

She didn't want to think of today any longer but couldn't stop the thoughts. Why did it feel like she had failed Simon and her family at the same time? Although hadn't she only failed Simon? She didn't owe her family any explanations. They would never get to dictate her life—they never would try either. She sighed, worrying her bottom lip with her teeth.

The inside of her thigh began to itch, and she had pulled at her restraints before she remembered her hands were bound by an expert. *Wonderful.* There was no way to reach the spot. She growled, leaving out a surprised gasp when Simon's hand touched her shoulder.

"Need a hand?"

"What do you think?" With a start, she remembered the game was already on. "Yes, I do, Master. My thigh itches."

Simon chuckled before trailing the pad of his thumb over her skin until she told him he'd reached the right spot, making the sensation a lot worse before scratching it. She let out a sigh when it began feeling better. "Thank you."

He withdrew his finger. "You're welcome. And now let's discuss how this night is going to proceed."

Sharon's heart began to pound as excitement cursed through her veins at the same time.

"First, I've decided you'll wear the nipple clamps I brought."

She bit her lip, her body remembering the pain this would inflict on her tender flesh. It should distract from any unwanted thoughts, as she was unable to move much.

"Next, I'll go down on you. I've waited for a taste of you all day."

A shiver ran over her body, and while she wanted this with all her being, she had no idea how to keep silent throughout it.

"Now, the thing is, you won't get to come. Our game is not about a quick release, and you won't have earned it. Anyway, I think it's about time all our anal training pays off, and to put it bluntly, I'm going to fuck your ass."

Sharon's eyes widened despite the blindfold, and she tensed. It was true, he had prepared her for this, bit by bit, with his fingers, a butt plug and vibrators. She had wondered when he would want to take her this way, had asked and not received an answer. She hadn't expected it tonight of all nights.

One of his hands came to lie on her stomach as if he knew of and was trying to soothe the nervous fluttering.

"I brought lube, condoms and time, and I want you to alert me whenever something feels uncomfortable, to use your safe word should it become too much."

It was a promise. One he would keep.

"If you behave very well, I'll make sure you come, too. Now, do you have anything you want to tell me, anything you want to ask?"

She took the time to calm her racing thoughts. She didn't have questions, just a good amount of trepidation, although if she trusted anybody to do right by her, it was him.

Taking a deep breath, she shook her head. "No, Master."

"Good. Then do you agree with my plan for tonight?" His hand was rubbing her stomach in concentric circles, spreading warmth, a measure of comfort.

"Yes, Master."

"Then I'll get out everything we need for tonight. It's going to be a long one, but I'm sure you'll agree it will be worth it in the end."

She couldn't say why but she believed him.

Chapter Three

Sharon's nipples hurt. Still, she didn't complain when Simon tightened the clamps a fraction, even though she couldn't stop her sharp intake of breath. She tensed and her hands balled into fists. She told herself to breathe in a steady rhythm to accept the hurt. The pain had to become a part of her, or she wouldn't be able to bear it for long.

Usually, she would moan, giving voice to the sensations running through her body. Tonight, she couldn't, so she focused on the way her fingernails dug into the palms of her hands, how the velvet cords cut into her wrists.

She had almost forgotten about Simon's presence while retreating into her own mind, and his hand cupping her cheek startled her.

"The clamps suit you."

She would never understand how he could be so calm and in control when she was about to fall into pieces the very next moment. They balanced each other well.

Simon pulled away, and the weight of his body dipped the mattress at the end of the bed, causing another ungodly sound. She would've flinched if she didn't fear making it worse.

"This is not going to work," he said. Getting up again, he began to untie her. "Let's settle on the floor. Stay still for the moment."

He was nothing but efficient as he freed her arms. She was startled when he went for the blindfold, too, and she had to blink a few times to adjust to the dim lighting.

"I want you to watch after all," he commented.

Taking the bedspread, he put it on the ground in the middle of the room, then he took the pillows off the bed. Walking back to her, he held out his hand. Sharon took it and let him help her up.

"I want you to lie down in the middle. Use a pillow for your head," he said, leading her over to the bedding.

Doing as he said, she wasn't surprised when he fetched the cords from the bed, taking her arms to tie them together over her head.

"Now remember that you've got to be very, very quiet."

Not wasting any more time, Simon ran his hands over her calves before they slid up the inside of her legs, his touch a caress sending shivers down her back. Once he reached her thighs, he applied light pressure, urging her to spread her legs, relenting when she could feel the strain.

"Don't forget to lie still," came his quiet command.

"Yes, Master," she whispered, even though he hadn't asked her to speak.

It was a lapse, and he pulled at the chain linking the nipple clamps together, stealing her breath while a fresh wave of pain made her body flush.

She waited for a verbal reprimand, but none came. Quite the contrary, as the next thing she felt was the sensation of his hot breath on her sex. A flash of instant lust caused her clit to throb in expectation of pleasure, made her want to clench her legs together, the need for friction fighting her ability to comply with his demands.

No matter how, she had to lie still but it seemed an impossible task when he licked the crease between her leg and her hip, first on the one, then the other side, his goatee scratching her sensitive flesh.

This had been a rotten idea. Why had she agreed to this torture when she could be fucking him right here and now?

"Do you know you're already wet for me?" he asked, slipping a finger between her labia, coating it in her wetness before sliding it into her.

Her inner walls contracted around the welcome intruder. He withdrew the next second.

She waited for him to repeat the motion, to move on or even to talk to her, but he didn't. Instead, seconds or even minutes passed while she waited for what came next.

It was too silent. As she lay there without anything to distract her, the muscles of her arms began protesting their position and the nipple clamps caused her tender flesh to pulse.

She wasn't allowed to move, to make a noise, and even with the pillow underneath her head, she couldn't see him well. Biting down hard on her bottom lip, she waited for anything to happen.

The tongue flicking her pleasure point without forewarning made her whole body tighten as the overload of unexpected sensations made her toes curl.

Again, he stopped almost at once, though this time he allowed her to take a deep breath before continuing his sensual assault.

Slowing down, he circled her clit a few times, trailing lower to dip his tongue into her sex. His touch was so light she wanted to curse him, to raise her hips for deeper contact. It would end the game, and by now she was too invested in it.

He had told her he wouldn't let her come this way, yet she wanted more, wanted all he was willing to give her. Maybe, just maybe, he'd grant her release, after all.

Impulse told her to close her legs a little, to wrap them around his head, to get as close to his touch as possible. Instead, she bit the inside of her cheek, the slight pain the distraction she needed to remain still.

Licking his way up her sex again, he sucked her clit before using his tongue to draw small circles on her most sensitive flesh. He was meticulous, relentless, driving her closer to the edge in a pace so slow, she was surprised when she was about to shatter in bliss soon. Her eyes fell closed.

The day had been too tense, and all she wanted was relief.

Maybe he won't notice.

Consequences be damned, she tried holding still, to keep her breathing even.

Close, so fucking close…

Chuckling, Simon retreated. "No, I won't let you come. This was for me. You might get to come later."

She cursed him under her breath. She opened her eyes to look at him. As he had sat up on his knees, she could see him better this time.

His face was impassive, but she knew well enough that it was a mask, hiding the multitude of emotions inside him.

"I think we better find a different position for you."

She was well aware what was up next, and trepidation waged war with excitement inside her. Even wanting this—being curious—she was wary.

He unfastened the ties around her wrists, then sat back. Meeting her gaze, he reached for the nipple clamps, tugging at the chain once more. He ran his fingers along the sides of her extra-sensitive nipples.

Hell!

She gasped, then met his cool gaze.

"Too bad they will have to go," he said. as he unfastened the clamps. The sudden blood flow pricked her skin as tears filled her eyes. Holding her breath, then releasing it, she waited for the pain to lessen. He waited until he had her attention again.

"Wait a moment, then I'll help you turn around."

He got up, and, after walking over to his bag, he got out a folded sheet. At her curious look, the corners of his lips raised.

"It wouldn't do to stain the duvet, would it?"

He had thought about everything, and she wasn't surprised.

He moved back, holding out his hand to her so she could sit up. It was difficult after she had stayed prone in position for so long, and her legs were cramping.

When she nodded at him, he helped her up and spread the sheet over the duvet.

"Next you're going to lie on your stomach, and we'll prop up your ass with a pillow."

She wasn't sure about this, not at all, although it was up to her to stop this at any point. As she turned onto her stomach, he helped her lie down so her behind would be elevated.

"I almost forgot," he said, more to himself than to her, reaching for her arms again to bind them once more.

Once he was done, he brushed the mass of her hair over her shoulder, then kissed her between her shoulder blades, causing her to shiver.

"Are you okay? Answer me, Sharon," he spoke.

"Yes, I am, Master." She wasn't comfortable, but she wasn't meant to be. Her nipples still hurt and the tension in her arms, radiating all the way to her shoulders, got worse with every minute.

"Good, then I'll get the lube."

She couldn't see more than his shadow while he moved.

"I want you to relax," he said when he lowered himself to the ground again. "Anal sex is not supposed to hurt. If it does, I need to know, all right?"

"Yes, Master."

He was unhurried while he massaged her behind with his hands, warming the skin, his touch confident, comfortable. She loved his hands, the surety of his movements. Even when she was a jumble of emotions, they were steady, in control, just as he was.

He continued for several minutes until she became sleepy, a yawn escaping her.

He pinched her ass, and she sucked in a sharp breath.

"You can sleep later."

The bottle of lube popped open, and she felt the trickle of fluid down the crack of her cheeks. Spreading the thick gel, he rubbed it into her sphincter, dipping in with just the tip of his finger before retreating, then adding even more lube.

It was not the first time he had done this, but the novelty of the sensation hadn't worn off and she had to swallow a tiny moan.

After a while, he slid in the whole length of his index finger. Thanks to his careful preparation, her body didn't offer any resistance, and she enjoyed the tingling.

Sliding in and out a few times, he added more lube, entering her with two fingers next. Though not uncomfortable, Sharon would've sworn this was all her body could take. She tried turning her head a little so she could watch Simon better, but the strain on her neck muscles and arms made her give up. She closed her eyes, trying to relax while he stretched her without hurry.

While this was not enough to come close to orgasm, she was fully awake again and still keyed up from his earlier ministrations. It was hard not to give in to the temptation to rub against the pillows underneath her in search of friction. Simon's free hand came to lie on the small of her back, warm and firm.

"I'll add a third finger now."

Even though there was utter confidence in his voice, his announcement made her clench her toes and bite her lip. She trusted him, but she wasn't sure if it was enough to try this. She remembered the first time he'd tried the butt plug, how she'd thought it would never fit.

The hand was gone and even more lube trickled down her ass and another finger slid in, careful not to hurt her. Instinct told her to hold her breath, but it would be the wrong thing to do, so she continued to take in air, pushing against his fingers, making them slip in easier.

"You're doing good, Sharon."

Stupid as her reaction might be, the compliment, spoken with the barest hint of warmth, made her smile.

Moving with deliberation, he almost withdrew completely with his fingers before sliding in again.

Again minutes passed, and she grew restless, wishing for more, wanting his hands on her, for him to take her without inhibition. Keeping still and silent, aroused without a chance of gratification, drove her crazy.

He had promised to take her mind off things, and God, he was. Stilling his fingers inside her, he bent forward, then began kissing a trail up her spine. Sharon moaned into the mattress as goosebumps rose on her skin.

She couldn't do this much longer. It had almost become second nature to retreat into her headspace while dealing with pain, to find peace and calm in midst of delicious torture. This, though, left her wanting. Need crawled up her veins.

His body was almost covering hers now. He bit her earlobe, whispering in her ear, "I think you're ready now."

Was she? Her heartbeat quickened, and she stiffened, which he had to be able to feel with his fingers still buried within her.

"Lie as still as possible, don't forget to breathe and speak out if it hurts."

How could he be so composed? Because he knew what he did—that was why. This was a common sexual practice for a lot of people, if not for her.

"If you want me to stop, you've got to tell me now," he said, waiting for a beat, pulling his fingers out when she didn't answer.

She wanted him to stop and to go on, but couldn't have it both ways.

"Relax," he advised once again, and he got up on his knees behind her. She felt his hand as he positioned his cock at her rear entrance. Not giving her time to worry, he began to push. Instead of letting fear dictate her actions, she exhaled, pushed back against his intrusion, and after a long moment, the head of his hard flesh slid inside her.

"You're doing great," he repeated, one hand on her hip now, the other sliding around her, his fingers trailing over her clit. She took in a sharp breath as almost forgotten lust raised its head again.

Her body hadn't forgotten how close it had been to climax, that it had been denied.

He rubbed her pleasure point in small circles, and she moaned as she neared the point of no return. Her body tightened in expectation of release, then… He stopped.

"Not yet," he said, then pulled back with his cock, sinking back into her again a second later. He moved, careful and slow. Although the sensation was alien, it wasn't bad, especially as his fingers still rested against her clit and the slightest movement of them created a soft, delicious friction that made her forget almost everything but her need to come.

"Is this still okay for you?" he asked after a few gentle thrusts, and she nodded before speaking out.

"Yes, it is, Master."

"Good." He picked up his rhythm, although it was still slow compared to some of the nights they made love. She was surprised when he stopped again, and she came close to asking him to go on.

"I want you to dictate the rhythm now. You're also allowed to come."

Finally. She bit back a sob of relief.

Taking a moment to compose herself, she began moving, feeling him fill her then retreat. Knowing she had full control over the act drained the rest of her tension, and he rewarded her with one hand stroking her back while the other still rested between her legs, applying the softest and most delicate of pressure.

Pressing into his hand, she squeezed his cock inside her, smiling when he groaned at the unexpected move.

Still, it was his game, and he wrapped her long hair around his hand, pulling to remind her of the fact.

She would always be an independent woman but a part of her enjoyed his possessive nature, which was possible because he confined it to the bedroom.

As she began to move a little faster, the sensation of him inside her ass became less and less strange, almost pleasant. All she could focus on was the caress of his fingertips against her most sensitive flesh.

She gasped as her climax hit her without fore-warning, her body shuddering under the impact. Biting her tongue so they wouldn't be overheard, she let her eyes fall shut. She was near to passing out as tremors shook her to her very core.

She noticed Simon tensing behind her. When she came back to herself, Simon had pulled out of her, and was stroking her with tenderness.

"How are you doing?" he whispered.

"I'm...good. Better than expected. This was...not..." She wasn't quite sure how to finish her statement.

"Not quite terrible?" he suggested, amusement lacing his voice.

"Yes. Not quite terrible."

He freed her arms and pulled her down onto the sheet, turned her toward him, so they could look at each other.

"I'm glad to hear that."

"So the game's over now?" she asked, surprised when a yawn slipped out.

He smiled. "If it weren't, you'd be punished right now for the lack of proper etiquette."

She rolled her eyes at him. "Of course. Anyway, thanks for taking the edge off." The feeling of unease that had plagued her the whole day was gone at last.

"My pleasure. And if I may say so, I think it was a good day. You've got a wonderful family."

"I do. And Mom looked happy. I'm so glad she got this second chance at love."

He laced his legs with hers, then kissed her shoulder. "I'm convinced they'll have a wonderful life together."

"I agree. And you know, I'm feeling very good at the moment, too." They had been dating for just a few months, and nobody knew what would happen in the future. Right now, she could see a future with him, and that was a feeling she hadn't had in years, if ever.

"That's good. How about we clean up a little and go to bed?" He made a face. Thinking about the creaking monster made her sigh.

"Agreed. And let's not move either."

Sharing a smile, they talked until she was steady enough to get up.

Chapter Four

The phone was already ringing when they entered Simon's apartment. Sharon and Simon exchanged a tired look, and he passed her to take the call.

She dropped her bag by the door, rolling her shoulders and yawning.

Thanks to the lack of sleep last night, all she wanted now was a hot shower and to fall into bed. She'd have to get up early, so there'd be time to stop by her apartment to fetch some fresh clothes. She could have always asked Simon to drop her off there tonight, but at the moment she wanted his company.

Meeting her family and breaching another boundary had left her exhausted. When she was with Simon, he would stop her from worrying too much and getting lost in her own thoughts.

She had just gotten out of her shoes, when he appeared in the hallway, holding out the phone to her, his hand covering the speaker.

"It's Jenn. She says your boss is on the lookout for you. He tried your apartment and your cell without luck."

Fuck. She had all but forgotten about her phone – she had thrown it into her bag with her other belongings this morning. Hers and Simon's, too. They couldn't have helped anybody on the highway anyway.

Taking the phone from him, she mouthed her thanks.

"Jenn, what's up? Who died?"

"And there she is. Damn, girl. I could've done without Kelly giving me the stink eye because he couldn't get a hold of you. By the way, apart from his call, you should have another five from me, and Simon should have a few, too. Anyway, Kelly didn't breathe a thing, but rumor has it there's a dead body that should be tackled by a different precinct and they want you to investigate it."

Sharon frowned, then looked at Simon who stood in the hallway, his arms crossed, waiting to learn what had happened.

"New case," she said to him, and he nodded, turning to leave for the kitchen.

"Why would they want me to meddle with another precinct's investigation?"

"I've got no idea, but do us all a favor here and call Kelly."

"I will. Thanks, Jenn."

"No prob. And don't forget to call me afterwards. I think I deserve to know what's the deal after playing call center all afternoon. Oh, and give Simon a kiss from me."

"Yes, to the first and a firm no to the latter. Talk to you later."

Ending the call, she let her arm drop, wondering what had happened that it couldn't be handled by the responsible precinct or any other officer of her own.

"What's the matter?" Simon asked, handing her a glass of water while taking the phone from her.

"The hell if I know. They seem to need me for a case that should be taken on by a different precinct, not that I have any idea why." She took a few sips, then drained the whole glass. He offered to take it from her, but she shook her head. She needed to move, to think and to call Kelly back.

Carrying the glass to the sink, she went to fetch her bag next, fishing out her mobile phone. Activating it, she flinched at the multitude of missed calls and messages. Instead of listening to those, she called her superior back. He answered after the first ring.

"About time. I need you at the precinct ASAP."

Sharon rolled her eyes. "Will you at least tell me what this is about, sir?"

"Yes, once you're here. It's a mess. Come directly to my office. How soon do you think you'll be here?"

Calculating the time, she told him she could make it in about half an hour, and he ended the call without another word. This couldn't be good.

She found Simon in his bedroom, sorting clothes, throwing most of them in the nearby hamper.

"I'm sorry, but I gotta leave. Kelly wants to see me now but didn't tell me a thing. I'll call you once I know more, but I think I won't be back tonight."

She was still tired, though the adrenaline would keep her going for a while longer. It had to.

Getting up, Simon stepped closer until he could enfold her in his embrace. "It's the job. Just call me when you can. I think I'll use the time and stop by the club."

He pulled back, and she sighed, raking her hand through her hair. "Does nothing ever faze you?"

He shrugged. "A lot of things do. But as I see it, you'll have your answers, or at least most of them within the hour, and it's not as if the two of us can change a thing about any of this right now."

"You're right. Still…" She looked at the hallway where her open bag was waiting for her. "Is it okay if my bag stays here for a day or two?"

"You don't have to ask. Now how about you call downstairs for a cab, I'll make us a coffee to go and we share said cab?"

"Sounds good." Almost too good, like life with him did from time to time. Would she ever stop worrying when the other shoe was about to drop?

Looking for the phone which he had already put back into place, she called the front desk, then Jenn. They were out of the apartment less than ten minutes after they had entered it.

* * * *

Kelly was sitting at his desk when she entered after a quick knock. He was frowning, his tie was rumpled and tufts of his thinning hair were standing up in all directions.

"Before I get down to business, do I have to remind you that we need to be able to contact you in case of emergency?"

She closed the door, then made a few steps into the office, stopping right in front of his desk. "With all due respect, sir, I was not on call, and I don't need to monitor my phone in my free time."

The expression on Kelly's face darkened, but she held his gaze and he leaned back in his seat.

"You're right. Although I could've done without trying to chase you down for hours. Take a seat."

She'd have preferred standing, yet didn't want to argue after seeing her boss's mood. Sitting, she waited for him to continue.

Kelly linked his hands on his desk. "Let's make it short as they want you at the crime scene as soon as possible." He raised a hand to forestall any protest. "Yes, I could've met you at the scene and spare you the trip here, but I thought you'd prefer a head's up as this is, pardon my French, a rather fucked-up situation."

He shook his head, then sighed. "The reason you're here is because the commissioner requested it."

"Pardon me?" Sharon sat up even straighter. *What the hell?* She didn't know the commissioner, and there was no reason he should know of her.

Kelly nodded. "That was my reaction, too. Anyway, everything that I know so far is that a man named Warren Rawlins was found dead in his apartment earlier today. He was naked, apart from a dog collar around his neck. He was stabbed multiple times, and beside his body they found the business card of Helen King."

Sharon hadn't heard of any of these names, so couldn't fathom what this had to do with her.

Kelly looked at his watch then continued. "Rawlins was found around ten hours ago, and he was bagged in the meantime, but they preserved the rest of the scene for you. So far, so good but here comes the fucked-up part. No one quite knows how it happened, but King got wind of the murder and that her card was found at the scene, and lo and behold, she's an old friend of the commissioner. Next the commissioner called me, asking for a favor. He heard about your successful and discreet investigation of the Davis case, and he wants you to be just as discreet now and help Second Precinct solve this case and fast."

Marlene Davis, the case during which she'd gotten to know Simon. A young woman had been shot inside his club, and Sharon had been the lead investigating officer.

She suppressed a smile. It hadn't been love at first sight between Simon and her. His arrogance had been annoying—still was from time to time. That day he'd been waiting in front of the door, his pose relaxed, his gaze piercing. One look at her and a hint of a smile had appeared on his face. She hadn't been comfortable with the location, and he had known it.

He had also been aware that she was trying to fight her curiosity when it came to the BDSM lifestyle. From the beginning, he'd been able to read her. She'd hated it and disliked him, or so she'd thought, as her strong reaction to him stemmed from an ever-growing attraction to him that wasn't suitable. At that time, he'd been a suspect on top of it all.

Pushing her memories to the side, she faced Kelly.

"Sir, don't you think they're just as qualified and discreet at Second Precinct?"

Her superior officer snorted. "To be frank, yes, I do. I've got no doubt in your abilities, but yeah, they could've dealt with this on their own. They think so, too, by the way, so don't expect a warm welcome."

"So, is there any chance to deny this request?"

Sharon didn't mind taking on a new case. It was her job. If she could prevent ending up in some political scheme, though, she would do it in a heartbeat.

"The commissioner called, so what do you think?"

Nodding, having expected nothing else, Sharon got up. "Thank you, sir. If you could give me the address, I'll make my way to the crime scene now."

Kelly got up too, handing her a piece of paper with a hard-to-read address scribbled on it. "Take Reynolds with you. I want someone to have your back, and she should be done with reassigning your open cases by now."

He shook his head, sat back down. "Well, one bit of advice. Be quick and…discreet." His voice was dripping with sarcasm he didn't try to hide.

Sharon bit back a comment. "Yes, sir."

Leaving the office, she tried to shake off the feeling that something was wrong here and that this concerned her on a personal level, even if it shouldn't. Well, time would tell.

Chapter Five

Jenn was waiting in their office with her jacket on, jumping up when Sharon opened the door. "What the fuck did you do that they requested you?"

"I won't even ask where you learned this now, but I've got no idea. Although I've got a bad feeling about it."

"Well, let's be honest, you'll either advance your career or scrub toilets next. Anyway, let's go and make some enemies." Grinning, Jenn passed her and waited for Sharon to follow.

On the way to their car, Jenn took her arm as soon as they were outside the precinct. "Now dish. How was the wedding? Is your family ready to adopt Simon yet?"

Sharon suppressed a sigh. Two days had passed since they had talked last, and it felt like a lifetime. A gust of wind hit them, and Sharon shivered, wishing she had put on a warmer coat. Within a month autumn would be in full force, and she hated the thought of the city being swallowed by coldness and dark nights that didn't want to end. While the change of seasons was beautiful in Vermont, it just meant rain, snow and a lot of mush driving people insane here. Still, she wouldn't want to go back, couldn't live in a place where she was part of a community tapestry rather than an individual.

She considered her answer before she spoke. "It was wonderful. Mom looked beautiful, and they were so damned happy. Henry, too. I'm glad she's got this second chance at love. I'll show you some pics later. And yes, they seemed to like Simon well enough."

Jenn looked at her from the side. "He's not your dirty secret, you know. It's not as if you're dating an escaped murderer or a modern-day slave driver. Hell, he seems to be a saint compared to your scumbag lawyer-ex."

"Yes, Michael was a scumbag, but Simon's not a saint," Sharon said, wishing she didn't sound so defensive.

"Nobody said that, but running a sex club doesn't make you a sinner by default."

She met Jenn's gaze. "Are you sure? So, what's Brian's take on this?"

If Sharon had trouble accepting she was dating Simon, it was even weirder to contemplate Jenn with a Baptist pastor.

"He thinks that God created mankind in his own image and that we all reflect the different parts of it. And he likes Simon, as do I."

"You think I don't?"

Jenn sighed. "To be honest, I think you want to be in love with him but are afraid that anybody could learn about your relationship. Would you be able to run for president if the *truth* came out? No. But correct me if

I'm wrong, I don't think that was your intention anyway."

Sharon combed through her hair with her fingers. She should have taken the time to brush it earlier. "No, it isn't, but I think my private life should remain private."

Of course she knew that she could never completely separate her business from her private life. It didn't mean she couldn't wish it were possible.

"It should, yup. But it never will be. Not all of it anyway. That's not everything though, is it? What else is up? Come on, girl, you know you can talk to me."

She gave Jenn a pained smile. "I know. It's just that I'm angry with myself. I wouldn't want Simon to be any different. I don't want to put my needs on a shelf and pretend they don't exist. Still, it doesn't mean I want to have fingers pointed at me, people talking behind my back and promotions passing me by because there's *scandal* attached to my name."

There. She had said it, not that it made her feel any better.

"You know, if you're not about to make the whole nature of your private life public to begin with, there's just one thing you can do. Live your best life and deal with any leaks when or if they happen. This all sounds worse in your head than it is. Would people talk? Yes. Be shocked? Yes, but then the next affair or divorce would take their mind off it in a hot second."

They had reached the car, and as Jenn had the keys, she let go of Sharon's arm, unlocked the doors then opened the driver's side, but she didn't make a move to get in.

"Come on, Shar, you know I'm right."

"No, I don't know. People might move on, but they won't forget, and it's different if you slept with your married boss or if they try to imagine you being whipped."

Jenn snorted, chuckling. "I tried to imagine it more than once and failed. It just doesn't fit the profile, but yeah, even serial killers don't look the part."

"Thanks for comparing me to a serial killer. "

"I didn't, but I've got to tell you that you make for a lousy submissive. Shouldn't you let Simon do the worrying?"

Sharon rolled her eyes. "Geez, do your bloody homework. I might like to submit in the bedroom, but I'm the master of my own life."

"How poetic." Jenn winked at her, then got into the car. "And now let's go and look at some blood and gore."

* * * *

When they arrived at the crime scene, they were met with the cold stares of one detective and two crime scene technicians. Sharon hadn't expected a warm welcome but damn those guys. It wasn't as if she wanted to be here.

The detective walked up to them, introducing himself as Bill Hannigan. At first glance, he was at least in his late fifties and Sharon was sure he'd seen it all one time too often. He looked tired and no wonder, as it was close to midnight by now.

Pointing behind himself, he introduced the crime scene technicians, who threw Jenn and her a quick look before continuing to dust a cabinet and a table for fingerprints.

Hannigan gave them a quick rundown of what had happened so far, then showed them some of the pictures taken earlier. It was easy to see the rage that had to have possessed the perpetrator. There was blood all over Rawlins and he lay on the ground in a fetal position as if trying to protect himself. It hadn't done him any good. In the meantime, Hannigan droned on, and Jenn raised an eyebrow when she heard about the business card found near the corpse. Sharon, too, would've loved to understand what it meant.

She was glad when Hannigan was finished. She didn't like this man and had heard most of the story from Kelly before.

Hannigan looked first at Sharon, then at Jenn. "Well, anyway, we were ordered to back off but give assistance when it's needed." He kept her gaze, and the anger in his eyes made her want to take a step back. Damn it, she wasn't the enemy here.

Hannigan scoffed. "Never mind, I'm sure you'll be fine, as you're our city's resident expert on deviant creeps."

It lay on the tip of Sharon's tongue to tell him that just because Rawlins' proclivities might have been different, it didn't make him a deviant. It would've been a waste of breath, and she curled her toes in her boots to keep herself from speaking out.

"Thanks. I appreciate that you waited here and shared your information," she said, trying to remain calm.

"Yeah, I hope we can return the favor someday," Jenn said, her voice dripping with sarcasm.

Hannigan snorted. "How about you solve that one for starters? Have fun interviewing half of the city's filth."

Sharon bit her lip, glad Hannigan's eyes were on Jenn. While there was no need to feel insulted, he had hit a nerve.

"We're well acquainted with filth," Jenn said, raising an eyebrow. Without another word, Hannigan turned and left.

Jenn turned to her. "I don't think we can expect much help coming from Prince Charming. Not that it matters. Let's find out what we got here."

She smiled at one of the technicians who had followed their little exchange with interest. "Did you find anything interesting yet?"

Sharon didn't catch the man's answer. Instead, she took in her surroundings. While the apartment wasn't as big as Simon's, it was larger than hers by far, although it felt smaller thanks to massive furniture taking up most of the space. At least that held true for the living room where Rawlins had been found.

Sharon looked at a mahogany cabinet on one side of the room and a bookshelf made of the same material on the other side. In the middle was a couch that was twice as big as hers and two armchairs that would sit two apiece. There were no rugs, but European floorboards instead.

Too many paintings cluttered the walls, most of them in bold colors, modern art with no sense or meaning Sharon could understand.

Rawlins had been found near the couch table and the amount of blood would've been sickening if Sharon hadn't viewed scenes like this too often.

Jenn joined her and kneeled. She shook her head, meeting Sharon's gaze. "This must have been personal. He was stabbed multiple times and with force. And it must've happened right here as there's no spatter anywhere else from what the guys told me.

Sharon moved, so she stood right beside Jenn. "We also know he was naked and wearing a dog collar when it happened. So where are his clothes?"

She called out to the crime scene technician next to her who told her there'd been a heap of clothes near the bed in the main bedroom.

Sharon met Jenn's gaze. "So, I guess this happened either at the beginning or the middle of whatever game he'd wanted to play."

"Whatever it was, I'm sure he'd have preferred a different ending," Jenn said. "Oh, look." She pointed to a spot on the ground where they could see the shape of a rectangle in a sea of blood. "This is where that business card must have been placed. Very subtle."

Sharon considered their options. "Three scenarios. Either the perp wasn't that smart and lost the card, they wanted to point us into the direction of Helen King for a reason only they know or it was Helen King herself, placing the card here because she knew her name would come up in the investigation, and this was her way of making it so obvious that she thinks we'll discard her on the spot."

Jenn stood up, her hands on her hips. "It's hard to tell. Do you happen to know her?"

Sharon huffed and looked behind her. The two crime scene technicians had moved on to another room, so she turned to Jenn. "No, and why would I? While Simon and I have an unconventional relationship, it doesn't mean I know everybody in the scene."

Jenn raised her hands. "Sorry. You're right. So, let's call King and go meet her?"

"Yeah. Now where do they have that business card?"

Sharon walked into the kitchen where the technicians were busy and asked the one who wasn't glaring at her for the business card. He didn't speak but pointed to the kitchen table where there were several open cases containing evidence bags.

Putting on gloves, flexing her hands at the uncomfortable feeling, she sorted through the different plastic bags until she found the one containing King's card. She turned the bag so she could read the number and after getting out her phone, she took off the gloves. Sharon dialed and waited for the call to connect. Under normal circumstances, it would be much too late to call anybody, but this was a murder investigation, and she doubted King would be asleep, seeing the woman was the reason she'd been dragged into this investigation in the first place.

"Yes?" A woman answered at the third ring, her voice smooth as velvet, self-assured.

"Am I speaking to Helen King?"

"Yes. And who are you?"

"Sharon Richards. NYPD. I'm calling…"

"Simon's cop. I see Quentin kept his promise."

The commissioner. Sharon swallowed her irritation. She hated politics. What the hell did King mean when she'd said *Simon's cop*? Why did she know Simon—and even more important—about Sharon's relationship with him?

Not in the mood to play games, Sharon shoved her questions to the side. "I need to talk to you about Mr. Rawlins, and the sooner, the better."

King chuckled. "But of course, you want to. Well, my address is on the card. I'm home."

With that, the call ended, and Sharon lowered the phone, glaring at the device in her hand.

"If looks could kill, one Helen King would drop dead right now," Jenn remarked, entering the kitchen. "You spoke to her, didn't you?"

"Yes, I did. I'll go over there now. I'm sure it's going to be an interesting conversation. Never mind, could you stay here and wrap this up? Find out if somebody spoke to the neighbors yet and if not, do it yourself? And get a hold of all the pictures of when Rawlins' body was still here. The sooner we've got all angles covered, the better."

Sharon couldn't explain it, but she'd rather not have Jenn with her when confronting King for the first time. For some reason Helen King knew about her, about Simon, and Sharon wanted to know why. If Jenn tagged along, it could end with King clamming up or with Jenn learning things Sharon didn't want her to know. It was a gut feeling, but Sharon had learned to rely on it.

Her partner frowned and gave her a long, hard look before she relented. "Sure thing. But if I don't get the whole inside scoop later, my ghost will haunt you forever."

"You're not even dead."

"Are you sure? Anyway, you can take the car, and I'll take the subway later." She handed Sharon the keys and went back into the living room. A few seconds later, Sharon could hear her talking to one of the technicians. As there was nothing to be gained from lingering, she left the apartment, wondering what she was getting into.

* * * *

Out on the street, she got into the car and put the key into the ignition, then stopped with her hand on the keys. She fumbled for her phone. There was somebody who might be able to answer at least a few of her questions.

"Hey, I didn't think to hear from you so soon," Simon greeted her.

"Yeah, me neither." She sighed. "Listen, I would love to chat but I'm on my way to an interview. Do you know a woman named Helen King?"

Some seconds ticked by, and Sharon's hold tightened around her phone.

"Yes, I do," Simon replied. The neutral tone of his voice made it clear Sharon wouldn't like whatever the story behind this was.

"Is she the one who died?" he asked.

"No, she's not." It lay on the tip of her tongue to ask if he would care if she had, but she chided herself not to be childish. "Her name came up. It's almost certain she knew the deceased, and I'm on my way to talk to her."

"I see," he said. For no good reason, it irked her that he wasn't more forthcoming on his own.

"Do you? Well, I don't. For one, after learning of this murder, King called the commissioner—a good friend of hers—and it was decided it had to be me tackling this investigation, and for another, she greeted me as *Simon's cop*. So, if you have any idea what this all is about, I'd love for you to enlighten me."

Simon sighed. "It's a long story, Sharon. We can talk about it later. But Helen hosts parties for people in the scene. She is also an ex, and you should know, she loves to play mind games. Don't let her engage you and don't show her any weakness as she'll have no qualms sinking her claws into you."

Sharon's grip tightened further around her phone. "You gotta be kidding me."

"I'm sorry about this, and I'd love to help you in any way, though as I see it there's nothing I can do for you right now."

He was right, and she appreciated that he didn't try to fight her battles. It didn't mean that his calm demeanor did anything to calm her nerves. Although would she even be fighting her own battle or his? She doubted she'd be in this situation if King and Simon hadn't had a relationship at some point.

"Helen's not a bad person," Simon continued. "She's just protective of her family and friends, of her business."

"And loves to play mind games. Well, I'm sure we'll have a great conversation over tea and biscuits. I'll talk to you later."

She ended the call. She didn't even want to know if there was something else that he thought she should know.

Deciding on a relationship with Simon had been one of the best choices she'd made in the last years but damn her, if it didn't cause problems she had never deemed possible.

Chapter Six

Making her way to Tribeca, Sharon managed to find a parking space a few blocks from where King lived. There were reasons she preferred the subway or a cab. Taking a car most often meant longer walks.

Tonight, she was thankful for the fresh air, the chance to collect her thoughts, even though they always circled back to the questions of what Simon's ex had to do with this case and why she was dragging Sharon along for the ride.

After a few minutes, she had reached her destination. She had her hands in the pockets of her coat, balled into fists to keep them warm. Stopping, she looked up King's residence. Much of Tribeca still had intact pre-Civil War architecture and King's building was no exception with its Neo-Greco design and the wrought-iron façades. It had four stories and the windows of the first three floors were obscured while there was a bit of light coming from the fourth floor.

Did King own the whole building? Sharon raised an eyebrow. If she did, she might be even more affluent than Simon was. And what was the reason for the obscured windows? Did Helen King value her privacy…or did she have something to hide?

In a way, this felt like a repetition of her investigation of the Davis case a few months earlier. Although she didn't have any confirmation as of yet, after seeing the nature of Rawlins' death, it was probable that both he and King were involved in the BDSM scene as well.

She would do a background check on King later, find out if she came from money or had worked her way up just as Simon had. Money had never been a problem between Simon and her. He didn't care about his wealth, and Sharon had enough to get by.

When they went out for dinner, they never went anywhere fancy, and they paid in turns. It was the same when they went to see a show or hit the cinema. Not that her job left her much time to go out anyway.

Knowing it was better to get this over with, Sharon crossed the rest of the distance. Once she had rung the bell, King answered after a few seconds, buzzing Sharon in.

Suppressing a sigh, Sharon stepped through the door. This was her investigation now, whether she liked it or not, and she couldn't avoid King. She had to find out which role the woman played in her current investigation.

The door swung closed behind her, and Sharon faced a long hallway to her left and a staircase to her right. The hallway ended with a closed door, and Sharon would have loved to take a look at what was behind it.

Her thoughts were interrupted when King came down the iron staircase, and she wasn't what Sharon had expected, even though she hadn't had the time to form any kind of clear picture in her mind.

The woman was tall, slender, yet not thin. Her dark brown hair fell straight down her back. Her piercing blue eyes met Sharon's gaze, giving nothing away. Although it was almost the middle of the night by now, King wore tight-fitting black jeans, a crisp white shirt with enough open buttons to reveal her cleavage, as well as high-heeled boots.

She was also a good five to ten years older than Simon.

"Simon's cop. That didn't take long," she said, not offering Sharon her hand.

"I'm Detective Richards, and I'd be thankful if you could address me as such, Ms. King."

King pursed her lips in a small, amused smile. "Come on up. I made some tea. Ginger."

She turned and walked up again, not glancing back to see what Sharon would do. Releasing her breath, Sharon followed her upstairs. This was another reminder of the time she got to know Simon. He, too, had thought he could decide for her if she wanted a drink and what it should be.

It became clear that King was another Dominant. How could Simon and she have ever worked out? Two Dominants had to clash, and their needs would remain unfulfilled.

Well, if she wanted an answer to that, she would have to ask him later, as this was nothing she'd discuss with King. She bit her bottom lip so she wouldn't growl her frustration. Discussing ex-relationships hadn't been on her list of things to do today, tomorrow or any time in the near future. If it weren't for this whole mess, she'd be in bed by now, untroubled by thoughts and questions that were bound to nag at her until they were answered. It was what it was and no internal complaining would change a thing.

King led her all the way to the fourth floor, all other floors having the same build—a hallway to the left, a closed door. The door on the fourth floor was open, revealing a little light.

Stepping into the room behind its owner, Sharon took a cursory look around. It was a big space with partitions sectioning off bits of it. There was a passage to the left, but from where she stood, Sharon couldn't see where it led. Right now, they were in a living room, one that was less than cozy.

One wall was painted in a dark green. It was hard to judge in the dim lighting as the few lamps on the wall were made to look like gas lanterns. The furniture was massive, dark, and there was a thick black rug covering most of the floor. For an insane second, Sharon asked herself who took care of cleaning it and what a hassle it had to be.

In the end, this was all a bit too much and an awful lot like walking into a cliché. She almost smiled at the thought that this was a lot like she had imagined Simon's living space when she had gotten to know him first.

King closed the door behind her, then sat on her couch. She had to hand it to the other woman—she knew how to strike an impression. King sat with her back straight, her hands on her knees and was watching Sharon, calculating. She didn't offer her a seat, but Sharon wouldn't have wanted one anyway.

On the couch table in front of them was a tea tray with two cups, and reaching for the teapot, King poured tea into one of the cups.

"No, thank you," Sharon said before King could start with the second one, not that her objection stopped King. *Well, what a waste of a perfectly good tea then.*

King looked up when she was done. "Before I ask if there's any kind of development in the case or even if you think I did it, I'll tell you that Simon and you won't work out." King's voice was deep and cold.

Sharon raised an eyebrow. Was this candid or brazen? After all, it was Sharon who had come here to conduct an interview and not the other way around. "As you might have guessed, I'm not here to discuss my personal life. Not Simon's either."

"You think you know Simon, don't you?"

Yes, she liked to think so. Not that it wasn't any of King's business.

She disregarded King's statement. "I'm here to find out how your business card ended up in a pool of blood beside the murdered body of Warren Rawlins."

A small smile appeared on King's face. Without wanting to, Sharon could see why Simon and she had been a couple once. The calm façade, the slight arrogance. At least on the surface, these two had more in common than Sharon had with him.

"Do you know how Simon came to own his club?"

What does this have to do with anything? Not trying to hide her annoyed sigh, she crossed her arms over her chest, wondering if they would spend their time answering questions with questions.

"I think it's safe to assume you knew Warren Rawlins, and I would like to know from where, what kind of relationship you had and if you have any idea why he was wearing nothing but a dog collar when he was found?"

"Let me guess, you know that Simon worked for an oil mining company and that he made some money in the stock market?"

Yes, that was what she had learned during her research early in the Davis investigation, and she still didn't see a point to any of this, although her gut told her she didn't even want Helen to make a point.

"So, your relationship with Rawlins?"

The blasted smile never left Helen's face. "Did you also know that the company he worked for was family owned? One patriarch and his two sons led the business, and they hired Simon, who proved to have keen instincts, excellent when it came to making deals."

"Warren Rawlins, Ms. King."

Helen shook her head, reminding Sharon of her elementary teacher when one of the children had disappointed her. Sharon's ire wanted to claw its way out but she couldn't show any weakness. She was faced with a huntress who thought she had scented prey, but Sharon was nobody's prey.

Helen spoke as if she hadn't even heard her.

"The old man was fond of Simon, and at one point Simon scored a big contract for the company. He got a big bonus out of it, too. In a way it almost sounds like a fairytale, doesn't it? The perfect career, don't you think?" She paused, but before Sharon could speak and try to circle back to her investigation King continued.

"Well, it was a fairytale à la Grimm. You know that the original tales were rather dark, don't you? Anyway, the younger son was a weakling, a drug user with no head for business. He hated Simon, so he cooked up a scheme with a similar-minded business partner, who then attested to the fact that Simon had leaked business secrets. Within days Simon was sacked."

This was all news to Sharon, and she gritted her teeth. Why had she never dug deep enough to know about this? Why had she never talked to him about his reasons for leaving his job behind? She had always assumed he had wanted to pursue a different lifestyle. She spoke before Helen could continue.

"Ms. King, of course, it's up to you if you want to waste your and my time. Although I think you have better things to do than to come to the precinct for a formal interview, which is the alternative to talking to me now."

She was ignored again.

"Simon had a girlfriend back then. She was the daughter of another oil dynasty tycoon. He had proposed a mere two weeks before he was fired. After he was let go, his girlfriend, or rather fiancée, decided that she couldn't be with a tainted man, and she left him without a second thought."

Sharon had heard enough—more than that.

"You've got no right to discuss another person's personal business with me. At least not when it doesn't pertain to the ongoing investigation. As I see it, the crime scene implies a connection to *your* business and not Simon's, so how about we find out if it will be worth digging deeper here?"

She was glad her voice was calm. Not that she was fooling King, and they both knew it.

"But don't you want to hear the rest of the story? You see, Simon was crushed. He thought he had a plan, that he had figured out his life. But here comes what makes this story interesting. Instead of letting this mess drag him down, he took the money he had made, invested it and was able to open his club a year later."

Sharon shook her head. "I see you're not willing to cooperate. Let's postpone this talk to tomorrow. I expect you to be at the precinct at nine o'clock sharp. It would be in your best interest to show up, too." She turned on her heel and had almost reached the door to the staircase when Helen spoke next.

"Simon might think he has feelings for you, but you're not cut out for this lifestyle and sooner or later, although I guess it will be sooner, he'll end this farce. This is his life, this is what he wants to do, who he wants to be. He won't change for you. And while this might hurt him, it won't destroy him. He's lived through worse."

Sharon didn't look back, opened the door then began to descend the stairs. Helen still wasn't finished.

"Yes, I know Rawlins, also not well and not on any deeper, personal level."

Sharon stopped, waiting to hear if more was forthcoming.

"Rawlins liked to attend my parties. He was at one around a week ago, a fact that several party guests will be able to attest to."

Helen had made her point, landed her blow and now she was willing to discuss business. Sharon closed her eyes for a second, her chest tight from holding her breath lest she release the bitter laughter stuck in her throat.

She didn't have to stay. She could leave right now, would have liked nothing better than to refuse to play this woman's games. Still, life was always about the consequences. If she left now, she would have to come back or have Helen come to the precinct.

Oh, there was also the option to go to Kelly and come clean about her relationship with Simon, his association with King, and claim bias. That would never go over well, and with the commissioner involved, Kelly would force her to finish this investigation before hanging her out to dry. Biting her lip so hard it hurt, she waited a beat before she turned around to Helen, made her way back to the top of the staircase.

"What kind of parties? And how about some names so I can verify your statement?"

King laughed, a rich, pleasant sound. "What kind of parties? Do I have to spell it out for you? Well, just think of it as casual meetings between people enjoying the same lifestyle. And names? You know better than to ask me that, and before you start with telling me you're going to ask for a warrant, I'll make you an offer. There'll be another party in two days. It starts at nine p.m. I'll have my assistant Angela send you an invitation. Feel free to stop by, and if you don't want people to run at the sight of you instead of talking, try looking less like a cop."

"How about..." she started but didn't get to finish her sentence as King's mobile rang. Taking a look, she smiled, then turned to Sharon.

"I'm sorry, but I've got to take this. I'll see you in two days then."

She looked down at her phone and pressed a button, her gaze holding Sharon's when she spoke. "Simon, how nice that you called. What can I do for you?"

Sharon's stomach turned into a knot, and although it should be her calling the shots here, she had to leave. Now. She hoped her face gave nothing away and turning again, she left for good this time.

Chapter Seven

"You didn't call me back yesterday," Jenn complained when Sharon opened her apartment door much too early in the morning. Stepping aside, she yawned. Jenn passed her by with a brown bag that smelled like it might contain pastries. Her partner made straight for the kitchen, and Sharon followed, another yawn escaping her.

Six a.m. wasn't the time of day she'd like to discuss anything, not when it had taken her until after three a.m. to fall asleep. Last night, after debating with herself whether to call Jenn or Simon or try to find Simon either at his club or his apartment, she'd just gone home to shower and fall into bed. Not that it had done her much good. She'd stared into the darkness for a long time, trying to fall asleep, to forget about King and Simon.

"Coffee?" Jenn asked, already having helped herself to a cup of the freshly brewed liquid.

"How kind of you to ask," Sharon said, sitting down on one of the stools at her kitchen counter. No matter what she wished for, Jenn wouldn't leave, and she owed her some answers.

"I'm very kind, as you should know," Jenn said, rounding the counter to take a seat beside Sharon. She put the bag between them. "Help yourself. Triple chocolate muffins."

Sharon hated her a little less when she opened the bag and got out one of the treats. She fished out a second one, placing it in front of Jenn who thanked her with a big grin.

"So, what happened? I was worried, you know," Jenn said before taking a big bite.

Sharon picked at her own muffin, taking a small bite and closing her eyes when the rich taste of chocolate hit her tastebuds. Swallowing, she pulled her coffee cup closer.

"How about a brief summary as I'm too tired to bother." She took a sip of the coffee, cursing when she burned her tongue. Turning her head to Jenn, she spoke, not caring if Jenn could hear her frustration. "Helen King is beautiful, composed and a pain in the ass. Yes, she was acquainted with Rawlins, and he attended a BDSM party at her house a few nights before his death. Of course, she didn't give me any names to verify her statement, but I can go and ask around at her next party in two days. Oh, she's also Simon's ex and thinks I better leave him the hell alone as I'm not the right woman for him."

She had gotten to Jenn with her last statement, and her friend's eyes widened.

"What the fuck?" she exclaimed, raking a hand through her hair, tousling it. It was almost reaching her shoulders now. It was a matter of time before Jenn lost patience and cut it off again.

Sharon circled the rim of her cup with a fingertip. "Yeah. What the fuck indeed. King likes playing mind games. Anyway, it would be great if you could try finding out more about her. I want to talk to Rawlins' family and his colleagues today. "

"Will do. Did she have any idea how her card ended up in Rawlins' apartment?"

Sharon shook her head. "Nope. I didn't get around to asking. There's another thing I'd like to know, too, and it's who told her about the business card in the first place."

Her friend snorted. "We both know she won't tell you. It must be somebody who knows about her parties and lifestyle. That much is for sure."

Somebody who wouldn't want to talk about their engagement in the BDSM scene. Sharon wasn't about to judge, although she wouldn't go as far as to risk compromising an investigation.

Wouldn't I?

She had slept with Simon for the first time when he was still high up on her list of suspects. She ended the train of thought before it could drag her down. While she was happy with the outcome, she wouldn't forgive herself for breaching protocol.

"Well, we might not find out who the idiot was who called her, but we should try to, at least."

Jenn touched her shoulder, waiting until Sharon met her gaze. "While I don't know this woman and have no idea what her agenda might be, I know that Simon makes you happy. He's also very much in love with you. Don't let this woman get to you."

Easier said than done. It had become clear that Helen King knew more about Simon than she did. Also, why had Simon called his ex last night, especially when he had to assume she would be there, too?

"I won't," she said, trying to smile.

Jenn shook her head. "Come on, Shar. You know the key to any good relationship, don't you?"

Trying her coffee again, Sharon found it had cooled enough for consumption. "Are you playing shrink with me now?"

"Yeah, I am. You know very well it's the way I was raised, and damn it, my parents were right with a lot of things. So, let's repeat after me—the key to every good relationship is communication."

"I know, I know."

"Good, then talk to Simon. You'll feel better for it, believe me. And now, let's enjoy these muffins. They're still warm. I also promise that when you make it back to the precinct later today, I'll have all the dirt on King."

Sharon smiled, then took another bite of her muffin. She doubted that anything about this investigation would be easy, but going crazy over it would solve nothing.

* * * *

Leaving the precinct's bathroom, Sharon wondered if she still had some Tylenol in her desk when her mobile rang. Fishing it out of her coat pocket, she answered without looking.

"Sharon Richards."

"Hey, have you been avoiding me?"

Simon, and his voice was calm in a way that told her he was trying not to let his own emotions show.

She winced, glad he couldn't see her. Yes, she had avoided him and on purpose. Knowing she should talk to him didn't change the fact she wasn't ready for whatever he had to say and never mind, it had been a busy day.

Talking to Rawlins' family had made her regret breakfast. Rawlins' mother had broken down and was then held by his father who tried to suppress his own tears. They had been informed the night before, but it all had been still so fresh. It had made her stomach churn, and that was even before she had the pleasure of asking them if they had any knowledge of her son's sexual proclivities and with whom he might have engaged in them.

They hadn't known and didn't want to understand what she was asking. She couldn't blame them. If they had never been part of the lifestyle, it would be hard to comprehend that their child had needs that were so very different from their own. All they could share was that Warren had told them he had been dating a woman named Amy for a while.

When speaking to his colleagues afterward, then the few people claiming to have been his friends, nobody had heard of any Amy. Sharon began to suspect she'd been nothing but a figment of Warren's imagination. One friend had even admitted to knowing that Rawlins had been into some kinky stuff but said he hadn't cared to know more.

From there she'd hurried right to the morgue where she attended most of the autopsy. Warren Rawlins had been a tall man, with broad shoulders and a fit body. His face, an impassive mask in death, had strong features and she tried to imagine him alive. Apart from his family, all accounts had pictured him as an unpleasant man, one who was cold on a good day and temperamental on a bad one. Looking at the washed corpse now, she saw the defensive wounds on his hands. He had tried to fight off the attack but had been helpless in the face of the murder frenzy.

Amaro—the ME—concluded that Rawlins had died from a stab to the heart. It was one of eighteen and the others had been of varying depth and intensity.

"Look at this wound," Amaro said, pointing at one near the kidneys. "I think it's safe to say it was a knife with a serrated edge." He gave her a small smile, and she was glad it was him who was doing the autopsy. They had worked on some cases together, and in contrast to others, he'd never minded that she was a woman. Times were changing but sometimes not fast enough for her liking.

"Maybe a kitchen knife?" she suggested.

"Could be, yes."

If it was, it would point to a crime that hadn't been premeditated but a spur-of-the-moment decision. It was said that everybody was capable of murder, yet how did one build up such a rage that it made them kill another human being in such a brutal fashion?

Finding out if Rawlins had been intoxicated at the time of his murder would become clear once they had the tox screen, which could take a while. Amaro estimated it would take the lab at least a week or two until they could expect results. Sharon didn't think it would matter in this case, although who knew?

"Sharon?" Simon asked when she'd been silent for too long and she snapped out of it again.

"No. Yes. Maybe." She answered Simon's question about if she was avoiding him, rolling her eyes at herself.

Having reached her office, she was glad Jenn wasn't in, and she sat down. Opening her desk drawer, she was even more happy when she found there were still two Tylenols left.

"Yes, I might've been avoiding you," she tried again, "but it's not as if I had any time to talk. This case is a mess, and your involvement doesn't make it any easier."

"What are you talking about? I'm not involved in any of this."

She raised her eyebrow at the hint of anger so subtle that she wouldn't have detected it if she didn't know him that well. "I'm sorry. Listen, I still have to deal with some paperwork here and talk to Jenn. How about I stop by later and then we talk?"

"I would appreciate it."

Damn, she hated it when he was so formal. It hadn't been like this between them for months, and even then, he'd never been cold with her.

"I'm not sure when I'll be able to leave here, but how about I give you a call once I do, and then I'll either stop by the club or your apartment?"

"Do that. And, Sharon?"

"Yes?"

"I'd like if you stay the night in either case."

His words, and more so his voice, gentler now, made her blink twice at the sudden onslaught of tears borne out of utter exhaustion. She couldn't explain it, yet his simple request had given her hope things would be okay. He wouldn't have suggested she spend the night if he didn't think they were good or would be.

"I'd like that, too."

"Good. Then we'll talk later."

He ended the call, and putting the phone away, Sharon got the two pills and swallowed them with the half cup of coffee she found on Jenn's desk. It tasted as vile as it looked, and she shuddered.

She was almost done with the paperwork when Jenn arrived about an hour later, looking as beat as she felt.

"I could sleep for a year," her partner said, more falling than sitting down on her chair, not trying to hide a yawn.

"Then go home and do it?" Sharon said, opening her desk drawer to get out a bar of chocolate for Jenn, which her friend accepted with a big but tired grin.

"Not a chance in hell. We're going to meet with Brian's parents later today. And they don't like me on a good day."

"Then there's something wrong with them. You know, and it's just a guess, but I think they have to get used to the fact that you're different from the women Brian used to date."

Jenn rolled her eyes. "What? I don't look like a meek kitten, just waiting to obey my Master's commands?"

Sharon made a face, and Jenn's eyes got big, although then she laughed.

"Sorry."

Sharon snorted. "Well, I hope I don't look like a meek kitten to you either."

Biting into the bar of chocolate, Jenn shook her head. "Nah, nothing meek about you. That said, I did my due diligence, and guess who is not a meek kitten either?"

"Helen King?"

"Jackpot. So anyway, do you want the long or the brief version?"

She didn't want either. Not that refusing to deal with King would make the woman go away or help her close this investigation any faster.

"Brief, please."

"Good. For starters, King turned forty-seven three weeks ago, which makes her a few years older than Simon. Seems he's diverse when it comes to his taste in women."

Just as Sharon had thought. Interesting. Where had these two met? How old had the other women he had used to date been? She was a few years younger than Simon herself. *Am I nothing more than an exception?* Although what did she know about him anyway? Well, this was not the time for self-pity, and if she wanted to know more about him and his past, she'd have to ask. She didn't think he would refuse to answer either.

She focused back on Jenn who had taken a bite of chocolate but was continuing now.

"King's from Rhode Island and her parents were filthy rich, like owning property on Martha's Vineyard filthy rich. After school, she studied architecture and worked for some firm whose name I already forgot for a few years. Then she quit, and it looks like she hasn't held any regular job in the last fifteen years. Although when you look at her tax reports, they state she's a party planner. We might want to look into party planning, too. Believe me, you and I don't make half as much with our income combined."

Having finished with the chocolate bar, Jenn threw the wrapper into the bin, pumping her fist when she hit it. She looked up at Sharon again.

"So much for the official part. Now on to the juicy bits."

Sharon leaned back in her seat, tried to smile. "I can't wait."

Jenn snorted. "Yeah, sure. Anyway, I had to call around quite a bit and a friend of a friend has heard that... Well, you know how this works. Word on the street is that King hosts parties for the rich who have specialized tastes."

Jenn grinned and continued in a sing-song voice. "You want to swing, you want to find somebody to hurt you good, or, and here is how Rawlins comes into play, you want somebody to lead you around on a leash like you would a furry friend? Well, if that hits your taste and you can afford the entrance fee, then King is a good bet."

Sharon was sure Jenn had hit the nail on its head when it came to Rawlins, that he had liked to be humiliated in public. Not her taste, and she would never stand for it, but to each their own. Rawlins seemed to have been extreme everything, an abrasive person in his regular life and a complete submissive in his private time.

"That all said, something arrived for you in the mail," Jenn said and opened her desk drawer, getting out an expensive-looking off-white envelope. "It's from King."

She handed the envelope to Sharon, who studied the handwriting as if it would give her a better clue as to who this woman was. Feeling Jenn's eyes on her, she opened it, not caring she was tearing the thick paper.

Inside she found a handwritten note and an invitation card with her name, King's address and a starting time of nine p.m. printed on it.

Putting the invitation card to the side, she read the note.

Sharon,

I'm not sure if Simon taught you the proper etiquette, but I'd like to inform you about our house rules.

Please be on time. Nobody will be let in after half-past-nine.

Make sure to wear proper attire at the party but to arrive in street clothes. Rest assured there's plenty of space to change on the premises.

Please don't talk to people involved in a scene.

Please don't take any pictures.

I'm aware of the importance of your investigation, but I have to ask you to be discreet when talking to people.

Last but not least, if you want to, feel free to bring Simon and join in.

Sharon huffed out a laugh and was hard pressed not to crumple the piece of paper in her hands.

"I guess she didn't send you the name of the perp with detailed information about where to find him and enough evidence for a conviction?" Jenn remarked with an edge to her voice.

Sharon looked up, finding the cop and not her friend looking back at her.

"She didn't. It's an invitation to her party and a set of rules for the same." Sharon sighed. "You can't tell me that she's not able to give me the names of people who knew Rawlins better or who he liked to engage with. If she wanted me to run a discreet investigation, she wouldn't want me anywhere near her party. She won't gain anything by dragging out the investigation. It's all just a bloody game to her. I wish she'd state the rules for this one."

"I agree, but let's not forget that while it's not impossible that King offed Rawlins, it still doesn't make sense. If she didn't, it's in her best interest for you to close this case ASAP. Yes, she seems to have a personal agenda, but she wouldn't have made the commissioner ask for you if she didn't think you could get her ass out of this too tight sling."

Jenn was right, and it was something Sharon hadn't considered yet. "Well, King must not have heard about the old saying. Don't bite the hand that feeds you?"

A slow smile appeared on Jenn's face. "That isn't quite the right metaphor here, is it? She's a Dominant, so biting might be right up her alley."

Sharon groaned. "You know what, I give up."

"Good, then let's see that we get out of here. I'm sure you've got somewhere better to be."

She had, even if she wasn't looking forward to it.

Chapter Eight

It was a bit after nine p.m. when Sharon arrived at the club. She ignored the look of a man in his twenties who was wearing all black and entered the premises ahead of her.

Greeting security, she all but ran into Simon who must have been on his way to meet with her outside.

"That was quick," he said, his smile not reaching his eyes. "Come, let's go to my office." He turned and didn't look to see if she was following him.

Most of the times she came here, he'd touch her, his hand resting on her arm, or sometimes it was an arm slung around her waist. Tonight, he was keeping his distance.

He, too, was on edge.

"Damn, what the hell is this all about? This case. Helen King. Us," she asked as soon as she had closed the door to his office.

She was glad he hadn't taken refuge behind his desk and was just leaning against its front. Tired, she moved his visitor chair so it faced him and took the free seat, looking up at him.

He crossed his arms over his chest. "I've got no idea. I also don't know why you avoided me all day and are now looking at me as if I committed that murder myself."

"I don't think anything like that," Sharon said, hating how defensive she sounded.

"Well, we already established that you were kinda evading me, so I guess I should be glad you're not thinking I'm a suspect in the murder of a man I've never met."

Sharon shook her head. "I'm too tired to play any games with you, Simon. Maybe it was a mistake to come here, and we should talk another time."

They kept their gazes locked. There was a storm of emotions brewing under the surface of his calm exterior.

It was a long moment until he spoke. "While that is up to you, it won't make either of us sleep any better tonight."

It wouldn't, and she almost smiled at the hint that this was affecting him as much as it did her. While he was never that expressive when it came to his feelings, he never denied them either. It shouldn't be so hard to trust him then, should it?

"You're right." She swallowed a sigh and got up, taking two steps until she stood right in front of him. "And I think you asked me to stay the night. So, let's talk, but not here. I would very much like to go home."

His expression softened, and he uncrossed his arms, slung them around her waist.

"Deal. Home?"

She gave him a fatigued smile. "I guess I got used to your apartment. It's all about the view, and your mattress beats mine every day."

He chuckled, shook his head. "It's good to be appreciated."

She got on her toes, brushing his lips with hers. "You are. More than you might think."

"Good. Just let me call a cab, shut down the computer and inform security, then we can leave."

She stepped back. "Take your time. But…I have questions, and I do need some answers."

He gave her the barest of nods. "Helen?"

"Yes." There was nothing else to say.

"Then we'll talk. At home."

They shared a tiny smile, and she sat while he got busy with wrapping up business for the night.

When they left the club, there were dim cries in the background, and if she hadn't been so exhausted and didn't feel the need to talk to Simon, staying would have been the right thing to ground her.

She hoped there'd be a chance to unwind soon, and if that made her a deviant in the opinion of most of the people in this city, so be it. At least she knew herself.

* * * *

Stepping out of her shoes as soon as she was in the apartment, Sharon hung up her coat and made her way straight to the living room where she sat cross-legged on the couch, releasing a deep breath.

Simon followed her a minute later, stopping behind the couch and putting his hands on her shoulders.

"How about a drink?"

She leaned her head back to look up at him. "I shouldn't. It's going to be a long day tomorrow."

He snorted. "Was that a yes?"

"It was, and make it a strong one."

"I will."

He left for the kitchen, and she turned back to the city, wondering if she'd ever stop feeling small at the sight of it. She wasn't special, just one of millions, her problems insignificant in the grand scheme of things.

She understood why he had placed his couch right in front of the big windows, why he didn't have a TV in here. This was a place to find one's inner quiet, to put one's thoughts into perspective.

She startled when he stood beside her all of sudden, holding a round glass with what she was sure was whiskey.

"Thanks." She took the glass from him. "God, I hate this stuff." Without thinking twice about it, she drained the whole glass, putting it on the couch table while she shook herself, making a face at the burning sensation in her throat.

Simon sat beside her, holding a glass of his own, but he put it beside hers for the moment. He looked far too amused, and she hit his arm.

"We can't all be hardened alcoholics, you know?"

"Yeah, I know."

She faced him, and from the look on his face, she gathered that the time to talk had come.

"So, Helen King," she began, not quite sure how to continue.

"Yes. What do you want to know?"

Everything. Nothing. Sensing her unease, he took both of her hands in his, stroking the back of hers with his thumbs.

"Just ask, Sharon. The answers can't be worse than what you're making up in your mind."

She allowed herself a moment to look at him, a man who had come to mean so much to her but who was still more of an enigma than she'd counted on.

"She's your ex-lover?"

He nodded once. "Yes."

She bit her lip. If she wanted to know, she had to ask. It wasn't that hard, was it? "Okay, where did you get to know her? How long were you together? And two dominants, how can that work?"

A smile played around his lips. "So you want me to tell you everything."

"It's not funny, Simon."

He sobered. "I know. So let's start with your first question. I got to know her when I moved to the city and was looking for an apartment. The realtor I chose is a good friend of Helen's. It happened that Helen was in her friend's office, waiting for her to finish up for the day when I had a late meeting there one afternoon."

And then what? Who had made the first move? The alcohol she'd consumed left her with a warm feeling in her stomach and she would be muddle-headed before long. That was what she got for skipping lunch. Once they were done talking, she should see that she got something to eat.

Simon was watching her, as if trying to gauge her mood.

"So how long?"

He made a face. "We were together for maybe two or three months but remained friends since then. We were never a good match."

"Because you two are dominants? Did she introduce you to sadomasochism or was that something you had enjoyed before? And how did you find out that both of you liked the same things?" The questions tumbled out of her, and she hated to show her blatant curiosity. She didn't want to pry, but she'd gotten dragged into a mess that wasn't hers, and she wanted to know why.

Taking a sip of his own drink, Simon held out the glass to her and despite her better judgment, she accepted the offer, then took a big gulp. She'd regret this so much. When she handed it back to him, he emptied it before putting it back on the table.

He held out his arms. "Why don't you let me hold you, and I tell you what I think you want to know, and if you still have questions afterwards, I'll answer them, too?"

She shook her head. "I don't need to be coddled."

He huffed out a laugh. "Oh, I believe you, but maybe in turn you'll believe that it's me who'd like to hold you close."

She didn't even have to think about it. "I do believe you."

This was not an interrogation, but it must feel like one to Simon. She wouldn't like it either if her past came under scrutiny because of a murder investigation.

Giving him a small smile, she turned her back to him and snuggled into his embrace as his arms came around her waist. Her head was cushioned by his chest and he rested his head on top of hers. He began to speak without further prompting.

"You met Helen. She's very enigmatic, and she already was when I met her. I told you, I like fascinating women, and back then, yes, she fascinated me."

She remembered asking him why he was pursuing her, that he had said he found her fascinating, that it was what drew him toward specific women.

"You asked her out?"

He chuckled. "Didn't we agree that I'll do the talking for the moment?"

"Yeah, yeah. And let me guess, if I talk again, I'll earn myself a spanking."

"I feel like it, yes," he said and goosebumps appeared on her arms.

This was a stressful situation for the two of them, and a scene would help them both to release some of it.

"How about soon but not today? I'm exhausted and halfway drunk right now."

"I know." He began rubbing concentric circles on her stomach, and in any other situation, she'd have closed her eyes and sunk into oblivion.

"To come back to the story, though," he continued, "no, I didn't ask her out. I concluded my meeting with the realtor, and when I left, Helen was still waiting outside. She welcomed me to the city, invited me for a coffee at her place."

He stopped, linking his fingers with hers.

"We started an affair almost at once, and there wasn't as big a reveal as you might think. It's not hard to spot the dominance in Helen, and her assortment of toys didn't leave much to the imagination either. But you're mistaken about her in one regard, and that's the reason we even lasted as long as we did."

"Which regard?"

"Helen's a switch and not a Dominant."

Sharon sat up and turned. It made her dizzy.

Simon steadied her and smiled. "Careful."

"So she likes to submit as much as she likes to dominate?" she asked, shaking her head. She couldn't see it.

"She does, although if push comes to shove, she prefers dominance."

He held up his hand when she wanted to speak. "Please let me finish. Helen and I never swore each other undying love, and while I can just speak for myself, I don't think she ever harbored any idea of us entering a permanent relationship. One day she began seeing somebody else and that was that. But she helped me build my life here. She was the one who pointed me to the property that became the club, and she recommended it to people attending her parties."

She couldn't remain silent for longer. "So okay, you were lovers, are friends and kinda business associates now. I get it. But why is she going after my jugular here? Why did she try to prove to me that she knows more about you than I do, and that I'm not the right person for you? And why the hell did you call her while I was with her last night?"

He tensed. "I didn't call her last night. I only spoke with her this morning. What gives you the idea that I did?"

When she told him about Helen picking up a call and addressing the caller by his name, he growled.

"Yes, she's my friend, but don't fall for her tricks. She's great at playing games. And I've got no idea what kind of problem she has with you. I swear I don't. "

"Did you talk to her about us? Before, I mean."

"Yes, I did. She knows me well, and she lent me an ear during your investigation. I told her about the interesting cop I met, how little I liked being a suspect. I didn't tell her any bloody details of our times together, though."

Sharon released a breath, hoping she could keep a lid on her temper. "She didn't need to know about me."

"You've never talked to Jenn about us?"

He had a point, yet it didn't sit right with her. "I did. But not back then. She guessed that I was conflicted, and I confirmed there was something to her prodding when I had decided I wanted to see where this could lead us."

Unable to sit still any longer, she got up and swayed. "Whoa. Damn. I know there are reasons I hardly ever drink."

Simon rose as well, then offered her a hand. "Come, let's get some food inside you. Then a shower and bed?"

She followed him to the kitchen, where she took a seat at his kitchen counter.

"How about scrambled eggs?" he suggested.

She smiled. "Sounds great. Thanks."

Neither was adept at cooking, just enough to manage a few simple dishes, but it was enough to keep them fed if needed. He opened the fridge, getting out eggs and a few vegetables before finding the pan in the dishwasher. Hoping she wouldn't feel woozy again, Sharon got up and made her way over to the almost overflowing machine.

"Don't. I'll do it later," Simon said.

"It's my turn anyway, and if I empty it now, we can use it later instead of playing Jenga in the sink."

"Thanks."

She took out a few plates, then stopped, looking at Simon, who had started melting some butter in the pan.

"You know that we're both atrocious housekeepers, don't you?"

He threw her a brief, amused look. "Yeah, but so far it's never bothered me."

They shared a small smile, and a few minutes later, the dishwasher was empty. They sat down with scrambled eggs and bread. When they were done eating, Sharon let out a content sigh.

"That was good, so good. Thanks. I needed it. And I'm sorry. It's not your fault that your ex is causing drama right now. She makes me uneasy, and I can't figure out her plan."

Simon turned around to her. "I wish I knew what her game is. That is why I called her this morning. I asked her why she wanted you to run this investigation, but she claimed it was because you did so well with the one in my club. I don't believe her, but I will find out what she wants."

"Don't. Let this be my problem. I can handle myself. I'm sure I'll know more after I attended her party on Friday."

Simon shook his head. "You gotta be kidding me."

Chapter Nine

Taken aback, Sharon raised an eyebrow. "Pardon me?"

"You're not going to attend one of Helen's parties," Simon said. His voice was colder than it had been in ages, if ever.

"Says who?"

"Says I. You're not ready for this, and I'm not sure this will ever be your cup of tea."

Biting her lip, she couldn't believe how fast things had taken a turn south. When she spoke, her anger was showing, and she couldn't care less.

"First of all, she invited me so I could get to talk to people who knew the deceased. Second, I'm old enough to decide where to go and third, you don't get to decide what I do. Who do you think you are?"

Simon stood stock still, yet there was no way to mistake his ire. "I think I'm your partner, and I've been at those parties, and you haven't."

"You think I was born yesterday and grew up in a cave in the woods? I might not have been at one of those parties yet, but I know very well that people with sadomasochistic tendencies meet there to live out their fantasies."

Looking at her for a long moment, Simon passed by her, making his way to the living room. He came to a stop in front of his windows. Following him, she caught his reflection in the windowpane, then held his gaze.

"There are a lot of things we don't engage in, things that neither you nor I are interested in. You will find them there. Breath play, ball gags and at one of those parties I passed a scene of people engaging in blood play. While there are things that Helen would never allow, even the rest of them can become overwhelming. And you can be sure that this is what she wants."

"Damn, give me a little credit here."

"I do. I know you're a capable cop."

"Then let me do my job. The faster I nail whoever did this, the faster we can leave it behind us."

She took a few steps toward him, then stopped when about two feet were separating them.

"I'm a murder cop, Simon. I've had to look at dead people mutilated in ways where I've almost lost my lunch. This won't bother me."

He faced her, shaking his head. "You're wrong. And if you go, I'll accompany you."

Sharon laughed at the incredulity of the situation. Oh, King might have suggested that Simon could come with her, but she never had any intention of taking her up on it. She still hadn't.

"You won't. This is my business, not yours. I don't interfere with your work, and you won't with mine.

Now, will you fight me or trust me and stop this bullshit alpha male display?"

For a tense moment, she wasn't sure what he'd do next. He looked as if he wanted to shake her, although he didn't move a muscle. He was fire and ice. Both would burn if she came too close. The muscles of his jaw clenched and unclenched, and he took a loud breath.

"I won't fight you. But I think you're making a mistake."

"So noted. So would you rather have me leave now?"

"No. Never." He spoke with utter conviction, his gaze softening. "I might hate this, but I don't have any right to tell you how to do your job. I'll ask you to reconsider letting me accompany you, though."

"I won't."

He sighed. "Yes, I know. So how about a shower and bed for good now?"

She was still annoyed and knew this wasn't over, yet she didn't want to argue any longer, didn't have the strength for it. "Will you keep me company in the shower?"

She had surprised him, though he rebounded within a second. "I'd like that, yes."

Bridging the last of the distance, she took his hand, beginning to drag him after her. "Please, don't let her win. I will find out what is behind all this. On my own."

"Just promise me to ask for help when you think you need it. I know this world, and I know Helen."

"I will. Promise."

* * * *

Sharon woke up to voices coming from the living room, and stretching, she wondered who it could be before she sat up with a start. One of the voices belonged to Simon, and the other was female. She wasn't sure, but could it be King?

Getting out of bed, she made a face at realizing she had worn Simon's shirt to bed and nothing else. It would have to do for now. If she took the time to get dressed first, the visitor might be gone, and she wanted to see who it was. The last thing she wanted to do was meeting King while wearing Simon's shirt, but if it was her, she wanted to know what had brought her here.

Walking into the living room, she found Simon in the kitchen, pouring coffee. There was a woman on his couch. It wasn't Helen and Sharon's eyebrows were climbing up her hairline. How many women were in Simon's life who she'd never met?

Simon spotted her first, then gave her a quick nod. She couldn't read the expression on his face, and he finished filling his guest's cup before addressing her.

"Sorry, I didn't mean to wake you."

The small Asian woman in her late thirties turned toward her, a smile on her face.

"I'm sorry, too. I'm Rose." She stood and walked over, holding out her hand to Sharon.

With an uneasy smile of her own, Sharon took her hand and to her surprise Rose's grip was strong, belying her petite figure and the fact she was almost a head shorter than Sharon.

"Hi, I'm Sharon, nice to meet you."

Rose let go of her hand and strolled over into the kitchen where she accepted the cup of coffee Simon handed her. Leaning with her back against the counter, she spoke again.

"Well, rumor has it that Simon's got a steady girlfriend now, and I guess you are it?"

She spoke in a quiet voice, and there was no sting to her words. Sharon relaxed, walking up to her, hoping to score her own cup of coffee.

"Yes, I am it. And sorry for the attire, but it's been a long few days."

"Here, for you," Simon interjected, holding out a cup which she accepted with thanks, glad for the warmth it provided, the enticing scent promising to wake her up for good.

"I heard about this case and that's why I'm here," Rose said.

"I don't understand," Sharon replied.

Rose smiled, holding up her hand. "Sorry, that sounded wrong. I'm a friend of Simon's. We met at one of Helen's parties, years ago, and I was one of the first clients of his club. I met my husband there. Now, my husband heard from another friend about Rawlins' murder and that the same cop investigating the murder in Simon's club is now investigating this one, too."

She took a sip of her coffee, letting out a happy sigh. "I'll never understand how some people can live on tea alone. Anyway, now it is also said that this same cop is Simon's girlfriend, and it was Helen's idea that she should be leading the investigation."

"Rumors, huh?" Sharon said, shaking her head.

"Listen, I hate gossip, and when my husband came to me with all of this yesterday, I realized it's been too long since I've spoken to Simon." She threw the man in question a fond smile, then faced Sharon again. "I'm not here to pry, and if you don't want to confirm or deny anything, then so be it. I just wanted to hear if Simon's doing okay. Nobody needs a murder in their own house, and nobody needs to be dragged into another investigation when it shouldn't concern them at all."

"I agree," Sharon said. Rose gave off a genuine vibe, helping to ease the knot of tension in Sharon's stomach. She was a friend of Simon's, simple as that. So far, she'd just gotten to know a couple of his acquaintances at his club, although she shouldn't complain. It wasn't as if she had introduced him to any of her friends apart from Jenn either.

Heck, she wasn't even sure she'd have gone that far if Jenn hadn't been around for the origins of their relationship. Maybe it was time they stepped out of the bubble of a new relationship. Her mother's wedding had been a beginning, but even there she could and should have done better.

Sharon snapped back from her musings, smiling. "Sorry. And yes, I can't say anything about the investigation."

"Didn't expect you to." Rose turned to Simon. "Now, care to tell me what's up with Helen? Yes, she knew Rawlins, he attended her parties, but a lot of people did. That's no reason for her to show any interest in the case apart from feeling bad that it happened in the first place. How did she learn about it anyway?"

That was the question, wasn't it?

Simon shrugged. "You've got to ask Helen about that. I've got no idea."

It was at least a partial lie, but Sharon was glad he hadn't told Rose about the business card they had found beside the corpse.

"Well, knowing Helen, she's got her connections. And we might learn in time why she wanted your girlfriend to be the one investigating." She looked at

Sharon, then at Simon. "I never knew Helen could pull such strings. Anyway, that said, can I expect to see the two of you at one of her parties in the future?"

Thinking of their argument last night, Sharon met Simon's gaze and he gave her a small, reassuring smile. She looked back at Rose. It was hard to imagine the delicate woman participating in any of the games Sharon thought were offered at these parties. Although Sharon didn't think she looked the part of somebody involved in BDSM subculture either.

"I'm not sure yet, Rose," Simon said.

Rose smiled. "Yeah, those parties are not for everyone, that's true. Well, anyway, enough of that. Now that I'm here, what else is new?"

Rose left over half an hour later, and when the door closed behind her, Sharon waited until Simon was back in the kitchen before addressing him.

"I like her."

"It's hard not to like her." He poured himself some more coffee, then offered the rest to Sharon who held out her cup to him. "We hit it off right from the start. She's the least judging person I know, always open and honest, and she cares."

She could hear he cared, too. Having lost her interest in her coffee, she put the mug on the counter, linking her fingers, meeting Simon's gaze.

"How long have we been dating now?"

He raised an eyebrow and put his hands on hers. "As in dating versus having a...*fling*? Around four months, as you well know. Why?"

"Because on days like today, or like the last two days, I wonder what I know about you. I had no idea about Helen, didn't even know Rose existed although she seems to be a good friend to you."

He stroked her hands. "Let's be honest, I've never even thought about you meeting Helen, and well, I've never had a doubt that Rose and you would meet. We should have dinner with her and her husband Marcus someday. You'll like him very much. Then there are also Gina and Carolyn. They have been a couple since college, which is where I got to meet them. We manage to see each other about thrice a year, but again, I think you'll like them. Apart from them, it's acquaintances as I like to keep myself busy."

Sharon sighed. "Thanks. Now I feel like an ass who doubted her boyfriend." Why was it that things always were so much bigger in her own head, that she was seeing problems where there were none?

He chuckled. "You're not. And please correct me if I'm wrong, but I think neither of us have the best track record when it comes to relationships. I like that we're moving at a pace that is comfortable for the both of us."

He brushed a strand of hair behind her ear, snorting when it fell right back into her face. He cupped her cheek.

"Is there anything else you'd like to know, anything you'd like to ask?"

Her eyes had fallen closed at his soft touch, and she opened them with a good bit of reluctance.

"There is, yes. Why is it always me with the questions and you with the answers?"

The barest of smiles flickered over his face. "Because I like to think ahead, plan ahead. In all areas of my life. And while you're meticulous in your job, you're not trying to anticipate every move in your private life."

He would always answer every rhetorical question, and she loved this about him.

"You've got a point, or a few of them. Anything you would like to know about me?"

He shook his head, and his expression became impassive almost from one moment to the next while she felt the tension in his hand still cupping her.

"When do you have to be at work?" he asked, and she took a quick look at her watch. It was just past seven.

"An hour ago with a case like this, but nobody will care that much if I make it in an hour or two. Why?"

"Then instead of asking you questions, I'd rather have you do something for me," he said, stepping back, watching her.

Right this moment, he was nothing more than a predator that had chosen his prey. The shiver running down her back was not unwelcome.

"What would that be?"

"I want you to get up, make your way to the middle of the living room and face the windows. Then I want you to undress and stay still."

She hesitated for a few seconds, then without a further word, she got up and took the few steps that would put her right in the center of the big room. Lifting his shirt, she shrugged out of it. What were the chances that somebody could see her like this, naked, facing the outside? While it wasn't outside the realm of possibility, she didn't think anybody could. Still, it made her somewhat uncomfortable which he would know and count on.

Thanks to the sun shining in, she couldn't see his reflection. She startled when his hands covered her shoulders, and she enjoyed the warmth of his hands on her skin.

"I think I'd like to spank you and here's the rules. If you don't move and don't speak, I'll make you come, maybe even more than once, but if you fail, you'll have to make me come and will have to spend the rest of the day very horny."

Although she had learned the value of being able to be as vocal as she liked, it would be possible to stay silent. Managing to stand still, though, was quite a different matter.

"So do you want to play? Consider it well."

She took a deep breath, debating the wisdom of giving in. Everything inside her told her to do it, but her endurance would be tested.

"Yes, I want to play, Master."

He squeezed her shoulders. It wasn't the first time he had displayed such a reaction when she addressed him this way. She liked that she could get to him this way. He might be in almost perfect control of himself, but she knew his ticks.

"Good."

He took a step back, smacking her ass with the flat of his hand. She hadn't expected this move so soon. Her breath caught, and she almost cursed as her pain receptors screamed in protest. Not giving her the time to absorb the sensation, he hit the other side as well, alternating sides at random intervals. It hurt, but each sting left a delicious warmth behind, and she got wetter with each passing second.

It soon became maddening not to be able to speak, to moan, and she bit down on her bottom lip, trying to focus on the outside world, the city that was as beautiful as it was mysterious.

Simon stopped and palmed her breasts instead, brushing her nipples which were hard and begging for attention.

"You should see your ass. It's all red now. Beautiful."

While his voice was quiet, almost dispassionate, he spoke the truth. She loved when he talked to her, described what he was seeing, what he was thinking, what he wanted to do with her.

He leaned down, biting the tender tendon of her neck, and she almost hissed.

"There are so many things I'd like to do to you now. Too bad we're on a time limit. When this all is over, let's take a few days off, just the two of us, no obligations."

Even through the haze of pain and lust, she loved the idea. It meant they'd have time to explore and get to know each other without life interrupting at the worst moment. It also made it clear he believed in their future, that they would come out on the other side of this mess all right.

He didn't give her further time for contemplation as he spread his fingers, and he explored her breasts, now and then gliding over her nipples, tantalizing and arousing, offering no relief.

Torn between wanting to spread her legs farther and clenching them together, she took in a sharp breath. There was no way she could win this game.

"Don't give up, Sharon. You can do it," Simon said, his remark as much encouragement as it was a command.

That was an easy thing for him to say. It wasn't him that—

Simon moved his hand lower, over her stomach, her body shuddering in response. He didn't linger and, covering her mound, then pulling his hand away, he smacked the soft skin of her thighs next.

Having expected pleasure but received pain, she came close to crying out, but swallowed the vocal complaint at the last second.

In desperation, she began counting the blows, but her mind trailed off while her body fought the conflicting sensations. She had to repress the sudden urge to laugh at realizing her biggest problem right this second was to be as still as possible lest Simon deny her release. Work, their relationship…it was all unimportant now.

Stopping the spanking without forewarning, Simon moved his hand to rest on her sex while he rolled her nipple with the thumb and forefinger of the other one in a way that made her ache and long for more at the same time.

Pinching the tender flesh, he stopped all motion just long enough for her to wonder what would be next before sliding his hand between her legs, his fingers spreading her labia while the palm of his hand rubbed against her clit.

The surge of bliss was so abrupt, she swayed, causing the man behind her to chuckle.

Damn this perfect jerk.

"Be careful, love or this will be over before you know it."

Without pause, the sweet dual torture of her breast combined with Simon sliding two fingers inside of her sex continued while the pad of his thumb rubbed her pleasure point in small concentric circles.

It was too much. So wonderful, but too much. Her heart had begun beating way too fast and she was panting, as droplets of sweat formed on her back, began sliding down.

He might have said they were on a time limit, yet he didn't behave that way. She envied his patience. It didn't take long for her legs to want to give out. Her whole body began to tremble.

He didn't stop, just slowed down a little more, his touches not more than feather light now. She bit her bottom lip again.

Hadn't he promised she'd get to come if she stayed still? She was, so why was he toying with her, testing her? Because that was who he was. By now she wasn't sure if it was anger or desperation making her want to lash out at him.

As he stepped closer, his belt pressed into her back. When he spoke, it was so quiet, she had to slow down her breathing so she could understand him.

"I sometimes dream of this, of taking you to one of those parties, so that all the world can see how beautiful you are. They would be allowed to watch, but never touch because you belong to me."

Without forewarning, he fucked her faster, rubbed her harder, and together with the picture he'd painted in her mind, she was close to orgasm within seconds. With a shock, she remembered he'd never said if she should come or not. Would he punish her if…

"Now, Sharon."

With a loud moan that couldn't be held in any longer, waves of delirious satisfaction washed over her, making her knees tremble. He didn't stop his caresses, didn't slow down, just prolonged the sensations until she was spent.

She would have collapsed into a heap if he hadn't one arm slung around her waist, holding her upright. As he pulled out of her, his other hand came to rest on her stomach, his fingers warm and wet.

"Fuck," she murmured, laughing the next moment.

"Later, love," Simon commented with a chuckle, helping her turn around so he could kiss her. "I think you should take a shower now and head into work."

She had her eyes closed, her head nestled against his shoulder blade. "Party pooper."

"Yeah, but you wouldn't be happy if you were too late for work. And you would blame me."

"I would be right to blame you."

She could feel his chest moving as he laughed. "Yes, you would."

He was stroking her back and, slinging her own arms around him, she wished they could stay like this for a while longer.

"And Sharon?" he asked, serious now.

"Yeah?" She wanted to pull away, but he held her close.

"I just want you to know that while I might have dreamed of showing everybody my beautiful girlfriend, I would never do it if you didn't want that yourself. Also, I don't think I'm ready for other men and women eyeing you with desire."

Amused, she tried freeing herself again, and this time he let her, his arms wrapped around her now.

"So you're the possessive kind of man, huh?"

He smirked. "Just in this regard, I assure you."

It was her turn to sober up. "Thank you. This means a lot." It did. She could be herself with him because he gave her a choice each and every time. He made her feel secure. "Oh, there's something else, by the way," she said with a smile. "What is it?"

Reaching out, she covered his visible erection with her hand. "I would very much like to take care of that tonight."

A playful smile graced his face. "I'm not sure it will last this long."

"I think I'll manage to get your interest up, no worries."

Chapter Ten

Entering her office half an hour later than she'd have liked, Sharon found Jenn was already in, staring into her computer, frowning.

"Morning," the blonde said without looking up.

"Morning." Shrugging out of her coat, Sharon sat down, glad that Jenn wasn't looking as she winced after her recent spanking. "How was time with the pastors?" she asked. While it was just Brian and his father who shared the profession, the nickname had stuck early. She reached for her cup, just to put it down again as she had had more than enough coffee for the time being. Work would be even less fun if she were jittery.

"Don't ask," her partner said, still not looking, although she typed with even more vigor now.

"Come on, spill it."

"Don't want to." Jenn refused to look at her but Sharon could see the tightness in her friend's jaw.

"Jenn, please. I'm starting to worry here."

With a small growl, Jenn leaned back in her seat, crossing her arms over her chest. "It was fucking fantastic. The pastors want to meet the shrinks."

"Ouch."

"Yeah, God damned ouch. Isn't it enough that Brian and I are okay, that we've both met each other's parents? Do they have to get to know each other? I mean, why? It's not like we're..." Jenn rolled her eyes.

"It's not like you're getting married?" Sharon finished for her.

"Yup. I don't even want to get married. Hell, we've not been dating for long. I'm happy, isn't that enough?"

"It's more than enough."

Jenn still looked unhappy, so Sharon got up again and walked to Jenn's chair, hugging her from behind.

"It's okay that you feel this way. This is a typical case of people wanting too much too soon. You don't have to like it, and you don't have to agree to it. The only thing that matters is that you and Brian are okay. What is he saying about this anyway?"

Jenn sighed. "He noticed I was uncomfortable. And he told his parents that with our schedules, such a meeting wouldn't be possible right now, but that we could make it happen at some point."

"You've got a good one there."

"Yeah, I do. But talking about good ones. What's with yours? Got a chance to talk?"

Letting go of Jenn, Sharon walked back to her place, deciding to go for the not-needed caffeine fix anyway. Smart choices weren't hers, at least not when caffeine was involved. Sniffing the pot, she crinkled her nose and filled her cup to the brim before topping off Jenn's.

"Yes, we did. And I got to meet one of his friends this morning. But how about I line up some interviews with those of Rawlins' friends we didn't get a hold of yesterday and when we go there, I'll tell you everything?"

Jenn's eyes lit up with amusement. "Everything?"

Sharon stopped in mid-motion of reaching for her writing pad. "Okay, what's that look for?" Taking a sip of her lukewarm beverage, she regretted her life choices while she waited for Jenn to elaborate. Of course, her partner didn't do her the favor. "Geez, talk now or be silent forever."

A grin formed on Jenn's face and despite her irritation, Sharon was thankful Jenn never stayed down for long.

"Well, for one you've got a nice little hickey on your neck. It's almost tiny, but...cop here. And then the way you sat down tells me somebody must have been a very bad girl."

Sharon snorted. Why did she think something would get by one of the best cops she knew? "Believe me, I was a very good girl."

Jenn laughed. "I think we've got to work on your definition of good and bad. Anyway, let's get this shit show on the road. Can't wait to hear what you've got to tell."

"Deal."

* * * *

It took Sharon almost two hours to set everything up, and to her chagrin, Second Precinct had called as well, asking for a meeting to compare notes and learn about their progress. They wouldn't make this easy on her. If she was honest, she wouldn't have either had roles been reversed. So, they would start with a visit there.

Hannigan was already waiting for them in the bullpen, leading them to his desk, but not offering a seat.

"Now tell me, what's new in the world of the perverted and deranged?" he asked without preamble. Another detective at a nearby desk laughed.

Taken aback, Sharon's hot anger made her want to lash out, but Jenn spoke before she could.

"We've got no idea what's new over here. But seeing that you asked us here, how about you tell us what there is to tell, and we decide if we have something to share as well?"

Her voice was ice cold, and it filled Sharon with satisfaction to see Hannigan turning red with anger.

"You think you're funny?" he spat out.

"No, I don't, but you're not funny either, pal. I get it. This sucks. We didn't ask for this case either, but guess what? We've got to deal with it now. You want to get rid of us? Then talk, help us when you can, and we'll see that we're out of your hair soon."

For a moment Sharon was sure Hannigan would explode in Jenn's face, though then he huffed. "Yeah, yeah. Let's see if you'll get this case solved at all. Anyway, one of our detectives heard back from one of the neighbors they talked to yesterday when they did a first area canvass. Some old bloke—living opposite of Rawlins—remembered something after all. He said that while nothing seemed out of the ordinary yesterday, he heard yelling a few nights before. Around midnight."

"Does he know who was with Rawlins that night? Did he see who he was arguing with?" Sharon asked, and Hannigan's head whipped around to her. If he didn't like Jenn, he had to hate her.

No wonder either. It was thanks to her that the case had been taken from them. It might have been King's doing when it came down to it, but Sharon could argue her case all day long without getting anywhere.

"If you want to know if he stood in front of his peephole and waited for some real action, then the answer is no. I'd say ask Rawlins, but I heard he's not inclined to talk to anybody at the moment."

Sharon had heard enough. She nodded at Jenn.

"Let's go."

She faced Hannigan. "Let me know when you decide to stop acting like an ass, and I'll share information then." Pivoting, she smiled when Hannigan shouted after her with irritation.

She stopped in front of the elevator and Jenn pursed her lips, amused. "And here I thought I was the true badass."

"You are and always will be. I still won't let a jerk like this one walk all over me."

"You know he'll run crying to his boss next and you'll get to talk to Kelly, right?"

Sharon shrugged. "In all honesty, I don't care. What's Kelly going to do? Take the case from me? Yes, please, let him, but somehow, I doubt he'll do me the favor."

"Oh, come on, you don't want to miss out on King's party, do you?" Jenn teased.

Sharon was spared an answer as the elevator had arrived, the opening doors revealing they'd have to squeeze themselves in.

Outside, Sharon took a deep breath, burrowing her hands deeper in her coat pockets. "Now let's see if any of today's interviews will turn out to be worth it."

They weren't, and a few hours later they had learned next to nothing. The last interview was with Rawlins' cousin who had worked with Rawlins on a few projects. The young man had been on a business trip last week, and he looked more tired than shocked.

"Listen, I don't want to lie to you here. Warren wasn't a monster, but he wasn't pleasant to be around either. He was...whiny and demanding. You know, the kind of person who thought the world owed him for a reason only he knew. In turn he was always disappointed by people, as nobody got how great he was and so on."

"Sounds like a real peach, good ol' Warren," Jenn said.

"Yeah, he was. And you know, he talked about this Amy you mentioned a few times, but to be honest, I don't think she existed."

"What do you mean by that?" Sharon asked, and the young man looked from Jenn to her.

"You know, she came up when he was asked about things you'd do with a partner, like, where will you go on vacation this year, and he answered that he and Amy planned to do a city trip. Or when I asked him about a play I've seen and he said that Amy made him go, too."

"And you think she was a figment of his imagination?" Sharon had heard crazier things in the past.

"Yup, because nobody ever got to meet her. Hell, Aunt Trish asked him to bring Amy that one time and you should've seen the look on his face."

"Why would he do that, though? Would his family frown upon him being single?" Jenn asked.

The young man snorted. "Nope, but they would've frowned upon him being gay."

Jenn whistled under her breath. "You think or you know he was gay?"

His lips curled into a smile. "Oh, I know nothing, and he would've never said a thing but my gaydar just knew, and mine is a good one, seeing that I'm as gay as the day is long. Anyway, if that is all, I need to get going. I have an appointment in half an hour."

"Sure, and thanks," Jenn said.

"Call us, if you…" Sharon began but was interrupted by Rawlins' cousin.

"Can think of anything else. Got it. And for whatever it's worth, I hope you'll find the bastard that killed him."

Sharon waited until he was out of sight before she addressed Jenn. "How come we spoke to about ten people today and nobody said the least thing about him being gay?"

"Because people like to see what they want to see."

"Geez, you're starting to sound like Simon," Sharon said, but with a smile, linking her arm with Jenn's.

"He's a smart one, just like me."

"Of course, you are. So anyway, if the cousin's right, we have to dig a lot deeper."

"Yup. And when you're at that party, make sure to ask if anybody has seen him with a guy."

"Will do."

They parted at the subway, with Jenn heading back to the precinct to tackle another case that she had delegated, thanks to it being all but closed. By now she was just waiting for DNA results to confirm what she knew to be true anyway, and she wanted to deal with the paperwork.

Sharon, in turn, would deal with the pleasant task of speaking to Rawlins' parents once more, asking if they had had any inkling their son could be gay.

She had just left the train station when her phone rang, and some passerby ran into her. Glaring at the oblivious woman with the headphones, who didn't even look up from her phone, she fumbled around for her own, grimacing when she read the caller's name.

"Mom, what's up?"

Her mother laughed. "Hi, darling. I'm doing good, thanks for asking, and may I ask how you are doing?"

Cursing herself for having been too harsh, she stepped to the side so she wouldn't be in the way of the throng of people having to be somewhere and tourists busy taking selfies or gazing up at the skyline.

With a wry smile, Sharon remembered her first trip to the city. It had been such a stark contrast to rural Vermont, she'd been sure she'd arrived in heaven. It hadn't taken long for heaven to turn out to be loud and obnoxious. Well, she loved it anyway, most days.

"I'm sorry, Mom. Somebody bumped into me. So how are you, and why are you calling me from your honeymoon?"

Her mother laughed again, the sound joyous and relaxed. Good. She deserved all the best in the world.

"My dearest daughter, I'm not twenty any longer, and come to think about it, neither are you. Although seeing that you're in love with a very attractive male specimen, you might still have more stamina than I do."

"Mom, please." She would never understand what it was with parents that made a grown-up feel like a teenager under their supervision years after they had moved out.

"What? I'm right, am I not? But anyway, I wanted to take the time to thank you again that Simon and you could make it to the wedding. Everybody was impressed with him, if I may say so. I heard everything from the aforementioned attractive, to good manners and charming, with two people calling him quiet and brooding."

Wrapping a lock of hair around her fingers, Sharon was glad her mother couldn't see her face right now. She was relieved people had mostly positive things to say about Simon. Still, she'd rather not discuss him at all.

"That's good to hear," she replied.

"And see, this is why I called in the first place," her mother said, her voice turning serious. "What's the matter, Sharon? I understood that you were tense the first time I met Simon. You two had just begun dating and you had no plans of him meeting your mother that day, but you still looked unhappy during my wedding."

Pulling at the strand of hair, she looked up at the sky that promised rain later today, wishing there was any way she could redirect her mom's attention. She knew better than to try.

"I'm not unhappy. I'm not," she said, speaking with what she hoped was enough conviction to make her mother believe her.

"You didn't look unhappy when you were dancing, that's for sure. You two seemed lost in your own world that moment. I hadn't seen you smile the way you smiled at him in quite a while. But every time somebody talked to Simon you looked as if you wanted them to stop."

Her mother would've made a good cop, too, although maybe it was just something that came with motherhood.

"Mom, I'm not unhappy, please believe me."

"I want to, hon. What is the matter then? And don't tell me it's because you got to know him over a murder investigation. You told me the case was closed months ago, and I believe you. So? Is he married to somebody else? Does he have another girlfriend at the side? Or are you fake dating?"

Sharon huffed out a laugh. "No, he's not married or seeing somebody else. And fake dating?"

"When Michael began to pack the stuff Connie hadn't taken with her when she left, I grabbed one of her novels. The main character was pretending to date her best friend, so her mother would stop trying to find a boyfriend for her. The book was crap."

"Mom! And no, Simon and I aren't fake dating either, and I feel deeply for him." She exhaled, then began to move again, unable to stand still any longer. Her mother was worried, and she shouldn't be.

"You know, with my last boyfriends, well, I knew they weren't good for me, that those relationships weren't meant to last. It's different with Simon. He's a good guy, not perfect, but good, and I'm beginning to wish for this to last but I am afraid it won't."

It was a half-truth at least. Sure, there always was the danger of unforeseen things happening that might kill their relationship, but she hoped it wouldn't be the case. Still, she feared it was her own inability to deal with the secret surrounding their life that would destroy it.

"Oh, hon, I wish I could hug you right now."

Sharon released a mixture of sob and laughter, thinking she'd always be twelve when her mother was involved. "That would be nice, yeah."

"Next time we see each other, I'll just hug you twice then. Never mind, yes, there are never any guarantees in life, we both know it, but how about you allow yourself to be happy with what you have and see how far it will take you? You deserve to be happy, and from what I've seen, I'm sure Simon is thinking the same."

"I hope so. But, Mom, could you please stop worrying about me and go back to enjoying your honeymoon? You deserve to be happy, too."

"And I am. Want to hear what Henry suggested this morning?"

"Of course."

They talked for a few more minutes, and when they ended the call, Sharon had calmed down again. She had known very well she had to work on herself. If even her mom was calling her about it, though, it was worse than she had reckoned with. Putting the phone away, she buried her hands in the pockets of her coat again.

How could it be that she wasn't ashamed of what she was doing with Simon and still felt panicked at the idea of people finding out and judging? Maybe she should ask Jenn if she could speak to her parents. Jenn wouldn't stop laughing if she told her about these thoughts.

She had reached the house of Rawlins' parents and didn't allow herself to hesitate before ringing the bell. They might not want to hear what she had to say, but she wouldn't do them a favor by dragging it out either.

Chapter Eleven

Leaving the precinct late in the evening, Sharon almost did a double take when she found Simon in front of the main entrance. She walked over to him, returning his smile.

"What are you doing here?" she asked. Happy to see him, she still couldn't stop herself from looking around to see if any of her colleagues were around. They weren't but Simon had noticed, and the flicker of irritation in his gaze made her stomach clench. She touched his upper arm. "Sorry. I'm happy to see you. So again, how come?"

"I was done with paperwork for the day and didn't feel like lingering in the club, so I thought I would ask if you were interested in having dinner with me."

"I'd like that. But you could've called. How long have you been waiting anyway?"

"About two minutes. I called your office before I left the club and another time when I arrived here. I also tried your cell phone."

She winced. "Sorry, I forgot that I put it on silent earlier. Second Precinct bombarded me with calls I didn't feel like taking. And then I had to talk to Kelly, who wanted an update on the case. Anyway, this is the best surprise."

It was. His mere presence was balm to her soul, and he made her smile even when she could fall into bed.

"Rough day?" he asked.

"Worse."

"Good that it is over then."

There was something about the way he looked at her, the way his voice softened when he spoke to her, that made her want to kiss him, to be as close to him as possible. With him, she longed to forget that she wasn't one for public displays of affection. Their gazes held, and she remembered this morning how she had promised him revenge for the sweet torture he'd put her through.

Without further thought, she took her hand from his arm, letting it comb through his short hair once.

"Why do I want you so much?" she asked, her voice rougher than usual.

His eyes lit up a bit and he looked much too pleased, but she couldn't find it in herself to be annoyed with him.

"I could ask you the same." He ran a hand over her arm, and the layers of clothes separating them weren't enough to stop the shiver running down her back. Something inside her had fallen for him from the very first moment, and she hadn't come to regret it yet.

"Dinner?" he asked, still not looking away.

Would it be bad to suggest they'd go for dessert instead? Worrying her bottom lip with her teeth, she chided herself not to be ridiculous. She wasn't a teenager any longer. "Yeah. Let's go."

He offered her his arm, and taking it, she let him lead her wherever he wanted to take them. She was more than happy to leave any decision-making to him for the rest of the day. As it turned out, they walked no more than a couple of blocks before he steered them into a small Indian restaurant.

"Wanna talk about your day?" he asked after they were seated and had gotten the menus.

"To be honest, no. Let's just say that we didn't make any significant progress if you discount the fact our victim might have been gay. Although almost all of his family and friends swear he wasn't."

"It might make for a motive if he was. If he wanted to go public and his partner insisted on keeping them a secret."

"Yeah. I hope somebody at this party might know something."

Simon was silent, waiting for her to meet his gaze. "This is still not a good idea."

She gritted her teeth. "And I told you it's my decision. That hasn't changed, and it won't change."

"I know," he replied, although she could see in his eyes that he wanted to argue further. This would remain a sore spot between them for the time being, not that she could change it.

"You could help me with one thing, you know," she said.

"Which is?" It was the way he spoke that told her that he was irritated.

She had learned to read his moods. He never made a scene, but she knew him now.

"I've got no idea what to wear. Or rather, what to bring that I could change into."

His jaw clenched, and he broke eye contact, then began studying his menu. He gave up after a short moment and sighed. "How about I give you Rose's number? I could give you advice, of course, but I don't feel like arguing this any further."

She hadn't considered asking Rose. "That would be great. Thanks."

"Sure. No problem."

She opened her own menu, then closed it again the next second. "I understand that this situation is a problem for you, and yes, it feels like an elephant in the room I could do without. That said, how about we meet after the party? At the club?"

"I'm not sure that's a good idea," he replied after a long look, although he sounded more like himself again.

"Because you could still be angry? Or angry again? Do you fear your control could slip?"

He smiled. "Yes, I do."

A BDSM scene would only work when the Dominant was in absolute control, and he wouldn't be if lingering resentment were festering inside him.

She tried for levity. "Well, do you have any other idea how to solve this? Ignore it all until we both feel better about it? Or what about some angry sex against the wall afterwards?"

He snorted, then chuckled. "Sometimes you're impossible. But you're also right, so let's do it and meet at the club. If we don't feel like it after all, we'll just go home."

"Deal. And now let's get something to eat. I'm starving.

* * * *

Sharon met with Rose early the next morning after calling her from Simon's apartment the evening before. If Simon's friend was surprised about Sharon's request, she didn't let it show, and she'd suggested Sharon stop by.

Entering the second-floor apartment in Greenwich Village now, Sharon was surprised to find Rose's apartment didn't reek of luxury. It was big for two people but nothing here screamed rich.

"What's the verdict?" Rose asked while she led Sharon into her kitchen.

"Verdict?"

"The apartment. You have taken in every detail. It comes with the job, I guess. My father is a retired cop. So coffee, tea or something else?"

Sharon could kick herself, but at least she didn't think Rose was offended. It was just that she was the first person in Simon's circle who wasn't affluent. "It does, yeah. And coffee would be great."

"Good. I could do with some, too. Please have a seat." Rose fetched the water tank of her old-fashioned coffeemaker and filled it with water before getting a filter and ground coffee. "I guess Simon's not thrilled," she said after she'd started the machine and sat at the small kitchen table opposite of Sharon.

"With what?"

"That you're going to attend one of Helen's parties." Her smile was soft, and this morning she wore jeans and what looked like a handmade sweater while her hair was in a cute ponytail.

It would take a bit longer for Sharon to connect what she saw with what she had learned about this woman.

People didn't wear their proclivities on their sleeves, yet she could picture Warren Rawlins at one of those parties, but not Rose.

"He's not. But this is about my job and not my private life," she answered. Knowing she had come off too strong, she apologized.

Rose waved it aside. "Don't worry. I can imagine that navigating your job and this relationship isn't easy. If you need somebody to talk to, let me know. I was glad for the friends I made in the scene when I first began participating in parties. They made me understand and accept that I wasn't an abomination of nature but just a human being with different tastes."

"Thank you," Sharon said, hoping Rose would be able to hear that she meant it.

"I know that it's unlikely that you'll take me up on it, but believe me, the offer's genuine." Rose smiled and her eyes lit up in a way that belied the calm outer façade. "And anyway, you can thank me later. Let's have that coffee now and then take a look at my closet. I'm sure you'll need a different size than what I have, but this can give you an idea of what you'd like to bring. We can go shopping afterwards."

"Sounds good."

"Wonderful, then that's a plan. Now, please don't mind me asking, but do you own a collar and if not, are you planning on doing so?"

Sharon blinked, everything inside her tensing at the thought. She was aware that in a lot of BDSM relationships, the submissive partner wore a collar as a sign of belonging to their Master. Simon had never brought it up, and it wasn't something Sharon had considered for herself. Yes, they were engaging in BDSM practices on a regular basis but no, it didn't define their relationship. She would never assume the role of a...a full-time slave to someone calling himself her Master.

Rose had read the expression on her face and put a hand on Sharon's arm. "Please relax. It was just a question. A lot of people in the scene don't wear one. To be honest I'd have been surprised if you did, at least on a regular basis."

Sharon looked down at the tabletop, giving herself a second to compose herself before meeting Rose's gaze again. "Why?"

"Why would I be surprised? Because I've gotten to know Simon as a man who appreciates strong women. Oh, he likes them to submit in the bedroom, but I can't see him liking to spend his time with somebody catering to his every whim. It wouldn't challenge his mind." She chuckled. "I'm sure you're challenging him quite a bit."

Sharon was not holding back when she had an opinion and so far, Simon had never minded. Quite the contrary, he enjoyed riling her up a bit from time to time.

"And coffee's ready," Rose said and got up. "Do you want cream or sugar?"

"Black, please. And I'm sorry," Sharon said. "That was a valid question. No, I don't own a collar, and I won't wear one for this party. This is not a social call but my way to speak to people who knew Warren Rawlins better. I want to fit in enough not to stick out like a sore thumb, that's all."

Rose poured the first cup, handing it to Sharon before she filled one for herself, sitting down again.

"I hate to say it, but you'll be noticed. Let's be real, at the end of the day, it's often the same people at

Helen's parties. New faces are not uncommon, but they stick out. It's not that bad a thing, though. People will be curious about you, and I guess it'll give you a chance to talk to them. Just know that there will be propositions."

Sharon took up the cup, then put it down again when the heat almost scorched her hand.

"Is there anything I can do to prevent that from happening? I can handle myself but the last thing I want is to cause a scene."

Rose smiled. "You won't. There are rules at those parties and one of those is that a no is a no, and people who don't accept that will be out within the minute. Safe, sane and consensual. This is never open for debate. But you're attractive and as soon as people realize you're Simon's girlfriend, you'll be the star. There was talk about the woman who captured the elusive bachelor's heart in a way he all but vanished from the scene. They will want to see and talk to you. In her own twisted way, Helen did you a favor by inviting you."

That would remain to be seen. Sharon was sure King was all about favors—when they were done for her. And what about Simon? Had he been a regular participant at those parties? When was the last time he'd attended one? It might have been after they had met.

She could ask Rose, but she didn't think that would be fair. If she wanted to know something about Simon's life, his past, he deserved the chance to tell her herself. It didn't matter anyway whether he had still attended parties after they met. She wasn't one to talk, not after she'd agreed to go on a date with her former boss back then. At that time, she'd already been involved with

Simon even if they hadn't been in an official relationship.

She should ask Jenn how Hastings—her ex-boss—was doing. They hadn't parted on good terms as he had accused Sharon of playing him, and in a way she had. A part of her had always known that she wasn't attracted to him, and she still had accepted his date invitation. Since then, she'd seen him once when he'd been at the precinct for a meeting with Kelly. Sharon had passed him in the hallway, and although he hadn't ignored her, there wasn't any warmth to the brief interaction.

If Rose had noticed her thoughts wandering, she didn't let on, just continued talking. "You know, I think I'd go with something lacy, in dark red, dark green or black. I have a bodice that might fit the bill."

Focusing back on Rose, Sharon pushed her private life aside. While it had become entangled with her professional life once again, it had to be the job first.

Chapter Twelve

Sharon got out of the cab at five minutes after nine p.m., ignoring the impulse to tell the cab driver to take her right home. This was work and her attendance was not up for debate.

Making her way over to Helen King's building, she followed a couple and a single woman to the entrance, all of them throwing her curious looks when they stopped in front of the door. Rose had been right. It was a small scene, after all, and she was the new girl on the block.

Smiling, she hoped to make a friendly impression, yet not too much of one. She wanted people to feel comfortable enough to talk to her while still respecting her.

The door opened, and they were let in by a muscled, somber man. Security. He checked their invitations and crossed them off a list. The music in the background, some electronic, sensual beat, was loud, and he almost shouted when telling them to go inside, pointing along the hallway, where the door was open this time. Of course, King wouldn't hold it in her private quarters.

Sharon followed the others, stopping upon entering the room, while the others crossed it, making their way to where Helen King stood beside a bar that was manned by two male bartenders.

Clad in a long black sheath of a dress, with a cleavage that almost reached her navel, her hair pinned up in a bun, King cut a striking impression. All cold poise and grace, she greeted her visitors who then disappeared into a room to the left after they had talked to her.

Knowing she had to acknowledge the host, Sharon walked over as well, ignoring the two-dozen people who already occupied the space, most of them in pairs or small groups. Sharon was curious to see how they were dressed but didn't take her eyes off King, who watched her every step.

Sharon might have been invited, but it didn't feel like it. She stopped in front of King, who gave her an icy smile.

"I'm impressed. I didn't think you'd come."

Sharon waited a beat, raising an eyebrow. "Why not?"

"Because you won't feel comfortable here and we both know it." There was a definite hint of amusement in King's voice that made Sharon want to grit her teeth.

Although she was smiling, Sharon's voice was cold when she spoke. "You might think you know me, but fact is, you don't. It was also *you* who wanted me to lead this investigation and to close the case. So you can work with me and we'll be out of each other's hair soon, or you can play futile games that will put my career in jeopardy while you'll be left with the reputation of a murderer. Your call."

King laughed. "The kitten has claws. Nice. That said, we won't be out of each other's hair, darling, at least until you see sense and break it off with Simon. He has been part of my life for far longer than he's known you and he will continue to be, so you better get used to it."

She broke eye contact and looked over Sharon's shoulder. Other guests must have arrived. Looking back at Sharon, she gestured at the room the others had disappeared into.

"There's a dressing room for men and one for women. You can get changed there. The rules are easy and were mentioned on your invitation. The most important one is to never barge into a scene. And as I told you, feel free to talk to my guests, but as soon as they begin to feel uncomfortable or questioned, you'll be out."

"Understood." Sharon turned on her heel, not caring if King had anything else to say.

When she crossed the room, she could see from the corner of her eyes that a couple who had been talking to each other a minute ago were looking at her. It made her skin crawl. If she'd been uncomfortable the first time she'd been at Simon's club, this was even worse. At that time she could fall back on her job, could set boundaries, and it had been only Simon she had to deal with. Now she might be here as a cop, too, but she'd have to be careful as she was surrounded by people who would treat her as part of a world she didn't think she belonged to.

She had almost reached the end of the room when somebody called after her. Stopping, she swirled around. Rose was approaching her, a tall, dark-skinned man following behind her.

"Rose? What are you doing here?" This was a surprise and a very welcome one.

"We were right behind you, but you didn't see us. Anyway, I think it's unfair of Helen to put you on the spot like that, so I got Marcus to score us an invitation."

She smiled up at the man who was now beside her, and it was easy to see the true affection between the two of them. Rose introduced them before she excused herself and took Sharon's arm, pulling her into the women's changing room.

Apart from them, one other woman was inside, and she didn't even glance up when the two of them entered. Putting on a pair of stilettos, the woman had an absent gaze and seemed lost in her own thoughts.

Still, Rose spoke in a hushed voice, while opening the small bag in her hand that contained her outfit for the night. "Don't worry, Marcus and I won't be in your way, but if you have a question, need help or Helen gets to be too much, we'll be there."

Lowering the zipper of her own bag, Sharon got out the lacy, almost see-through bodice, the stockings and a pair of heels. If her boss could see her now, he'd have a stroke. Maybe Simon was right, and this was a mistake. She should have found a different way to obtain information.

She looked up at Rose. "Thank you."

"Sure. Well, you see, we didn't know Warren well, but he was one of our world. Also, I want to know who killed him. I want to feel safe again and not live in fear I could be next."

So far, Sharon hadn't considered this could be a serial killer who had it out for people in the scene. There was no indication this could be the case, and she hoped her instinct wasn't wrong here. She put her hand on Rose's arms.

"I'm sure you don't have to fear a thing. From what I learned so far, Rawlins wasn't the most pleasant person around and there aren't many people sad he's gone. This doesn't read like a hate crime but like somebody with a personal agenda."

Rose took in the information, then nodded. "Thank you, Sharon. And you're right with your assessment. The few times I met Warren, I didn't want to have any prolonged contact with him. He seemed…driven in a way, angry when he thought nobody was looking."

It fit with what Sharon had learned so far. Whatever Rawlins' demons had been, they had lived close to the surface.

"Do you happen to know if there were people he often spent time with at these parties?" She could kick herself for not asking sooner.

"No, I don't. When I'm at one of these parties, I might see people I know, say hello to a few of them, but Marcus and I are in a monogamous relationship. We enjoy the atmosphere here, the thrill of being able to watch some scenes unfold, but we don't invite other people to play with us."

So it could work? Being a part of this world and still in a committed relationship? Would she ever want this…and what about Simon?

"I hope you don't mind me saying this, Sharon, but you think too hard," Rose said.

"Yeah, I know."

That was something that Jenn told her all the time and that Simon had remarked upon more than once. She shrugged and began to unbutton her shirt. She was uncomfortable even though she couldn't say why.

Changing in the NYPD locker room never was a problem for her. She met Rose's gaze who had shrugged out of her own shirt by now and held a corset in one hand.

"I don't know why, but that's just who I am."

"I understand. And it's always good to know who you are, what you want and to accept yourself that way."

It was, although Sharon still had to work on herself if she wanted her relationship with Simon to thrive. Ignoring Rose and her wayward thoughts for the moment, she didn't linger and changed into the bodice, the stockings.

Looking down at herself, she sighed. This was ridiculous. This wasn't who she was, yet it had to be if she wanted to pass muster tonight. Rose had fallen silent, too, and when Sharon turned, dressed, she watched the other woman putting on a collar. Noticing her curious glance, Rose lifted her hand to the studded leather band.

"I don't wear it in daily life, but during these parties, I want the world to see that I belong to Marcus."

"And people leave you alone?" It might almost make it worth it putting one on.

Rose shook her head. "No, it doesn't work like that. Sometimes there are still people asking if I'm open for a scene with them, most of the time newcomers who I haven't met before. A no is always accepted, though. This collar is a token, a sign of my total submission to my husband for the night. I trust him to provide me with what I need, to not to go too far and in turn, I'll heed his commands, put my pleasure and my pain into his hands. And you know, he has never made me regret submitting to him. Not once."

So far it was the same with Simon. She had trusted him with her body almost from the very beginning, and in time her heart had done the same. For a second, she wished he was here right now, that he could see her. His face would be a stoic mask, but she'd be able to see the restrained passion, the want and yes, even the love.

Too bad this evening was not about that, and she better not forget. Well, Helen King wanted to mess with her, and it was up to Sharon if she let her or not.

She freed her hair from its ponytail and donned her heels before she got up. At least she could walk in them. They weren't her regular footwear, but she had a few pairs she liked to wear when she went on dates or out with friends. She resisted the urge to look at herself in the man-high mirror on the other side of the room. Rose still wasn't finished dressing, but Sharon didn't wait for her. She had to navigate this situation alone. Still, it was good to know a friendly face was here.

"We'll talk later," Sharon said, and Rose nodded.

"Good luck."

She would need it. Leaving the locker room, she almost collided with two other women who wanted to enter. One of them had a leash in her hand, and she didn't let the other woman out of her eyesight. She wouldn't be surprised if these two were a couple. *What about Rawlins? Did he like being led around on a leash and was the person who held it the one who killed him in the end?*

Outside, she took a moment to get used to the dim lighting. The music was louder, too. By now, she estimated there were at least thirty people in the main room and a few more in the men's locker room. She spotted a group of five that was with King and there were several other small groups or couples. One couple rounded a partition at the end of the room to obtain some privacy.

Feeling eyes on her, she scanned the room until she saw one of the two bartenders smiling at her. She had to start asking questions somewhere and bartenders often saw and heard more than people gave them credit for.

When she made her way over, the man's smile widened. It was almost out of place in the otherwise somber yet charged atmosphere. When she neared him, she could get a better look, and she estimated him to be in his late twenties. He wore a pair of tight leather pants and a vest, and his body was muscular but not in a way that made it seem too much. By all accounts, this was a very attractive young male, and she couldn't be less interested. She was amused by herself.

"Hi, what can I get you?" the young man asked. His voice was deep with an accent she couldn't quite place.

"Just some water, thank you."

He raised an eyebrow but didn't comment, handing her the drink a minute later. "You're new here, aren't you?"

"Yes, I am. You're not though, are you?"

His smile widened to a grin. "I've been bartending for Helen for a good two years now. And I think you must be the cop."

Caught by surprise, Sharon laughed. "Well, I am, but how did you know?"

"Well, for one, Helen told me and my colleagues that a cop would be in tonight." He lifted a finger. "Then, you weren't making small talk just now but interviewing me." A second finger joined the first. "And last but not least, there are quite a few rumors about the club owner and his cop." He raised a third finger. "Anyway, so you are Simon's cop, aren't you?"

If Sharon got a dollar for each time somebody called her Simon's cop, she'd soon be rich, although there was no sting or even curiosity to the young man's statement.

"I'm nobody's cop, but yes, I work for the NYPD and yes, I'm in a relationship with Simon," she said, in a quiet voice but with conviction.

Her opposite raised his hands, but his smile never faltered. "No offense meant."

"None taken."

"Good. My name's Marco, by the way."

Introducing herself, Sharon took a sip of her drink, then took a look at the space that had become even fuller in the meantime. "How many people attend these parties?"

Marco followed her gaze, then looked back at Sharon. "I'd say around fifty, sixty, give or take."

A woman in tight leggings, a bra and a collar stepped up beside Sharon, ordering a drink. Sharon waited while Marco fixed the beverage, taking the time to scan the crowd.

At first glance, it could have been a regular party if it weren't for the different style of clothes. Most people had chosen black or dark colors, many were wearing leather and a lot of the women wore stockings just like her.

Hearing a harsh cry even over the music, she looked in the direction of where it had come from. It was from somewhere behind the partition. It seemed a scene had just started. A few other guests looked over as well, though most didn't react at all.

Rolling shoulders that were way too tense, Sharon looked after a couple, holding hands, followed by a young man disappearing through a door at the far left.

"The dealer's room," Marco said from behind her.

She turned around to him. The young woman was gone, and raising an eyebrow, Sharon looked from him to where the group had disappeared, then back at him. "Dealer's room?"

"Toys and other paraphernalia. It's a nice side business. Helen's parties are nothing but professional."

Yeah, yeah, the other woman was a goddess of the BDSM community. Knowing her snark was misplaced, she decided it was time to see about her own business.

"Marco, did you know Warren Rawlins?"

The smile on his face was replaced by a scowl. "I was waiting for you to ask. Yeah, I did. He attended a lot of parties in the last year."

"And?"

Looking into the distance for a second, Marco's gaze met hers again and the expression in his eyes was hard.

"He was an asshole, sorry for saying that. He tried propositioning me a few times, seemed to think he could order more than drinks here, and when he learned that wouldn't fly, he turned into a jerk, telling me I'd be worth nothing more than a quick pity fuck anyway." Marco snorted. "I didn't even get around to telling him I'm into neither BDSM nor men."

"Then what are you doing here?" Sharon had asked before she could stop herself.

Marco chuckled, and the mood lightened again. He pointed at the other bartender who was helping a man who was in the company of a much younger man.

"That one is not just my colleague but my older brother. He's active in the scene, and he got me this gig.

It's good money. You know the costs of living in NYC, don't you?"

"I do."

"So, yeah. Anyway, after my pleasant run-in with Rawlins, I saw him a few more times, although he made sure to get his drinks from Stephen. Rawlins was into the heavier stuff. He liked to be someone's pet, you know, to play with somebody that would drag him around like a dog. And that wasn't enough for him. He loved to be humiliated by his Doms, too."

This confirmed her thoughts after hearing Rawlins had been found naked with nothing but a collar around his neck. She was sure King knew everything about how Rawlins was found and what her conclusions would be. Still, she hadn't breathed a word to her. She was helping nobody—least of all herself—by omitting information.

"Isn't that allowed here? Humiliation, that is," she asked Marco.

"It's not forbidden, but it's a question of not taking things too far. I know that Helen took him aside at one of his last parties and had a little chat with him. I don't know any of the particulars as everything happened in the back room but there was a big argument and Rawlins left in a huff."

Another thing that would've been helpful to know. It just made King look more guilty. What was the other woman thinking or hiding?

"Thanks, Marco," she said then took a sip of her water.

"Not for that. Now, will you tell me how you caught one of the most wanted bachelor's hearts?"

Sharon wasn't sure whether to laugh or sigh. Gossip, a potent currency wherever she went. "You know, if I ever find out myself, I might tell you." She drained her water and pushed her glass toward Marco. "To be honest, something just seemed to fit, and it still does."

"I don't know Simon well but he's one of the good ones. Treats you like a human and not just the hired help." He held up the glass. "Another one?"

Sharon shook her head. "No, but thanks. I want to talk to a few more people."

"Well, then I hope I'll see you around again."

An older man appeared beside Sharon, and she took it as her cue to leave. Having no idea who to talk to and if it would be impolite to join a random group, she made her way to Helen to ask her about the incident with Rawlins when she stopped dead in her tracks at the sight of Simon in a pair of tight jeans and a black shirt. He had just joined Helen and was greeting her with a kiss on her cheek.

What the hell was he doing here? Hadn't they agreed that she could handle herself? Ignoring the hot anger cursing through her veins—as showing it would just play into the other woman's game—Sharon walked over anyway.

King's gaze met hers before she could reach them and following the other woman's gaze, Simon spotted her. There was a bare hint of a smile on his face but it was replaced with a frown when he met her gaze.

Everything inside her screamed to ask him why he had come when she had asked him not to. Still, she didn't as she wasn't inclined to give King a show.

"Sharon, were you able to get any useful information so far?" the older woman asked her with a smile on her face that contradicted the look in her eyes and the cold tone of her voice.

"As I've been here for less than half an hour, no." Everything in Sharon itched to look at Simon and demand an explanation. It was something they would talk about, just not now. "I'm wondering about one thing though. Did you know that Warren Rawlins was a submissive that was into humiliation?"

There was an amused glint in King's eyes that Sharon would have missed if she hadn't paid close attention.

"Yes, of course. Didn't you?"

"So far you've spoken to people that knew his everyday persona, haven't you?" Simon interjected.

"Yes, until tonight, I had only spoken to his family, friends and some colleagues," she answered him. She might've been annoyed, but she wasn't a small child about to stomp her foot because things hadn't gone her way.

She watched Simon looking from her to Helen, and despite his amiable greeting from before, he looked irritated now.

"How would Sharon have been able to learn about his inclinations from those people? Damn, Helen, shouldn't you of all people want this case closed as fast as possible? Sure, nobody should know that your name popped up in the investigation, even you shouldn't, but they do. Right now, people are too curious to bother thinking that you could be the killer but what if the case won't be closed in a week or a month?"

Helen smiled and put her hand on his upper arm. "I'm sure it will be closed before then, but I thank you for your concern. And never mind, during the Davis case your business didn't suffer either, did it?"

Simon kept his frustration in check, though to Sharon the tension in his body said more than a thousand words could. Helen would know him that well, too.

"Don't try playing games with me. You know it did."

Sharon swallowed her surprise. She hadn't been aware that the time it took to solve the Davis case had a negative impact on Simon's business. At least at the beginning, the curious had flocked to the club. It seemed that had changed over time. He hadn't told her and what was more, she hadn't asked. Was she afraid that when she learned more about him, she would become a part of his world for good, that she could no longer pretend that engaging in BDSM play was just something that happened sometimes? Would it be so bad to admit for once and all that this was a part of her life that wouldn't change? A long hard look at herself was overdue.

"And you survived the ordeal quite fine," Helen said, her voice so much warmer when she spoke to him. "Don't worry, Simon. I will make it, too."

Having enough of the way her questioning had derailed, she spoke before King and Simon could continue their own personal battle of wills.

"Ms. King, I heard that Warren Rawlins caused a scene one of the last times he was here. What happened?"

King looked from Simon to her, her eyes narrowing. "That's what you heard? Interesting."

"Tell me what happened?" Sharon was done with being polite. She needed answers and was one pair of missing handcuffs short of dragging King to the precinct for a formal interview. At least it made for a nice fantasy. In reality, that woman would call a lawyer and be out of there before Sharon could voice her first question.

"Yes, there was an argument," King answered a long moment later. She looked away from Sharon and to Simon, then back at Sharon. "You see, Warren had a temper. And that one time, he wasn't… Let's just say, not quite happy with his partner's performance." She shook her head. "At one point in the scene, he broke character and told his partner that he shouldn't call himself a Dom, that his mother knew better insults than him."

A nasty scene and nothing that King would've wanted to happen during one of her parties.

"What did you do?"

"I took him to the side, told him to leave for the night and that he'd be suspended for the next two parties. Then I spoke to his partner and offered him a few drinks."

The man must have been livid, humiliated, something that didn't sit well with the average person. That had to be even more grating for a Dominant.

"I need the name of Warren's partner for the night."

King scoffed. "You think he did it? Over that? By the end of the night, he was engaged in a scene with another party participant, and he didn't seem unhappy. And anyway, Joseph left the country a few days later. He's with the military and started a new posting. His name is Joseph Aetos. Go, check the facts and waste your time and mine right along with it."

With a last look, she turned to a group of people that had arrived. By now it had to be the time that the doors were closed for new arrivals.

"Brody, Annie, how great you could make it," Helen greeted the couple, and like that Simon and Sharon were excused.

It figured that she wouldn't get around to asking more questions about Rawlins. Well, if that was how Helen liked to play the game, Sharon would invite her to the precinct next. In the end, King would be wasting nobody's time but her own.

For now, there was Simon who shouldn't be here, and she had no idea how to deal with him. She startled when he took her arm and began leading her away. She pulled her arm away, then glared up at him.

"What do you think you're doing?"

He clenched his jaw, and when he spoke, it was in a clipped tone. "Let's talk but somewhere more private."

Instead of trying to take her arm again, he began walking in the direction of the partitions, without looking back once. It was tempting to let him walk away and take care of her own business.

What would it help? This investigation would be over at some point—one way or the other—while she had to live with the decisions she made in her private life. Right now, her resentment for Simon wanted to cloud her thinking, but nothing would get better if she ignored him.

Taking her time to follow him, she was surprised that there were several cubicles behind the partition. The light was even dimmer here, and her eyes needed a moment to adjust. Looking into the first few cubicles—looking for Simon—she spotted one with a living room setting, one with nothing but a big bed and one that featured a St. Andrew's cross. There was something for every taste. Their host knew how to keep her customers satisfied.

There was a couple in the second cubicle. A Dominatrix in leather pants and a black sports bra had bound her male companion's limbs together in a way that looked uncomfortable, although Sharon was sure it had happened with the man's full consent.

It wasn't any of her business, and she moved on, finding Simon in the seventh and last cubicle, this one featuring a spanking bench and an assortment of whips and floggers on a table.

Simon leaned against the wall beside the table, his arms crossed over his chest. Anger radiated off him and Sharon hated herself for the thought that he looked hot, for wanting him right then and there. Something about him still made her better senses short-circuit. This was neither the time nor the place for this.

Stepping into the cubicle, she wished there was a door she could close and that the loud moans from the other cubicle would stop for a moment. This would have to do.

She stopped at the other side of the table, fighting the impulse to cross her arms as well. She met Simon's gaze, hating how impenetrable he was. Of course, he had to be in fucking control of himself and his emotions while she was brimming with emotion. Waiting a moment for the wave of anger to pass, she spoke. "Would you mind telling me what you're doing here?"

His eyes narrowed, and he looked at her as if he had questions himself. She waited for him to speak. She wouldn't ask again. He relented.

"Helen's assistant called me. She told me that you had asked her to call to see if I were free to join you after all."

Sharon opened her mouth, but nothing came out, and she shook her head before she closed her eyes and focused on her breathing. Opening her eyes again, she locked gazes with Simon. She should've known it was another one of Helen's games. What did this woman think she would gain by this? Sooner or later, her deceit would have come out anyway.

"I never asked anybody to call you, and I've neither met Helen's assistant, nor would I know where to find her."

Simon uncrossed his arms, and he straightened a bit, his fingers flexing before his body became still again. "I see," he said, his voice hoarse from repressed anger.

Right this moment, his curt answer irritated her even further. She hated that phrase as much as he seemed to like it. She didn't want him to change, but wasn't this a situation that warranted more of a reaction than a simple *I see*?

"Tell me what you see?" Her voice dripped with sarcasm, and she didn't care. "That your beloved friend is trying to throw a wrench into our relationship? I mean, I must hand it to her, she's good. Hasn't she proven that I should've known better than to suspect you'd come here unbidden?"

Rounding the table, Simon walked up to her, putting both of his hands on her shoulders.

The warmth of his skin, coupled with the subtle scent of his cologne, made her want to close her eyes again, though for a very different reason this time. Would her body always want him, no matter what her mind was telling her? She wanted to look up at him, but found she didn't have the strength, fearing her body could betray her further. Although staring at his chest, knowing what she would see and feel if he stripped out of his tight shirt didn't help either.

"Listen. She can only prove a point if we let her."

The thumbs of his fingers were caressing her shoulders now. It was meant to be comforting, yet it was everything but. The stress of the last days, together with the tense atmosphere of this place, sent her hormones into overdrive. Not the time. Not the place. If she could hammer the message into her brain, she would.

"I'm sorry I fell for her ploy," Simon said, his voice warming.

"It's not your fault." She met his eyes. "I should have trusted you instead of assuming the worst."

"Let's agree we both could've handled this better," he suggested, and in a final betrayal, her gaze wandered down to his mouth, her tongue sneaking out to wet too-dry lips.

With effort, she took a step back, then looked up again. While his gaze had been ice before it was fire now, and she clenched her hands as her body throbbed with sudden need. "Okay, let's also agree we must find a way to deal with Helen. Together. Not tonight, though. Right now, I need to talk to more people and find out who Rawlins was with when he was here."

Simon shook his head and took a step toward her, reeling her in by her hips.

"You won't find your answers here tonight. Nobody will admit to having been with Rawlins. Not with people looking, judging. If they didn't know before, people will know now that you're a cop having come to investigate."

Not *a* cop but *Simon's cop.*

"But..." she began, and he stopped her with a finger across her lips.

"No but. I might consider Helen a friend, but I won't let her toy with you or with me. This investigation needs to end, yes, but it won't if you try finding answers on Helen's turf. If she had wanted to help you tonight, she would have. She didn't, did she? And I think what you need now is something else."

Her body shuddered at his words and the implications. "No, we can't. Not here. And it's not what I need, it's what I want."

He smiled. "I'm sure your body disagrees."

"It does, but it is not my master."

She hadn't used the word on purpose, yet Simon's eyes darkened nonetheless.

"You're right. It's not. I am. So will you trust me with your body and your mind tonight?"

Here? Where people could come and barge into their privacy at any moment?

And wouldn't it be unethical, seeing she was here about the job? He tightened his hold a bit, just enough to bring her back from being lost in her own thoughts.

"Time to decide," Simon said, his voice the one of her Master and not her partner.

Could she do this? Did she want this? What if somebody came to see her writhing in pleasure and pain and what if it were Helen?

Want was turning into pure need as her body throbbed at the idea of release and people seeing that she was Simon's and Simon was hers.

"I want this, and I hate that I do," she said, her voice quiet.

Reaching up, he cupped her cheek. "If I've learned one thing in this scene, it was that I wanted to be able to look into the mirror the next day and still like what I saw. Let's get out of here, and I'll take care of you elsewhere."

Overwhelmed by the sudden wave of emotions crashing down on her, she blinked back tears. "Damn. I love you. And I want you more than I can say."

"Same."

He trailed his hand over her neck and her shoulder, all the way to her breast where he stroked her nipple through the sheer fabric of her bodice, then squeezed the sensitive flesh between his thumb and forefinger. A shiver ran down her back, and she swallowed a moan.

Her eyes had fallen closed, and she startled when he let go of her to take her hand.

When she looked up at him, there was a hint of warmth in his eyes that helped ease the knot in her stomach a bit. They were a team, and she would do well not to forget it. Helen's plan might be to cause a rift between them, but it would only happen if they let her.

Together they moved out of the cubicle, making their way back to the main room. Unable to look away, Sharon stole glances at the other cubicles, her step faltering for a second when she spotted Rose and Marcus in one, Marcus being in the process of fastening Rose to the St. Andrew's cross.

Memories of the times she had found herself in Rose's place flooded her memory, and her body began craving the intense sensation that would make her forget all about the jumbled mess of this investigation and an ex-girlfriend who was trying to manipulate them even if the purpose wasn't clear.

"Soon," Simon said, squeezing her hand.

One team!

Entering the main room, she felt Helen's gaze on her, and it took everything in her not to turn into the direction. She would've loved to know if Simon was acknowledging Helen, still she didn't look at him to check either. Instead, she kept her head high while they made their way to the changing rooms.

"I'll wait here," Simon said in front of the women's changing room.

"What about you?"

A small smile graced his lips. "I was in a hurry. I changed as fast as I could and was on my way."

He had thought she needed or at least wanted his help. Turning to him, she kissed him, her lips lingering on his. With reluctance, she pulled away, ignoring the thrum of desire. "I'd have done the same."

Not wasting any time, she changed back into her earlier clothes. Outside, Simon was talking to another man who gave her a curious smile when he spotted her.

Excusing himself, Simon faced her and they left the premises. In front of the door, Sharon stopped, then took a deep breath.

"This is insane," she muttered.

"It's a game we didn't want to play but will win anyway," Simon said.

Sharon nodded. "We will, but playing with people's feelings, messing with their lives, should never be a game."

"It shouldn't be. But Helen thrives on manipulation."

"She needs a different hobby. I heard knitting's all the hype right now. Anyway, let's call a cab?"

"The cab over there is ours. I paid him to wait."

Sharon was thankful that Simon's money didn't influence their everyday decisions. Today, she was grateful for his foresight.

"Thank fuck."

Raising an eyebrow, his eyes twinkling in amusement, he led Sharon to the waiting car.

Chapter Thirteen

"You choose," Simon said, closing the dungeon's door behind them.

Halfway inside the room, Sharon stopped and swung around to him. "Choose what?"

Shrugging out of his coat, placing it over the lone chair, he made eye contact. "You will choose what toys we will use tonight, I will choose how I will apply them. Choose with care."

He sat on the chair, watching her. He'd said his piece, now it was her turn. He kept her gaze, and for a moment, Sharon was frozen. She had counted on the fact he'd take over for the night and make the decisions until she felt she could breathe easier again.

He would, *after* she had decided what kind of distraction she needed. If she told him to take over from here, he might give in, but she wouldn't back off from a challenge.

Breaking eye contact, she walked over to the rudimentary shelf holding various toys.

She remembered her first time in the room Marlene Davis had died in as well as her first time in a dungeon. The various toys in both locations had fascinated and terrified her at the same time. After a few months, she knew how most of them would feel if they were used on her, had learned what would make her help forget best.

Throwing a gaze over her shoulder, she found Simon hadn't moved, was still watching her. Having never engaged in sadomasochistic play before him, she couldn't imagine doing so with anybody else. Submitting to somebody was the ultimate intimate act.

She trusted him like she did nobody else, and he understood her body even better than she did. Returning her focus to the toys, she picked up one of the leather floggers, running her fingers over the soft strands that if used on skin would make her synapses scream out in pain, a slight hurt that would increase bit by bit as the spanking continued.

Without further thought, she picked up a paddle next, knowing that the broader strokes would make warmth replace the hurt caused by it almost at once. The prickling sensation left behind would make her squirm with need as wetness would have her long for physical release along with the emotional one. At least until the pain became so intense that it threatened to consume her and the simple act of breathing was a chore.

Passing the assortment of ball gags, something she'd never consent to, she chose a pair of metal handcuffs instead of the padded ones. Tonight, she wanted to feel the pain, even knowing they would leave marks she'd have to cover the next day.

Pleased with what she had chosen, she walked over to Simon who had gotten up and held out his hands to receive her selection.

He nodded once, and he was towering over her.

"You will undress now, and then I want you to walk over to the spanking bench."

She looked over to where the bench stood, biting her bottom lip. They had used it twice in a scene so far and something about the position it put her in made the sensations of the spanking more intense than they usually were.

The spanking bench had two padded knee rests that were angled away from each other so she would have her legs spread wide open. The chest rest—also padded—was angled down, and she knew she would cling to it for dear life while he took her mind off everything.

Sharon faced Simon again and began to undress under his never wavering gaze.

"I'll start with the flogger, then use the paddle later. We'll just replace the handcuffs with the restraints of the spanking bench." He put the handcuffs on the chair, then met her gaze.

"Do you agree to this? If not, please speak out now."

"I do agree, Master."

He ran a hand down the side of her neck, and she shivered, the pleasurable sensation spreading all through her body. How was it possible that the lightest of his touches aroused her in a way that reduced her to the point of asking him to take her right then and there?

Stepping back, he didn't say anything but waited for her to continue peeling out of her clothes.

When she was naked, she met his gaze for a moment, but he said nothing. He had given her a command, so there wasn't any need for communication now. Silence. A powerful tool, and he knew how to wield it.

Walking over to the spanking bench, she took a deep breath to compose herself before she got into position with her lower legs on the knee rests and her upper body pressed against the chest rest. The leather padding was cold against her skin. It would warm up, although the room was too cold to be comfortable.

She swallowed, hating how vulnerable she was in this position. If it were anybody else but Simon with her here now, she wouldn't go through with this. She was surprised when he kneeled in front of her.

"Last chance to reconsider."

His voice was calm, devoid of any warmth, but it was a serious offer. He knew her well.

"No. Do it, Master."

A hint of a smile ghosted over his face. "Good. Then we'll begin. Be as loud as you want."

He got up, then he applied the ankle and wrist restraints.

Now she was helpless, and her well-being was in his hands. For a second, she could see the flogger in his hand before he walked around her until he came to stand behind her. Bracing herself for the first hit of soft leather strands against her back, she flinched when there was the telltale sound of the flogger parting the air. To her surprise she didn't feel any impact and understood Simon hadn't aimed at her skin and was moving the flogger in a circular motion…

He did it a second time and this time she could feel the movement of air against her back. He was taunting her, making her wonder what would happen next. Would he swing the flogger again, or…

This time, the end of the tails connected with the point between her shoulder blades, and she moaned at the sharp sting, her body tensing at the initial shock. With all but no time to process the sensation, the toy met her skin again, and her breath caught in her lungs.

After two more times Simon moved on, applying the flogger to her buttocks next, again and again making contact. Making measured, equal strokes at first, he then alternated between applying less pressure one time and more the next. She lost count of how often the toy had met her skin.

The burning feeling began morphing into pain that couldn't be ignored any longer, and she cried out, not caring who might hear her or not.

When Simon stopped, she took a deep breath. Her arms were shaking from being so tense. Her ass had begun feeling numb and it was her thighs that protested the abuse the loudest.

"You're doing very well," Simon complimented her, and he lowered the flogger, caressing the inside of her thighs with the fine leather in a soft motion. A quite different kind of sensation that made her moan as lust mingled with pain.

"Hmm, I wonder if you're wet for me."

She was.

Slipping a hand between her folds, he brushed a single finger along her vulva, dipping inside her wet core. Her sex clenched around his finger. She wished he would slide it in further, that he'd add another one. Of course, he withdrew and stepped back before hitting her upper thighs with the flogger a few times more.

Retreating into her own mind, she allowed the sensations to pass through her, and she was calming as her body continued to deal with the impact of the flogger that alternated between hitting different spots.

She couldn't say how much time had passed when he stopped, and his cool hand made contact with her ass. She hissed at the intense sensation of discomfort that was replaced by want when his fingers stroked the area with tenderness.

He bent down over her and placed a kiss between her shoulder blades.

"You look beautiful. I'll be back in a moment."

Too caught up in the conflicted feelings and a bit detached from reality at the moment, she didn't register him leaving. Her pain receptors were reeling from the spanking and she tried to slow down her breathing, her heart rate.

She startled and hissed when something cold made contact with her back. After a few seconds, she understood it was a chip of ice Simon had let glide down her back.

Groaning, she couldn't say if her body liked this or not.

"Here, take one," Simon said, offering one of the chips to her, and she opened her mouth so he could place it on her tongue. God, she was parched and hadn't even been aware of it.

He took another chip and ran it all over her body. She shivered, half from the cold and half from arousal. The next chip caressing the parts he'd just struck with the flogger made her cry out as her body remembered the harsh treatment that she had asked for.

She twitched and became aware of how uncomfortable her position was. Her legs began to feel the strain of their unnatural position and her breasts pressed uncomfortable against the chest rest. Even padded, the spanking bench would always be uncomfortable after some time had passed. She tried moving a little but it was to no avail.

Simon appeared in front of her face again, offering her another bit of ice, watching her suck it. From her position she couldn't quite meet his eyes. Too bad, as she had learned his tells and would've liked a clue what he might be up to next. As if reading her mind, he lowered himself to her level once more.

"Are you sure you want me to use the paddle, too?"

A justified question. Her body was already sore in various spots, and it might become too much. Could she bear it? And what about him? Were his needs met by their play?

"Sharon, answer me now?"

Should she end this now? God, her mind was too sluggish for a decision. She took a deep breath. What did she want?

"Yes, I want you to use the paddle, Master."

He inclined his head before he got up. While he fetched the paddle, she tried to focus on keeping her breathing quiet, to accept and thus let go of the discomfort. She had all but forgotten about Simon when he spoke.

"We will start with ten strokes. Five on each cheek."

It didn't happen often he told her in detail what he was going to do. It was appreciated in this case as she could brace for the impact.

The first stroke wasn't hard. It touched the middle of her buttock, yet she screamed out. The skin was too raw, and the hurt made her whole body go taut. He did the same on the other side and again, she had to give voice to a sensation that was too intense right this moment.

Each stroke was worse than the one before, and she'd been wrong. She wasn't ready. Whether it was her body that couldn't bear more or her mind that couldn't retreat into the necessary headspace, she didn't know. Everything inside her was protesting the pain. Her eyes fell closed and her hands balled into fists.

She lasted until the eighth stroke when she couldn't deal with even one more hit. Her voice was rough when she cried out. "Phoenix."

Simon stopped at once and took a step back from her. "It's okay, you'll be okay," he said. "Let's get you untied." Simon's voice had warmed up and within seconds, the first ankle restraint was gone, then the other. As he moved around her, the wrist restraints were next. She tried sitting up, and his arms around her waist steadied her, helping her get up. She was wobbling a little and Simon held her against him.

Tears of pain and frustration ran down her cheeks.

"I'm sorry," she said, hating being a sobbing mess.

Simon's hold on her tightened, although it still was a gentle embrace. "Don't apologize. You never have to apologize for using your safe word." He kissed her temple. "Do you think you can walk? I'll look at your bruises upstairs."

She pulled away, tried to smile but failed. "What would you do if I said no? Carry me?"

"Yes."

He was serious. Shaking her head, she leaned into him again, took in his scent, his warmth.

"No, I can walk."

"Okay, but if it's too much after all, let me know. And now let's find a robe for you."

Walking over to a wooden cupboard, he got a robe out of one of the drawers. He helped Sharon into it. She was shivering and the thin robe didn't do much to offer any warmth.

Simon wrapped an arm around Sharon's waist, and together, they made their way upstairs. A woman in full leather gear, including a face mask, passed them, and she nodded at Simon. She was a young woman who worked for Simon as a Dominatrix. Sharon had met her once when the woman had come in early. She had smiled at Simon and Sharon, and had seemed to have a bubbly personality. She hadn't fit the picture of a Dominatrix. It never did any good to judge people by their appearances, something that had never been clearer than here in the club.

Sharon was exhausted by the time they reached Simon's private room and didn't protest when he suggested she lie down on his bed. Getting out of the robe, she let herself fall onto her back and had to grit her teeth. Turning around with her arms in front of her, she closed her eyes, waiting for the painful pulsing of her body to stop.

Simon was rummaging around in the background, and she refused to open her eyes when the mattress dipped and he sat down beside her.

"I've got something for the bruises here. You'll still be sore tomorrow."

His hand was cold, and he rubbed some kind of salve into her skin. For the moment it hurt, but she bit her lip.

"All done," he said after a while.

"Thanks." Knowing she couldn't avoid this forever, she opened her eyes again. "I know you don't want to hear it, but I'm very sorry."

He sighed. "I don't want to hear it. You did the absolute right thing."

"Yeah, for me. But what about you? What about your needs?"

"I got to do a scene with the woman I care for. What more could I want?" He stroked her cheek. "And life sometimes doesn't work out as it's supposed to and neither does sex or BDSM play."

She wanted to tell him that he was right, that she was glad he understood, yet the words didn't want to come. The day had been long, their session intense, and her body and mind were tired.

"Sharon, it's good that you know your boundaries and that you're willing to enforce them. It helps me with trusting that you *will* speak up when things become too much, and it should help you to understand that you are in control of what is happening."

She met his gaze. "Yes, I know. I just hate to fail."

"You didn't fail. Quite the contrary. I'm proud of you."

She sighed. "Can we agree that I know you are right, but that I still need to process?"

He leaned in to kiss her. "That's more than okay. But you know, I've seen you around others, and you are always kind to the people in your private life. You tell them not to be so hard on themselves. Don't be so hard on yourself either. You did the right thing."

She growled. "Can you stop being so fucking considerate?"

He laughed and she couldn't help but smile back at him. He didn't laugh out loud often but when he did it was an unexpected treat. "I'll try, but I can't promise anything."

For a minute, they didn't speak, and she just enjoyed looking at him. He wasn't angry with her. He had kept his word to stop when she asked him to. Had anybody ever been so good to her? For her?

"I'm glad I've gotten to know you, Simon Carter."

He smiled, his knuckles brushing against her cheek. "Same. What do you think? Let's call a cab and heed home. A warm shower or a bath will do you a world of good."

"And if I don't want to move?" she asked, contemplating the effort of getting up.

"Then we'll stay."

It was appealing to close her eyes and fall asleep, and she almost gave in. Her body would pay the price tomorrow if she did, so she sat up even though it was a fight.

"All right, let's get going but just because your mattress is so much nicer."

He chuckled and held out his hand for her to take. "Of course."

Chapter Fourteen

Slowing down from a jog to a brisk walk, Sharon took a deep breath, ignoring the rain dripping down on her. Her clothes stuck to her body, and she blinked to clear her vision. This was not the weather for a run, but she had needed to get out of work. She had hoped the exercise would dissolve the anger simmering inside of her, and when the dreariness of the day meant that few people would be around, all the better.

Rolling her shoulders, she reached for her phone and chose a different playlist. The cheerful tunes might've been good for running, but now they rubbed her the wrong way.

The last three days had been nothing short of torturous, and she might be damned if she had any idea how to make the next ones better. She had hit wall after wall trying to find out who might have been Rawlins' partner.

She and Jenn had re-interviewed the family and all his colleagues in vain. Next, she had called Rose, asking the other woman whether she could contact some of her friends in the scene to see if they had any intel. Simon's friend hadn't just agreed but had called her back a day later. Too bad that all Rose could report was that while a few people had seen Rawlins with a man at some of the parties, everybody had claimed something different when it came to age or appearance of this man or these men. Either some of these people's memories were false or Rawlins only had casual relationships with these people which wouldn't warrant a personal motive for murdering him.

This was personal, even if she couldn't prove it yet.

By now Sharon was convinced that the one person who could help her now was Helen King. The woman had to have more than a few contacts in the scene who would've known Rawlins better.

Would King even tell her if she asked or would she try to toy with her again? Sharon could always go to Simon for help, but the thought didn't sit right with her. So far, she'd been able to solve her own problems, and she would always go the extra mile to keep her professional and private life separate…all the more so in this case when her relationship could be a danger to her career.

Adding to it, she was sure there'd been an argument between Simon and his ex. She hadn't asked, but she knew Simon well enough—something wasn't sitting right with him. The last days he'd been more distracted than usual, brooding.

She was convinced he had done as he'd said and called Helen the day after the party, but when Sharon had spoken to him on the phone that evening, he'd been tight-lipped. If he didn't want to talk about it, it was not up to her to question him.

If she didn't want to contact Helen herself, it left her with the option to send Jenn for an interview. Her partner wouldn't be rattled by any of the woman's antics. Too bad Sharon carried no hope that Jenn would return with any usable information. If King wanted to help, she'd have given up the information ages ago.

Growling, Sharon stopped, looking up at the gray sky, the cold rain pricking at her skin like fine needles.

What to do now? In the end, it was her investigation, her decision. One thing was for certain—Second Precinct wouldn't stop calling at least twice a day, asking for updates in a snotty tone. She also wasn't fond of Kelly becoming a steady resident in her office either.

Sick and tired of her own hesitancy, she swore to herself that she would come to a decision and stick to it by tomorrow morning.

Walking in a fast pace, she reached Simon's apartment building a few minutes later, and Leon, the doorman, raised an eyebrow when he spotted her. He worked here part-time, and Sharon and he had talked a few times since Simon had introduced them. Leon, who attended college classes at night, had asked her a lot of questions about her job as he was considering applying to the academy.

"Don't tell me you went running in weather like this," he said, opening the door for her.

Stepping under the awning, she realized she would drip all over the expensive floors and elevators, something she hadn't considered when she'd donned her running clothes.

"Well, it seemed like the perfect weather to enjoy some quiet and solitude out there," she said with a pained smile that Leon returned with a bright one of his own.

"Good point. You're expected, I guess?"

Sharon nodded. "I am."

Simon had called her very early this morning, asking if she wanted to spend the night. She'd agreed without a second thought, and when she decided to go running, she'd been sure he wouldn't mind if she took a shower and redressed at his place. By now quite a few clothes of hers had found their way over there.

"Sorry, about the mess," she said to Leon, who waved her concerns aside.

"No problem. I'll take care of it. It'll give me something to do. You know, it's one of these days when not many people want to go out. You're the first person I've spoken to in over half an hour."

"Thanks, Leon. I'll make it up to you."

She hid a smile at the young man's light blush and made her way to the elevator before a few drops would have turned into a puddle underneath her feet. She was lucky as the elevator doors opened at once, and half a minute later, she rang the bell at Simon's door, hoping he'd be quick as she'd begun shivering in her wet clothes.

He was and raised an eyebrow at her appearance. "Who tried to drown you?" he asked, stepping aside to let her enter.

"Funny. I was running, and I hope you don't mind if I make a beeline for the shower."

"Better than catching pneumonia," he replied. "Want me to prepare you a coffee or a tea in the meantime?"

Sharon stopped with her hand on the bathroom door handle. "If you laugh now, I might have to kill you, but could you make it some hot milk? For some reason it warms me up faster and better than tea or coffee does."

She could see his lips twitch. "Sure, no problem. I'll even add some cookies."

"Simon, I swear…" she began but stopped when he laughed.

Although she was a bit miffed to find it was at her own expense, she was aware she'd brought it on herself and that she would've done the same if roles had been reversed.

"Sorry," he said a moment later, his eyes still twinkling with mirth.

"I might forgive you. But only if the cookies are worth it." A shudder ran down her back, and she opened the bathroom door. "Anyway, I'd better have that shower now. I'll be with you soon."

She was done a few minutes later, and when she left the shower stall, reaching for a towel, she found a small bundle of clothes on the closed toilet seat. She smiled and was thankful for Simon's foresight. Wrapping herself in one of his big sinful towels, she picked up the black leggings he had chosen before she donned one of his blue sweaters that she had worn a few times before. Sometimes he was too good to her.

After dressing, she found him in his kitchen and to her surprise there was more than just her milk and indeed some cookies out on the counter. She raised her eyebrows at the sight of flour, yeast, pepperoni and some vegetables.

Sitting down on a stool, she reached for the cup of milk, closing her fingers around it, sighing at the scent and the warmth. Simon watched her, shoving the small plate with sugar cookies toward her.

"Here."

"Thanks. I'm surprised. I didn't know you had cookies," she said, taking one.

"I usually don't. My brother sent them a couple of days ago."

She bit into it. "They are good."

Simon smiled then took one himself. "He baked them himself. Baking's one of his hobbies. He says it relaxes him. A few times a year I'll receive a care package. He says I'm too serious for my own good and could do with some sweetness in my life." He snorted.

Sharon ate the rest of her cookie, then brushed the crumbs on her hands off over the counter.

"You think he's right?"

Simon finished his own treat before answering. "Let's say he wasn't quite wrong. For a long time I used to live for my job. It was true for my old job and even with the club, I tended to get lost in work."

Sharon reached over the counter, covered his hand with hers. "What changed?"

He raised an eyebrow. "Somebody shot one of my customers, and the cop they sent to investigate was the most stubborn person I had met in a while. She was also beautiful and needed somebody to help her unlock her hidden desires."

Sharon slapped his hand, then shook her head. "What is it with you? Did they weave arrogance into your genes?"

He smiled. "Is it arrogance when I'm right?"

"Unbelievable," Sharon muttered, taking a sip of her milk. "Let's change topics before I start to wonder what I'm even doing here. What's with all these groceries?"

He took up the package with flour and met her gaze. "What do you think?"

"That you want to cook? You don't cook, and I don't either."

He put the package down, then shoved it over to her. "Time to change this, don't you think? And I want us to cook together. Remember when we talked about pizza and that we could try to make our own at some point?"

She did. On the first night she'd spent here, she'd woken up hungry and Simon and she had shared a frozen pizza and childhood memories, and he'd suggested they could make their own one day.

"And you think some point is today?"

She didn't mind preparing simple dishes like pasta, but she didn't have an idea how to even start with making her own dough.

"Yes, I think we should give it a try." He turned serious, then sighed. "I hate these words more than most others, but I think it's overdue that we talked. And I thought we could do that while doing something productive."

She tensed. All the things she could think that were worth talking about were things she'd rather not consider right now.

"Relax, Sharon." Simon went around the counter and coming to stand behind her began to rub her shoulders in a soothing motion. "I hate what happened at Helen's party last week." His voice had hardened.

"I did, too. Still, I don't see what it has to do with this, with cooking. And didn't we kinda talk about it?" She turned her head so she could meet his gaze.

"It's not just about that. It's that when it comes to you, I've been egoistic these last months. I should've taken the time to tell you more about the scene, to find out what you want. What we share can be a—let's say—

private lifestyle but there's also a community to experience it with if you want."

His hands stilled, and he leaned down to brush a small kiss against her lips that made her long for more. She was of half a mind to turn around and pull him close again when he straightened.

"I should've asked if you wanted to attend a munch, if you wanted to go to a party, if you wanted to experience this with a different Dom." He scoffed. "It's just that it seems I'm not all that good at sharing, and I wanted to keep you all to myself."

She turned on her stool, shaking her head. It made her wet hair fall into her face and she brushed it back. Simon's hands came to rest on her hips, anchoring her into place.

"What the hell is a munch? And no, I don't want to submit to another man."

She was sure he didn't realize that his hands had tightened their hold, but she didn't feel like complaining. His expression had darkened, too, and for a moment neither of them spoke. It would be so easy to give in to the tension, to exchange this conversation for feeling him inside her. It would make her forget this day. Although he had a point—they should talk about their expectations when it came to their relationship.

"Simon, what is a munch?" she repeated.

It took him a second, then his hold on her loosened. "It's an informal get-together from people in the scene, most often at a bistro, a diner. Those are good when you're new in the scene. You get to know people, make connections. It's where you learn where the next party will be held, where you'll find advice when needed and might get to know people you're interested in engaging in play with."

It made perfect sense.

How was I unaware of this and why didn't it come up in my research early in my acquaintance with Simon? Although back then she'd looked up tools and techniques. She hadn't considered herself part of the scene. If she was honest with herself, she still didn't think she was.

"You said these are informal?"

"Yes."

"Okay, then I might be interested in going to one, just to get a better feeling for the scene and the people in it."

She put her hand on his shoulders, wondering when it had happened that being with him had become something she looked forward to, that made her feel calm even when the rest of her life was littered with frustration.

"Right now, I don't want to attend any more parties if I don't have to. I don't want to be put on display, I don't thrive under humiliation like Rawlins did and I sure as hell don't want to experiment with other partners."

"Good."

She had to smile at his brief response even though she could see a wealth of emotion in his eyes. He loved to be in control of his emotions, his environment.

This wasn't a one-way lane, though. He had his own needs and desires, and if they wanted to move forward together, she needed to know about them.

"How about you? Do you miss being with other partners or going to parties? Is it enough for you to be with me and to reduce play to the club and your apartment?"

"It's perfect," he answered without hesitation, and he began to play with a strand of her hair, let it glide between his fingers. "I've never needed more than one partner, and I didn't have one so compatible with me before."

Letting go of her hair, he cupped her cheek, his touch sure yet soft. "I like my life as it is right now. Our life. I would want to attend a party now and then, but to stay in contact with a few people, not to play."

She leaned into his touch, allowing her eyes to fall shut. "I understand."

It was good to know they were on the same page, that her feelings aligned with the reality of the situation. By now this thing between them was more than dating or a casual relationship and she wanted it, even when it meant she had to face her fear of being found out.

She opened her eyes again. "Can you promise me that if your needs change, you'll talk to me? I'll promise the same in return."

"I will."

She couldn't predict the future, but she'd be damned before she'd let another man cheat on her or feel the life drizzle out of her relationship bit by painful bit.

"Good."

"Very good." He leaned down to kiss her, but she shook her head, putting her index finger over his lips. "No time for that. You wanted to make pizza, so we will, or at least ruin your kitchen in the process."

He snorted. "I'm touched by your trust in us."

"Uh-huh." She got up. "Less talking and more ruining, Carter."

Chapter Fifteen

Sharon had just picked up the phone as Jenn entered the office.

"You're on the warpath, I see," her partner said after one look at her. "Who do you want to kill this time?"

Putting the receiver down, Sharon waited for her partner to shrug out of her coat.

"Nobody. Yet. But I decided to call King. I've about had it. Either she'll receive me this morning, or she'll get acquainted with our lovely premises here. And she can threaten to call the commissioner all she wants."

Sitting, then getting up again to find her mug and the pot of fresh coffee, Jenn threw her a look. "Good plan. Although you know the commissioner has the pull to fire you if he wants to."

Sharon nodded, taking up a pen to start doodling on the piece of paper in front her. "I know he does. But let him. I'll find something else. I love this job, I would hate if it ended this way but I refuse to be a pawn in this game."

Jenn poured herself a cup, though then she handed it to Sharon. "Just in case this might be the last cup we share."

"Geez, now who's being dramatic?"

Jenn sat down. "I am. But you know, apart from your suicide mission, you look good. Did your boyfriend work some magic on you?" She raised an eyebrow and Sharon was tempted to stick out her tongue at her.

"I wouldn't call it magic. We spent the evening trying to make pizza."

Her friend's eyes widened, then she laughed. "Tried to?"

"Yeah. He bought all the ingredients, but something was wrong with the yeast, so the dough remained a small, grainy lump. And guess what? Fresh pizza doesn't need as much time in the oven as frozen pizza does. Dinner was a crispy affair."

Jenn snorted. "What were the two of you thinking? And what did you do? Go hungry?"

Realizing she'd doodled King's name, Sharon crumpled the sheet of paper and threw it into the nearby bin. "Nope. We ordered Chinese because by then I'd had enough of pizza. "

"Understandable, but why did you do it anyway? Does Simon plan another change of careers?"

"No, not that I know of. But it's a long story—kinda—and anyway, we used the time to talk about the last months, where we want to go from there."

Jenn's mirth turned into a softer smile. "And you admitted that you're in it for the long haul."

Sharon half-shrugged. "I don't know about that, and no one can predict the future anyway, but yeah, we both want the same things, at least right now."

Her partner took a sip of her coffee, sighing. "I get that you're cautious, hon, but have you considered trying to trust that things will turn out okay for once? If it all comes crashing down, you'd notice it anyway, so enjoy what you have now, make the most out of it."

It sounded so easy, and Sharon wished she could relax enough to embrace all she had. It was a good life with a job she wanted to do and a partner who supported her. Simon accepted her for who she was and still didn't find her lacking. It didn't come much better than this. Still, she wasn't ready yet.

She pointed her pen at Jen. "Sometimes you're a wise woman, and this is one of these times, but for now I've got other things to worry about, and it's time to bite the bullet."

"Have fun. But if you go to visit her, I'll go, too." Her gaze hardened. "We're partners, Shar, and we were both tasked with solving this murder. And you should know that you can trust me. King can't tell me anything I don't know about you. This woman won't get to me."

Jenn was right, and Sharon nodded. Picking up the phone again, she dialed.

"Sharon, what can I do for you? Did you find out who killed poor Warren?"

She gripped her pen so tight it hurt. "It's still Lieutenant Richards, Ms. King, and I'm sure you'll know before me when this case is closed."

King laughed and Sharon continued before the other woman could speak. "I need to talk to you. Today, and it's up to you if we talk at your home or if you come here. You can choose the where but not the when."

"Trying to show your claws? Well, well, then why don't you come over? I'll even make us fresh tea. I couldn't help but notice that you didn't even try yours last time you were here. You should know that you have to try it to find out if you enjoy the taste."

She wouldn't engage in the game, but rolled her eyes at Jenn.

"I'll see you in about half an hour then." Ending the call before King could get another word in, she faced Jenn. "You better hurry with your coffee, as we'll go and see King now. And you're in luck. She's going to make tea. You can have mine, as I sure as hell won't want it."

Downing her cup in one go, Jenn was already on her feet again. "I noticed you didn't tell her that you won't come alone."

Sharon smiled. "No, I didn't. I think it won't hurt if she's in for a surprise for a change."

"It can hurt to show her that she's not in control all the time," Jenn agreed. "Anyway, let's go."

* * * *

Sharon's gut feeling proved to be correct as King's eyes narrowed when she saw Sharon had brought reinforcement. While it lasted not longer than a second, it gave Sharon satisfaction to know she had gotten a rise out of the other woman.

"Now who are you?" King addressed Jenn, not bothering to offer a hand. "I'm afraid Sharon didn't mention she'd bring company."

"Why should she have? This is an interview and not a tea party, isn't it?" Jenn replied. Sharon almost snorted while the expression in King's eyes turned ice cold.

"I guess you're Sharon's partner then. And may I also conclude that you consider yourself the funny one?"

"Since when is there anything funny about murder?" Sharon interjected. "And Detective Reynolds is right. We're not here to exchange pleasantries but to make some overdue progress."

"You still haven't? Hmm, somehow I'm not surprised." King turned and led the way up to her living quarters.

Sharon exchanged a look with Jenn who rolled her eyes. They all remained silent until they had made it upstairs. It was almost a repetition of the time Sharon had been here the last time, as King took a seat on her couch while not offering a seat to Jenn or herself. A tea tray was ready, and King picked up one cup.

"If I had known to expect more visitors, I'd have made more tea."

"Nobody cares about the tea," Jenn said, crossing her arms over her chest. "So how about you tell us who can give us information about Warren Rawlins and his partner? Or do you know who it is? It's time to part with some answers." King didn't speak for a long time, her gaze resting on Jenn while she ignored Sharon. Tilting her head, she spoke while picking up her cup from the table.

"I'll answer one of your questions if you answer one of mine."

Jenn shook her head. "I won't play any games with you."

King scoffed. "It's not a game, but as I see it, you want something from me while I want something from you. I also know you both care about your jobs and that you need my help if you don't want to patrol the streets next."

Sharon had enough and she hated the fact there was an edge to her voice when she spoke. "You're aware that you're our number-one suspect right now, don't you? You want us to drag you in for an interrogation? You want rumors to circle that Rawlins had some pull over you and you murdered him in an attempt to shut him up."

She had all of King's attention now. "And of course, you believe I was stupid enough to drop a business card in a pool of blood. Business cards I hand out at parties but don't carry around with me. If that's your only evidence, all you'd achieve is making yourself, your partner and your department look stupid."

King's gaze was piercing but this time Sharon didn't mind. "It might surprise you to hear, but I don't care. I love my job, I wouldn't mind advancing my career at some point but what I care most about is solving cases, not politics. If politics turns out to be all that is left, then it's time for me to move on. Yes, naming you our prime suspect would make us look stupid, but you know about the power of rumors. You'd go down with us."

"I don't think so." King turned to Jenn. "She's cute when she tries to show off her claws, isn't she?"

The nerve of this woman was unbelievable. If she thought she'd get a reaction out of Sharon, she was mistaken. The same was true for Jenn who laughed.

"Believe me, you wouldn't want to see her if her claws came out for real. Anyway, enough with the foreplay. Do you want to talk to us now, or shall we continue this at the precinct?"

King put down the teacup she was still holding. "All right, here is my question. Do you think your partner is with Simon for the thrill of trying out something new or because she's made for the lifestyle?"

Jenn sighed, shook her head. "I'm sorry to tell you, but this whole back and forth is tiring. And regarding

Sharon, well, she's my partner and my friend. While Simon and she make for a great couple, I don't think this has anything to do with Warren Rawlins."

King raised an eyebrow but otherwise didn't react while seconds stretched into what had to be a whole minute without anybody speaking or moving. Then she nodded once, got up and walked away. "If you'll excuse me for a minute."

She left for another room and Sharon looked over to Jenn. "This is fun, don't you think?"

"As much fun as the time I tried waxing my legs, yes."

Sharon gave her a brief smile. "Shall we leave and make an appointment for tomorrow morning?"

Jenn shook her head. "Nope. Let's see what she's up to first."

"I just don't get her angle. If she wants to get back with Simon, she should know better than trying it this way. Simon's less than amused by her antics."

Jenn looked to where King had disappeared then back at Sharon. "It's clear as day that she dislikes you. Although until she tells you what her problem is, you'll have to wait and see. In the…"

King entered the room again, holding a small piece of paper. Looking at Sharon for a moment, she went over to Jenn and handed her the slip.

"This is the address of André Desoto. He met Warren at one of the parties, and they hit it off, as they say. They were together for close to a year, I think. Not openly, mind you. André works for a very conservative lawyer firm and hopes to make partner. I heard he got engaged to a woman not that long ago. Make of that what you will."

"And you didn't tell us about this why?" Jenn asked, pocketing the piece of paper in her jacket without giving it another glance.

"Because I thought you'd be able to do your job," King said with a cold smile.

As King had her back to her, Sharon shook her head. What was there to gain with playing dumb? "Are you enjoying this investigation so much you fear it could be over?" she asked the other woman.

King turned. "No. I didn't want any of this to happen, and no, I wasn't keen on meeting you. I know that Simon and you aren't meant to last, so why bother? When the chance presented itself, though, I took it. I was and am still holding on to the belief that your dislike for me will make you try to solve this case as fast as possible."

Sharon didn't want to speak, yet couldn't hold her tongue either. "What is your damned problem?"

King pursed her lips, delighted by the fact she had gotten under Sharon's skin. "I dislike impostors, naïve women who see a good-looking man and think they want to try being an *oh so bad girl* for a little while. You might think BDSM culture is part of your being now, but soon enough you will run and find somebody else to warm you in a cushy bed." She made a few steps toward Sharon, then stopped herself. "We don't need tourists in our world."

She gave Sharon a long, hard look, then turned back to Jenn. "Now that I know your name, let me tell you that I did my own research. I know that you're the only child of two psychiatrists, a child who has a big mouth to overcompensate for her vulnerability."

She faced Sharon again. "And I also know that although you've been in a relationship with Simon for months now that my contacts in the NYPD don't even know you're dating anybody. You're just another pillow princess that fears her naughty secret could become public. To be honest, you're both pathetic, and now I'll ask you to leave. Just do your job and be gone, will you?"

She turned her back to both of them and left for the same room she had gone to before. Hot anger made Sharon's pulse race, and she opened her mouth to give King a piece of her mind, then shut it again. It would solve nothing.

Jenn walked over to her and touched her arm. Sharon focused on her partner instead of the door King had disappeared behind.

"Come on, there's nothing more to learn here."

Jenn was quiet while they walked downstairs. King's words had hit home for both, wrong as they were. Sharon was glad they had gotten a parking space almost in front of the house, and she waited until they both were in the car before she addressed Jenn. "None of what this woman said is true. It's not worth thinking about."

Jenn put the key in the ignition and faced Sharon, her facial muscles relaxing and a small smile breaking free. "You know, that's what I wanted to tell *you*. Although don't tell me you won't be thinking about it. You will and so will I."

"I don't want to think about it," Sharon said, breaking eye contact to look out of the side window.

"And you will anyway. Good old Helen wasn't quite wrong with what she said about me. I'm sure my parents' constant analyzing made me as loud as I am, because while growing up, I wanted to block them out, wanted to live instead of always inspecting my every move, every choice." She laughed. "I once had a phase where I started to sing every time my poor mother opened her mouth as I was so done with her understanding and her always trying to guide me into the right direction." She gave Sharon a small smile. "Anyway, King's wrong when it comes to you. She just knows about your insecurities when it comes to disclosing your relationship with Simon and she tapped right into them."

Sharon looked at Jenn again. "I'm not with Simon because of his looks or because of a rebellious phase."

Jenn's smile became natural again. "You know it, I know it and King knows it as well, and she hates it so much. But that said, Simon's looks don't hurt at all."

Sharon hummed. "Hmm, he's not all that shabby."

"Yeah, right. Let me know if he's too shabby for you."

"So you can cheer him up? Forget it. And your very own Brian doesn't look all shabby either. Anyway, let's get going."

Jenn started the car. "What? We don't want the witch to think twice and come down to have another word with us? But yeah, let's get back to the precinct and find out what the name she's given us is worth. We could do with a solid lead."

Chapter Sixteen

Splitting the work, Jenn called friends and family of Rawlins, inquiring if they'd heard the name André Desoto before while Sharon tried finding out more about the man himself.

At one point, Jenn slipped out of the office, and when she came back, she carried two wrapped sandwiches. She placed one right onto Sharon's keyboard. A glance at her watch told Sharon it was way past lunchtime and her stomach growled at the smell.

She took it up, beginning to unwrap the foil. "What did you get?"

"Caprese. I thought something light couldn't hurt."

"You're right. Thanks, hon. Let me fetch some coffee to go along with it." Sharon got up while Jenn flopped down on her chair.

"You know that the stuff's been in the pot since this morning, don't you?"

Sharon poured the first cup, then walked over to where Jen's was sitting on her desk, still not empty. She topped it off. "Since when do you mind? And I'm sure it will make us value the sandwiches even more."

Jenn took a sip and made a face. "Yeah, no. I'll make a fresh one after lunch, but tell me, does your Simon know you're a girl with such refined tastes?"

Sharon sat back down again, grinned. "He does. And don't forget he's a Jersey boy at heart."

"Bad boy from the suburbs turning billionaire. Sexy."

Sharon rolled her eyes and bit into her sandwich. It was good, and she stretched her legs, wishing she had time for a walk. "I think he's just a millionaire. Sorry. But guess whose family are billionaires and who will become even richer with his wedding?"

"André Desoto?"

"Bingo. He's forty-three, comes from a wealthy family and has a younger brother and an older sister. He went to Yale, although his grades were mediocre. While he took the bar, nobody will sing his intellectual praises anytime soon. Rumor has it, his father was and is not impressed. Well, Desoto Junior worked for a few firms until Daddy got him the job at Miller, Burton and Owens."

Sharon took another bite of her sandwich, and Jenn did the same, waiting for her to continue. "Desoto's main deal is take-overs. There's not much to be found about his personal life, but yes, he got engaged to a young socialite. She's fifteen years younger than he is and the heiress of a fashion dynasty, just finished her fashion design studies."

"Desoto should be keen to make this marriage happen. I'd love to know if he had to sign a prenup," Jenn said.

"Most likely. Although he just got engaged two months ago. The last thing he'd want now is for the world to find out that he likes to run around with naked men on a leash."

Jenn snorted, then coughed, reaching for her cup to take a sip of the offending coffee. "But it's such a pretty picture, isn't it?"

A tomato had fallen out of Jenn's sandwich and Sharon opened her drawer, getting out a napkin she handed to Jenn. "Yeah, it's very cute. What did you find out? Had any of Rawlins' family heard of Desoto before?"

Jenn picked up the tomato, wiped the spot then crumpled the tissue. "Nobody had. Not his family, not his friends. But that was to be expected. So, what do you say? Shall we pay André a visit this afternoon?"

Sharon was about to answer when her phone rang. She had seen the number too often not to know that it was Second Precinct once again. Putting the sandwich away, she reached for the receiver.

"The sooner, the better," she said to Jenn before taking the call.

* * * *

André Desoto wasn't happy to have a cop on the phone, and even less so when Sharon insisted he had to talk to them in person. When she left him with the choice to meet at his office or the precinct, he asked if it were possible to meet at Central Park in an hour.

Sharon, swallowing the comment that he had to be very afraid of them if he wanted to meet outside at temperatures near the freezing point, agreed instead. It would be good to get out, even if it was for a short while.

When she hung up, Jenn made a face before telling her she couldn't come along as she'd have to meet with the prosecutor in an upcoming case.

"This is ridiculous," her friend said while she wrapped up the rest of her lunch. "But Thomas said something about new evidence, and that it all relies on my testimony now. Even so, I can only tell the jury what I told him before. And he should know me better. I won't wilt like a flower in front of the DA either. But you know him. If he can't control everything, he isn't happy."

"He's thorough, that's all," Sharon said, feeling just a little bit bad that she'd get to enjoy the rest of her lunch. "I'll tell you everything afterwards. "

"You better," Jenn grumbled, then got into her jacket, wrapping a new, thick blue scarf around her neck.

"Where did you get that?" Sharon asked, pointing at the scarf. It looked warm and comfy and was something she hadn't seen Jenn wear in all the years she'd known her.

"Oh. Brian's mother. I didn't have the heart to tell her that I'm not one to wear scarves."

Sharon smiled. "Seems she likes you after all."

"I'm not so sure. But she made it herself, and Brian says she never gave one to his other girlfriends, so she either likes or hates me more than those."

"I'm sure she likes you. You're the natural catastrophe nobody knows they need in their life."

Jenn scoffed. "Don't flatter me too much. Anyway, see you later."

She left. Sharon spent the next few minutes finishing her sandwich and ordering her notes, so she wouldn't have to spend too much time with paperwork later. Forgetting the time, she cursed when she glanced at her watch.

Arriving five minutes late, she could already spot Desoto near the Bethesda Fountain. The park was more deserted than usual, and Desoto looked just like his picture, a very good-looking man in his mid-forties, wearing an expensive suit, his dark blond hair just a tad bit too long, gelled back to make the too smooth look complete.

He was pacing up and forth, but stopped when he spotted Sharon approaching him.

"Mr. Desoto. I'm Detective Richards. Thank you for making the time."

While he took Sharon's offered hand, he looked less than happy to be there. "Listen, I don't have much time. I'm expecting a client soon."

Of course, he was. She gave him a smile. "I understand, and I don't have more than a few questions. It's about Warren Rawlins. I heard you and him were in a relationship for close to a year."

Desoto froze. It was obvious, he had not expected Sharon to go right for the jugular. It lasted for a second, then the expression in his eyes hardened. "I've got no idea where you got your information, but…"

Sharon interrupted him as she was in no mood for any more bullshit today. She had also forgotten to don her own scarf and gloves and would be glad to get out of the cold soon. "I think you said you were pressed for time, so let's not waste yours or mine. If you don't want to talk to me, okay, but it wouldn't take me long to find enough people to corroborate the story and to drag you in for a formal interview."

The coldness of his expression turned into one of hot anger, and Sharon wasn't surprised to see the temper. This was the type of man who wanted things to go his way, who didn't like opposition.

"What do you want to know? And believe me, if you spread any rumors and smear my reputation, I will come after you."

Sharon rubbed her hands against each other to keep them warm. "Mr. Desoto, you're a lawyer and while you aren't working in criminal law, you should know better than to threaten a police officer. So anyway, where did Warren Rawlins and you meet and why, and when did you end the relationship?"

A muscle twitched in Desoto's face, and he almost spat out the words. "We met at a…party. We talked, found out we had common interests, so we *saw* each other on a regular basis for a time, until I thought it was time to move on."

"You met at one of Helen King's parties?"

She had taken Desoto by surprise, and his whole body became as tight as a bow.

"Yes, we did."

Sharon brushed back some strands of hair that had blown into her face. It wasn't even the temperatures that made being out here close to unbearable—it was the wind that felt like it was peeling the skin right off her face.

"Listen, I don't care about your personal proclivities. I'm not here to judge or to spread rumors. I want to know who had a motive to kill Warren. Help me out and you'll be rid of me."

Desoto huffed. "Yeah, of course. You're looking for a scapegoat to take the blame."

"With no evidence to support this? I don't think so. Anyway, was your relationship a pure sexual one or more?"

Desoto didn't want to answer, and he turned away from Sharon, staring into the distance. "I'd say it was more for Warren than it was for me."

"He took it hard when you decided to break it off?"

Desoto looked back at her, and his stony expression turned into one of anger. "He was livid, called me every name in the book."

That rang true. After all that the people in Rawlins' life had said about him, it fit the profile.

"Wasn't Rawlins the submissive in your relationship?"

Desoto straightened, his gaze piercing, and while Sharon had sympathy about not wanting to talk about a BDSM relationship with a stranger, in this case it had to be.

"Yes, he was. The worse you treated him, the more he liked it." He laughed but it was a sound full of bitterness. "For a while it was great, you know. Warren was an attractive man and so obedient when he wanted to be. I'm a lawyer and at work I've got to mind every word. The same in my social circles. One misstep and you're out. So it was perfect. When I was with Warren I could say whatever I wanted to. I could unleash all the anger, and he would soak it up, beg for more even."

His gaze turned piercing. "It was all part of the game, and I never mistreated him. I was in full control of the physical act."

As much as a strange concept it would be for most people, it made perfect sense to Sharon. When he'd been with Rawlins, Desoto could let out all the negativity he had bottled up inside of him, so he could be professional and all smiles when he needed to be. Rawlins, in turn, had been able to deal with his own demons. Whether it was low self-esteem or feeling confined by a life that didn't fit his personality that made him crave intense humiliation, she had no idea. In any case, it was clear he'd have soaked up the praise he'd have gotten when he performed well in a scene. It was different than what she shared with Simon but in a way the same as two consenting adults filled each other's contrary but compatible needs.

"Just to be clear here, did Rawlins want to be humiliated or did he enjoy pain, too?"

Desoto bristled. "Do you want a detailed recount of what we did and when? What does it matter? But yes, he liked pain. He liked sex, too. For a while we wanted the same things in life."

Until they didn't. Or rather until Desoto changed his lifestyle and began dating a woman, to keep up appearances.

Desoto straightened. "Enough with that. You have your answers now. I've got better things to do than to discuss my private life with you." He turned his back to her and began to walk away.

"What did Warren do when he heard you got engaged to a woman? Did he threaten to out you?" Sharon called after him.

It had the desired effect, stopped Desoto cold. He was back with Sharon within seconds and his anger had turned into naked hatred. "This is none of your fucking business."

"*This* could be a motive." Taking a page out of King's book, Sharon gave him a cold look, a small smile. "You see, while I don't have concrete evidence you killed Warren, it's still like this—I don't have to convince *you* why there could be credit to the theory that you killed Rawlins, but you have to convince *me* that you didn't. You want me off your back, then convince me."

"You..." Desoto began.

"Don't interrupt me, please. I wasn't finished. Again, if you want me to be gone, then you'll answer my question and also tell me what you did the night Warren died between two and ten p.m."

He wanted to argue—she could see the storm brewing behind his eyes. Not being able to control his emotions would make him a bad dominant, although maybe he needed the game to stay in control in the rest of his life, and now that he'd lost his preferred way to unwind, he became unhinged.

"You are treading on thin ice here, Detective. It wouldn't look so good if I went and complained to your superior, would it?"

Sharon's smile came naturally. "Oh, please, do. You wouldn't be the first one to do so either. And you know as well as I do that if it's not me asking the questions, it will be somebody else. But it's your choice."

"You think you're so smart," he spat out. "Anyway, Warren was... Let's say rather unhappy with my decision, and yes, he tried to threaten me. I reminded him I was still in possession of a few pictures he wouldn't want his parents to see. He backed off. And for where I was the day he was murdered, well, I was with my fiancée. And if you dare go to her and tell her anything about this, you'll regret it."

Sharon shook her head. "Threatening a police officer is still not a good idea. You should start to listen. And we'll have to verify your alibi."

"Then ask my fucking brother. We spent the day on his yacht."

Without another word, he turned and stormed off.

Sharon didn't try to stop him this time. There wasn't anything more to be gained here. They would check his alibi and go from there.

As much as she wanted to, she didn't believe he was the perpetrator as his anger was too close to the surface. Had he killed his ex-lover, he'd have tried to be more composed instead of raising red flags with the way he acted.

While she couldn't condone his behavior, a part of her could understand his reaction. If she became entangled in an investigation and her relationship to Simon was about to become public knowledge, she'd be agitated.

She blew on her fingers that had started turning blue. The thought she wasn't all that different to a man like Desoto didn't sit right with her. Their social circles might not be the same, but the way they dealt with their relationships was. She had never made a big deal out of her relationships, yet she had mentioned her boyfriends now and then. Sometimes one had fetched her from work at the end of the day.

With Simon, it was as if he didn't exist outside of the bubble of their time together. He should be more than a well-kept secret.

Another cold gust of wind made her shiver. As there was no use in lingering here, she made her way back toward the park's exit. Desoto might not be the solution to this case, but at least it was a fresh lead, and it even might keep Hannigan and Kelly off her back for a day.

Chapter Seventeen

Watching as Jenn left the office close to eight p.m., Sharon suppressed a yawn before stretching her arms. While her reports could wait until the next morning, she hated starting her day with paperwork and an hour more would hurt nobody.

She had spent most of the afternoon on the phone and a slight headache made her long for a window she could open. First, she had spoken to Desoto's brother who had confirmed the alibi. He said they had left for his yacht in the early morning and hadn't returned until late evening. It had been no surprise when he inquired why the police wanted to know whether his brother had been with him, but Sharon had managed to end the conversation without disclosing any details. If there was no reason to, she wouldn't drag Desoto's private life into the limelight. *Treat others like you'd want to be treated yourself.*

Once she'd hung up, she brought Jenn up to speed before calling Hannigan, then Kelly, the former wondering why she hadn't put the *pervert* in chains yet, the latter glad there was a trail to follow.

If it hadn't been Desoto, then who? Desoto's fiancée, who might know more than her beloved was aware of? Maybe it would be worth investigating her after all. Rubbing her temple, she decided this was something to worry about tomorrow.

She opened a new document on her computer and began typing, then stopped. Sitting back in her chair, she reached for her phone, smiling when she had guessed right and reached Simon at the club.

"Sharon, what can I do for you?"

Sharon's eyebrow rose. This was not the way he used to greet her. While his tone of voice wasn't cold, he was distracted.

"Nothing. I wanted to hear how you are, how your day was."

This morning, she'd told him that she didn't think they would see each other today, and he'd said he had a few things he had to take care of himself. Still, she liked talking to him, although now she felt stupid for assuming he even wanted to talk to her, then chided herself for her reaction.

It took him a moment to answer, making her even more worried—or should she call it paranoid?

"It wasn't all bad. I had a meeting with my tax accountant. And my brother called to inform me he'd come to visit me next week. He's got a meeting with a business partner in the city. If you feel like it, there's the chance to meet the one person who has all the dirt on me."

"That sounds great. Count me in."

"Good, then we'll make it happen. So how was your day?" he asked. Paper rustled in the background.

Telling him about her day, she was sure he was listening, though not in the same way as he normally would. Something was off, even if she couldn't put a finger on it. She wrapped a strand of hair around her finger. Either it was him or it was the case that was getting to her. King had gotten under her skin, whether she liked to admit it or not, and she was playing right into the other woman's hands when she worried and began to question Simon and herself.

When she stopped talking, it took him a moment to reply, and she heard him shuffling papers once more.

"If you don't think he did it, where do you want to go from there?" he asked.

"I've got no idea, and to be honest, I'm almost too tired to think. I'll go over everything again with fresh eyes in the morning."

"Sounds like a good plan. Don't stay at work too long."

"You neither. We'll talk soon."

"We will." He ended the call.

What is going on? She growled in the silence of her office. Damn her, if this wasn't like an itch she couldn't scratch. Knowing that her concentration was shot, she saved and closed the document on her computer

Things might look or sound different the next time they saw each other. Now she'd go home, take a hot shower, eat something and go straight to bed. Whether she'd be able to sleep was a different question.

Having to pass her boss's office on her way out, she sighed when the door opened. It wasn't Kelly who left, and when she realized who it was, she wished it had been him after all.

Luke Hastings—her former boss—closed the door behind him, stopping when he spotted Sharon. She watched the expression on his face change from tired to neutral. He had to have seen the same transformation on her face.

Speeding up a little, she gave him a nod before she passed him. She couldn't change the past. If she thought an apology would help, she'd give one again. He wouldn't want it, so she would do them both the favor to be gone as fast as possible.

"Richards, wait."

Dammit. She didn't want to stop, to talk to him. As there was no good reason to ignore his request, she turned around, waited for him to catch up to her.

"I heard about your case," he said when he stopped in front of her.

For the first time in months, she gave him a long look. He was still a good-looking man, and he sported a tan that he couldn't have gotten on its own. Not here. A vacation maybe? He had also lost a bit of weight and the dark circles underneath his eyes could rival hers. Was it the stress of his job or his private life?

"Is that what brought you here?"

He shook his head. "No, it was something else I had to talk about with Kelly. But he told me about the case and that Second Precinct is putting a lot of pressure on all of you."

Sharon shrugged. "They're pissed. Wouldn't you be, too, if we swept in and took over one of your cases?"

A smile broke free on his face, taking years off him. "I'd be livid and fight you tooth and nail."

He would, and knowing him, he'd have won this particular fight. Even though they hadn't been compatible in private life, he'd been a great boss—in fact, the best she'd worked for so far. She gave him a small smile back. "See? So yes, I get where they're coming from. It still would be nice if it got into their heads that we never asked for this case in the first place."

He nodded. "Politics. It would be nice if people remembered that this job is about solving crimes and finding ways to prevent others."

"You're expecting too much of humanity, especially a bunch of territorial cops," she said, the tension draining from her. She had never meant to be at odds with him, and this gave her hope she might be forgiven after all.

He snorted. "Indeed. I do. I'll be heading outside, how about you?"

"Yeah. Me too."

"You never learn, do you? All this overtime isn't healthy. Anyway, let's head out together?"

He began to walk, and she followed him. "Sure." She heaved a sigh. "I'd have loved to leave earlier, but I want this case closed and the angry mob off my back."

"You will. I always knew I could count on you and Jenn. You two won't rest until this case is solved."

They passed two of her colleagues and the two men greeted their former boss. Hastings had been popular among most of them. For a second, she wondered what the rumor mill would make out of him being here at this time of the day and the two of them leaving together. If two and two amounted to five in their minds, and they thought there was something going on between Hastings and her, at least nobody would even think about connecting her to Simon.

Appalled by her own musings, she almost stopped dead in her tracks and Hastings gave her a quizzical look.

"You don't have to answer, you know."

She looked up at him, realizing he must have spoken. "I'm sorry, sir. What did you say? I'm afraid I was lost in my thoughts for a moment."

He sighed. "Not only did I think we were over the whole *sir* thing, but I asked how you're doing otherwise."

It was a peace offering, one she didn't hesitate to accept. There was not much of a chance they'd work together again and they'd never be true friends, but she didn't want her first instinct to be to run when she saw him. "You're right, and I'm sorry. I'm doing fine. My mother got remarried not long ago and it was good to see her so happy. How about you?"

"That's good to hear." He made a face. "I'm thinking about transferring again. The job's okay most of the time but there's a lot of unrest within the team. We'll see."

They chatted for the rest of the way and once they were outside, Hastings paused. "It was good seeing you again, Sharon."

She smiled. "Likewise, Luke." She considered adding an apology then kept silent. It wouldn't change what had happened, and it didn't feel like the right moment to offer one.

He, too, looked as if he wanted to say something, but instead he nodded once and turned toward the parking space. "Stay safe."

"You, too."

Making her way to the subway, she almost ran into people twice as she couldn't stop the wheels in her head turning. There'd been a breakthrough in her case that might not help them after all, the man she was in love with was distant and the one she'd shunned earlier this year had softened his attitude when it came to her.

Right now she was on edge like she hadn't been since before she'd met Simon and he had shown her a way to deal when the turmoil inside herself became too much. She could still call him, though she'd feel even worse if he rejected her or agreed to meet with her and still behaved so unlike himself.

Her original plan of a shower and sleep had to do. The rest would wait until tomorrow.

Chapter Eighteen

Waking up before five a.m. thanks to the garbage cans outside being emptied with a noise that would wake the dead, Sharon got up and was out of her apartment within half an hour, deciding even coffee could wait until she reached the office.

This early, it was quiet outside and the harsh wind made sure she was wide awake within minutes after she left the warmth of the subway behind. She was startled when her phone rang and prayed it wasn't about another case, or even worse, a murder related to her actual one.

She hadn't expected it to be Simon, and she answered, annoyed with herself for being worried. It was instinct, one she couldn't shake off. Her job, then the death of her father had told her that life could change in a heartbeat and that any call this time of the day could not mean a good thing.

"Hey. Are you okay? It's not even six a.m."

"I am. I didn't wake you, did I? I thought half-past-five was your usual get-up time. I can call later." Now he sounded worried. *Fantastic.*

"No, it's okay. I woke up early and am on my way to work. What's the matter?"

He sighed. "It's about yesterday. I know I was curt with you and thought I owed you an explanation."

It was good that her gut feeling had been correct. Still, she shook her head even if he couldn't see it. "You don't owe me anything."

"Maybe I don't owe it to you, but how about you deserve more than receiving mixed signals?"

He knew how to read her well, and maybe it shouldn't surprise her. *So is he more empathetic than the other men I've dated or were my last boyfriends jerks all around?*

"I think I can agree with that. What is or was up? If you want to tell me, that is."

"I do. How about we meet tonight?"

If this day turned out as the last one had, it would be another long one. Not that it mattered. It was Friday, and it would hurt nobody if she arrived a bit late at work tomorrow. If nothing shook loose today, there might not even be something to investigate.

"Sure. Where do you want to meet?"

"The club."

There was an edge to his voice, and it sent a shiver of anticipation down her back. So often, they were of a similar mind when it came to their needs.

"I'm looking forward to it," she said.

"Me too. And Sharon, I didn't mean to drag you into another mess."

She had almost reached the precinct and stopped, turning her back to work for a moment longer.

"Helen? Or the investigation."

"Both?" he replied, chuckling.

"Well, you didn't. Would I still be lead detective of this case if I hadn't investigated the murder in the Davis case and become entangled with you? No, but I don't mind paying this price. At all."

"Good."

Did he sound pleased? "Don't become too full of yourself."

"I won't. But I'm glad you became entangled with me."

She almost snorted. It was good to know he didn't stay down long, but it was still too early for witty banter. She didn't even have her first coffee yet.

"As much fun as this conversation is, I've reached work. I'll text you when I leave, although I've got no idea when that will be."

"I'll be here."

They ended the call, and Sharon made her way into the warmth and chaos of work.

* * * *

When Sharon reached the club, it was after nine, and she was still deep in thought. She and Jenn had spent most of the day trying to make a comprehensible puzzle of the kaleidoscope of facts that didn't want to go together, and she was beat.

Warren Rawlins had been an unpleasant man who had tried to hide that he'd been gay and into BDSM. He had invented a girlfriend named Amy who they were sure didn't exist, although maybe it had been Desoto he was talking about.

Desoto in turn had as much to hide as Rawlins had and gave the impression of not even liking his lover much, that he'd used Rawlins to fulfill his needs and nothing else.

Nobody they had spoken to, not friends, not people from the party scene, remembered having seen Rawlins and Desoto together, although when they spoke to Rose, the other woman had offered the theory that Desoto might have been masked when he was with Rawlins.

So Desoto had a clear motive and a lot to lose if his affair came out. Until this afternoon, it hadn't mattered as it looked like he had an alibi. That had shattered the moment his sister-in-law called to tell Sharon that while it was true that she and her husband had spent the day with Desoto, her brother-in-law had left for a good two hours in the middle of the day. The yacht had never made it to the open sea and had remained in the harbor the whole day.

So where had Desoto been? She would ask him tomorrow and he better have a good answer, or she'd book him without a second thought.

When she entered the club—everything so familiar by now—she made her way to Simon's office, almost bumping into a guest leaving one of the rooms down here.

How would I react if somebody threatened to out me to my social circles? Well, she wouldn't resort to murder, but she didn't have that much to lose either. Her family would still have her back and she could find another badly paying job. The fall would be far worse for André Desoto.

Squaring her shoulders, she made her way toward Simon's office. There was nothing she could do right now, and it was time to leave the day behind.

When she opened the office door after a quick knock, it was easy to see that something was off at once. Simon was sitting behind his desk, his face was drawn taut, and she could smell cigarettes at once.

He smoked when something had gotten under his skin, never otherwise. Twice she had caught him right before a date. Back then it had been the uncertainty of where they were heading, but as far as she was aware, he hadn't smoked in months.

Closing the door behind her, she leaned against it. "That bad a day?"

He took a deep breath, and it was as if she could touch his anger if she reached out.

"I'm sorry, but I think we should postpone our plans. I'm not in control tonight," he said, and even his voice couldn't suppress his frustration.

She gave him a calm smile. "No problem, but will you tell me what this is all about? I'm worried."

When he looked at her, his eyes almost black, she was sure he'd reject her, though then he spoke.

"I'm fucking angry."

Which wasn't hard to see. He was willing to talk, so she swallowed the quip.

"What happened?" she asked instead.

"What do you think?" he asked, getting a cigarette out of the pack that lay on his desk, before putting it back in again.

"Helen?" she ventured a guess. In almost all of his life he kept a cool head, but he'd been close to this woman, and was fond of her in a way.

"The one and only."

"What did she do this time?"

He took another deep breath and opened the first drawer of his desk, putting the cigarettes away.

Shoving it closed, he met her gaze. "After the stunt at her party, I called her the next day and told her in no uncertain terms that I wouldn't accept her trying to play us. As I was in no mood to hear any explanations, I ended the call then."

It was good to hear she hadn't been alone in being rattled by the situation. She had seen he'd been pissed and figured he'd told King as much. Now she had the confirmation, and, yes, it felt good.

King was an old friend, a former lover, and Sharon understood that there was a bond between Simon and her. It didn't mean that it gave the woman any right to try to ruin Simon's new relationship.

"I figure she didn't take it well," she said with no inflection in her voice. This wasn't about her feelings but his. She had asked, and now she would listen.

He scoffed. "Of course not. She called back several times that day. She tried the club, the apartment, my cell phone. She left voice messages that I never listened to but deleted."

He leaned back in his chair and folded his hands on his desk but his fingers were still twitching, fighting the need to reach for the cigarettes again.

"So anyway, I found out that Helen is doing her best to destroy a business deal in the making yesterday."

"What kind of deal?"

He leaned back in his chair and spoke in a clipped tone, making her consider walking over to offer a hug, but she remained in place.

"I'm about to acquire some property in Queens, or at least I was. You know that the club is my life, but in the last months, I've realized that I created a playground for the wealthier parties of New York. In a way it makes sense even, as the business has to finance itself. There's property taxes, utilities, equipment and personnel that must be paid. You know I insist on everything being top quality, so the fees people have to pay are hefty ones."

"How much is it?" She wasn't green behind the ears, had known that the clientele was a well-off one. It didn't mean she had ever thought about the costs involved.

"More than you'd be able to afford on a regular basis. Although in the end, the cost depends on what you need. We have people that want to give BDSM a try, and they pay a fee for their session, and we never see them again. Then we have members who pay a monthly fee as well as a reduced session fee. Our Doms and Dominatrixes receive their salary as well as a part of this fee."

It sounded fair. "And now you want to open another club in Queens?"

He shrugged. "I'm not sure yet. Either it'll be a club for those who can't afford the fees here or it could be a meeting place for people in the scene with options for seminars and the likes. Maybe it could be both. People have needs independent of their income. And there are too many people who think they'll buy a few toys and have a go at it. I've got an acquaintance, an emergency room doctor, who was a regular customer before he moved to Los Angeles a few years ago. He could tell you some horrific stories from play gone wrong."

Sharon winced. "Ouch. I don't think I want to imagine that. But I like your idea." She still wanted to go over and offer a hug, but this wasn't the end of the story, or he wouldn't still be so tense.

"Then let's discuss ideas soon?" he asked, offering her a tight smile.

"Sure. I'd love that." If he wanted her input, she'd give it. "But what's the rest of the story? What did Helen do?"

His eyes darkened and as much as she hated to cause his frustration to rise to the front of his mind once again, he'd feel better for letting it out.

"See, to find a suitable property I called the realtor through which we got to know each other. It seemed the easiest. She must have told Helen, as all of sudden I got a call that there was another bid on the property which was substantially higher than mine."

Anger rose in Sharon, and she had to oppress the urge to curse. "Are you sure that Helen was the other bidder?"

"Well, I called the realtor and let her know that she better tell me if it was Helen or not, because if I ever learned the bidder was Helen, I would make sure that word went out that her company wasn't as discreet as it should be."

He wouldn't have shouted, wouldn't have insulted the woman, but his ice-cold demeanor would have done the trick.

"She confirmed your theory, I see. Did you speak to Helen next?"

"I tried to. Guess who ignored my calls then. Not that I called more than twice." He broke eye contact with her, looked down at his desk before looking up again. "She called me back maybe an hour ago and was oh so polite. I told her to stop her bullshit games and to stay out of your and my private life."

This wouldn't have gone over well. Not with King. While Simon liked absolute control in the bedroom, King wanted complete control in all areas of her life.

She made a face, trying a smile she knew was failing. "And then she apologized and told you she'd never do this again?"

"Yeah, right," he all but spat out. "She started to list all the reasons why I'm mistaken and why I don't need you in my life."

They just looked at each other, two people united in anger.

"And did she make you see the light?" Sharon asked, not able to hide the edge in her voice. God, she was tired of this woman and this shit.

"I listened until she was done, wished her a good day and ended the call. She didn't want to listen, and I was too angry to even try to discuss this any further with her."

"You know that this is still not over?"

"Yeah." He opened the desk drawer, then took out the pack of cigarettes.

Straightening, she walked over and stepped behind him, putting her hands onto his shoulder, feeling the tension in her fingertips.

"Helen's not worth risking cancer." She began with applying soft pressure and she felt more than heard him sigh.

"It's better than wanting to beat something into a bloody pulp."

A close friend had betrayed him, had tried dictating his life. Of course, he was livid.

"I think there must be a better way than both of those options."

"I'm sure you're right, but tonight I don't see any. How about you go home and we talk tomorrow? I'm in no way good company right now."

"I don't care."

He looked up at her over his shoulder. "I care."

She almost gave in. If he truly wanted to be alone, she'd respect his wish, although she didn't think he would make good company for himself right now either. And wasn't it part of a relationship to be there for her partner when they were down? Not that the both of them had much experience with a good relationship. Still, it was never too late to strive for a better one, was it?

"If you're sure that you want me to go, I will. But do you trust me?"

"I do." He spoke without thinking twice, and her decision was made. If he was too agitated for their preferred way to unwind, there were other options to distract him from the jumble of his emotions.

Letting go of him, she walked over to the key box that was on a shelf behind his desk and got out the key to his private room inside the club.

"Sharon, not tonight."

She closed the key box, faced him again. "I know. Come on." She held out her hand, and waited until he had come to a decision and got up, taking her hand.

"What do you want with those then?"

"You'll see." She led him out of the office. They made their way through the club in silence that was interrupted by sounds coming from the other rooms, the dungeons downstairs.

Opening his room, she switched on the lights – dim as they were – and let Simon proceed before closing the door behind him.

He stood still, watched her, and she crossed the distance between them, putting her hand on his chest. Simon locked gazes with her, and while he didn't speak, it was easy to see he wanted to know what she was doing here.

She gave him a brief smile, then spoke. "I know you're not into pain, and I'd have no idea what I'd be doing playing a Dom either, but I suggest that tonight you leave the thinking to me. My game, my rules for a change. But only if you agree to this. It's your decision."

Curiosity struggled with his need for control, and she waited for him to make up his mind. In her job she had to be in control of herself, stay calm even under pressure. When it came to the bedroom she liked to submit, but it didn't mean she couldn't take the pressure off him for the night.

"Do I need a safe word?" he asked, a trace of amusement back in his voice.

"I don't think so, but better be safe than sorry. So what will it be?"

It took him a minute to answer. "Queen."

"Agreed. Any reason for this choice?"

A self-deprecating smile appeared on his face. "Yes. It seems that now that I've got a problem with a King, my Queen is coming to my rescue."

She suppressed a smile. He had a way with words when he wanted to, could command as well as seduce.

"I see."

He put a hand over hers where it still rested on his chest. "Sharon, I…" he began but she interrupted him.

"Do you agree that this is my game tonight?"

He inclined his head. "I do."

"Good. Then you will only speak when I allow you to. Understood?"

The stormy expression in his eyes made it clear this didn't sit right with him.

"Understood," he answered her, his jaw tight.

Scanning the room, she considered her next move. Letting go of him, she took a step back. "I want you to stand in the middle of the room. Then get out of your shirt and T-shirt."

She didn't wait for him to comply and walked over to the bed, where she shrugged out of her coat. Folding it, she looked back at Simon who had done as she had asked. Standing in the middle of the room, wearing a pair of dress pants and a pair of black shoes, his chest bared, he made for a nice view. His shirt, tie and T-shirt were lying in a heap beside him.

She wouldn't lie to herself. The sight of him woke her desire, tore at her discipline. There was something about his deep gaze, his slender body that was muscular nonetheless, that made her crave to touch him. While she worked out in the gym or went running, he preferred swimming, and his workouts paid off. She didn't think she'd ever tire of looking at him.

Strolling over to where he stood, she gave him a once-over, and he cocked an eyebrow in response. She smiled. Oh, he'd lose the attitude before long. He wasn't in charge and she'd drive the lesson home soon enough.

"You're not allowed to speak. *And* you're not allowed to touch."

He didn't look all that pleased, but obedience was not in his nature.

"If you comply with my demands, I'll reward you in a way you will enjoy. A lot."

Putting both of her hands on his collarbones, she began to trail them all over his chest, enjoying the feeling of his strong upper body, the tickling of his sparse chest hair and how her caresses made goosebumps rise on his skin.

They made love far more often than they played the game. She had explored every inch of his body before, yet tonight was the first time she was in charge. It was something she could get used to now and then.

When her fingertips glided over his nipples, they hardened, and Simon took in a sharp breath. When Sharon looked up, the heat in his gaze made her breath hitch, and for a moment, she was tempted to get on her toes and kiss him.

Not now.

Brushing his nipples once more, she studied his reactions, how his pupils dilated and his body shuddered.

"You feel good, very, very good," she whispered, allowing her hands to trail lower, right to the waistband of his pants, where she followed its outline with a fingernail. His hips twitched forward, and there was no way she could miss his erection straining against the confines of the fabric.

It was tempting to reach lower and feel his hardness underneath her hand. No, she wouldn't rush the game.

Letting go, she rounded him so she could map out his back just as she had his chest. His breathing had sped up, and his hands had curled into fists at his side.

Withdrawing for a minute, she just looked at him. Simon stood still, his body tense in anticipation of what would happen next. Making her wait for his next move was something he often did, and Sharon knew the frustration of biding her time, wondering what he had in mind. It was hell in a way—it didn't leave room for all the other things that had her on edge in the first place.

When the fingers of his right hand began to twitch, she moved in again, placing a fingernail at the base of his neck before making her way down his body until she reached his pants again.

He moaned, a shudder running through his body.

"Hmm, I think you like that," she murmured. "So no more of that."

Stepping around him, she looked up at him and he met her gaze, defiant and less than amused. There was nothing reserved about him now.

His lips were parted, and she was tempted to give in for just a second and brush his lips with hers. If she did, the game would derail. Her own hunger for his touch was almost too strong to be ignored.

When she cupped his cheek, the coarse hairs of his goatee stubble pricked against her skin. His gaze was challenging her, and for a second she wasn't sure who was in control here.

This wouldn't do. Letting go of him, she walked over to the wooden table where his selection of toys waited. As his back was to her, he had to guess what she would go for.

Picking up a blindfold she had worn more than once, she went back to him, then stood behind him.

"Don't forget not to move."

Getting on her toes, she secured the blindfold, making sure it was tight enough he wouldn't be able to see but not tight enough he'd be uncomfortable. She noticed the slight flinch, then put a hand on his back.

"I'm too distracted when you look at me," she said, and he chuckled.

He wouldn't be amused for long. She stepped around him and let out a squeak of surprise when strong arms gripped her, pulling her close, his mouth finding hers in a kiss that was pure heat. With his tongue penetrating her mouth, his hands trailing lower to cup her ass, her simmering desire became a roaring fire of want that threatened to consume her.

One of his legs parted hers, and the slight friction against her pleasure point made her whimper. Oh, hell no, this was not the game they had agreed on. With effort, she broke the kiss and stepped back, smacking his ass.

"No way. You're not in charge tonight."

"I could…" he began, but she didn't let him finish.

"I'm sure you could do a lot of things. But this is a last warning. Either you behave, or I'll leave you here to deal with this yourself."

She ran a hand from his stomach to where his hard cock strained against his pants.

He opened his mouth, but she applied just a bit of pressure with the palm of her hand and whatever he wanted to say was drowned by his moan.

"You won't speak. You won't move," she said, her voice hard. "I mean it, Simon. Try me and you'll see."

She removed her hand, waited for over a minute, and when he remained pliant, she spoke again. "Wait for me here, will you?" Walking back to the table, she grabbed an item she had handled at least as often as he had. Holding it in one hand, she returned to him, taking his hand.

"I think we'll relocate you. Don't worry, I'll lead you."

Together they made the few steps toward the four-poster bed.

"Now turn around."

He did so, although taking his time, and once he had his back to the bed, she used his pair of handcuffs to cuff one of his wrists. Next, she wove the chain behind one of the posters before cuffing his other wrist. That should prevent him from trying any other stunt.

Simon pulled at the chain, his body tense.

"Not used to this, huh? Well, that happens when you're a bad boy and misbehave. Now, if you show me you can be very good, too, you'll be rewarded. If not, I'll have my fun with you and go home."

She watched how he stilled, straightened, and she wished she knew what was running through his head at this moment. At least he wouldn't be thinking of King right now, and she would make sure he wouldn't think of anything before long.

"Let's try this again, shall we?"

Breaching the small distance, secure in the knowledge he wouldn't be able to interfere, she began with placing a tiny kiss on the side of his throat, right over his pulse point, then kissing her way down to his collarbones. He moaned, and she mirrored her actions on the other side.

Wanting to taste more of him, she showered his chest with small kisses for minutes, licking and nipping at his skin now and again. When he took a shuddering breath, she upped the ante and closed her lips around one of his nipples, running the tip of her tongue over it a few times.

He moaned more loudly, and there was the slight clank of the chain as he moved his hands to no avail. Tugging at his tender flesh with her teeth once, she let go, switching sides, rubbing the abandoned nipple with the pad of her thumb.

He shuddered and pressed forward, seeking more contact.

Deciding she had teased him enough for the moment, she pulled back. Passing half of the room to where a lone chair stood, Sharon sat, thinking back to the many times he had made her take his place.

Like those other times, she was aroused, but this time she'd decide the next course of action, not him. Feeling too hot in her sweater, she stripped out of it, glad she had decided to wear a tank top underneath, then watched her partner and lover while sitting still and silent. This was a useful technique in interrogations and in the bedroom.

Had he ever had the roles reversed on him, even in such a soft variation of a scene? Given how he wanted and needed absolute control, this had to cost him. It also spoke volumes about his trust in her.

Wasn't she crazy that she worried about people learning about this relationship when it was the first time she felt like herself in one?

Minutes had passed, and Simon shifted his weight from one foot to the other. She took it as her cue that he was nearing the end of his patience. Getting out of her shoes, she moved over until she stood in front of him. Without touching him, she could feel his body heat and her hands curled into fists.

Her fingers itched from wanting to feel his skin underneath her fingertips, and she would like nothing better than to bury her nose in his neck and inhale. There was something arousing and comforting about his scent.

Giving in to her need, she put her arms on his shoulders, closing the distance between them. Taking a deep breath, she hummed, then closed her lips around his earlobe, tugging.

She smiled when he shivered in reaction. Kissing a trail down his neck, a thought made her stop halfway. "Would you mind if I marked you? Answer me?"

"No. Do it," his answer came at once.

Not wanting to analyze this urge, she began sucking at the skin underneath her lips, enjoying his low moan, and she increased pressure. He groaned and the handcuffs rattled. She released his soft flesh when she was sure he'd see her mark for the next few days and shook her head at herself. This was primal, unlike herself and she loved it.

Not giving him time to settle, she began unfastening his belt, then lowered his zipper. Hooking her fingers into the waistband of his pants, she dragged them down until they fell to the ground, then kneeled to help him with his shoes, so he could step out of his pants.

Being done with patience for the day, she shoved the pants aside with her foot, giving herself a moment to admire his strong legs, the shape of his hard flesh contained by a pair of black boxer briefs.

Tracing the outline of his cock with one of her fingers, she spoke. "As I've forgotten to mention it earlier, you're only allowed to come when I allow you to."

He tensed, and she smiled. Turnabout was fair play, wasn't it?

"Don't worry. I will make it feel good for you, believe me," she teased, kissing his cock through the barrier of fabric.

Not wanting to deny him or herself, she helped him out of his boxer briefs, and wrapped a hand around his erection, stroking it from its base all the way to its head.

Simon's hands jerked forward, and he growled out when they grabbed thin air.

Sharon laughed. "That's not being a good boy. Consider this a warning. If you behave, I'll get you off—eventually. If you don't, I'll sit back and watch you get yourself off. Whatever sounds more enjoyable to you. I will enjoy myself anyway. Oh, and if you misbehave too much for my liking, I'll unchain you, go home and get myself off thinking of how much I like the view of you chained to this bed."

He bit his bottom lip but didn't speak. She loved when he was in control of a scene or when they were equal participants in a game of give and take, but to see him now, restrained to the bed, a blindfold on his face, gave her a jolt of pleasure and satisfaction.

Not letting go of his cock, she began stroking it up and down with one hand while she engulfed the head in the warmth of her mouth, her tongue trailing along its side, the slit on top.

Much too soon, his ragged breaths were interrupted by long, drawn-out moans. Releasing his warm flesh from her hand, Sharon took his cock even deeper inside her mouth. It twitched.

If she continued like that now, the point of no return would be reached in no time. With reluctance, she withdrew, sitting back on her haunches. His whole body was taut, his hands curled into tight fists.

Sharon herself was wet, longing for his touch, and her heart was beating faster than it should from the light activity. It was harder to stay in complete control than she'd have thought.

"Tell me how you feel," she commanded.

He took in a deep breath, and when he spoke his voice was hoarse. "I'm fucking aroused."

The pure frustration in his voice made her smile. Under normal circumstances, it was up to him when he'd find his pleasure. Now he had to rely on her willingness to even let him come.

"I can see that," she said.

Getting up on her knees again, she licked a path with her tongue from the head of his cock down to his balls, circling them with soft touches. "Well, I've decided to let you come once you ask me nicely. You may speak when you're ready."

When she next sucked the head of his cock, he didn't react, and she was sure he was holding his breath. She had done the same several times before when the need to come became so strong it was close to impossible to hold back, when her whole focus was on controlling a body that screamed for release.

She let go and stopped touching him, giving him a few minutes until he had relaxed before beginning to tease him anew by taking him as deeply inside her mouth as possible while stroking the underside of his testicles with her fingers.

He groaned, his hips moving forward a bit, though then he stopped, still mindful not to make her take more of him than she could handle. Still a gentleman even though his control was tested in a way he wasn't used to.

She loved his thoughtfulness, but it wouldn't spare him more sweet torture.

Twice more, she brought him close to the brink of orgasm, then stopped, letting him cool off before starting again. His legs had begun trembling, and his breathing was heavy.

She had just run a hand around his body, making her way to the tight entrance of his anus, circling it, her touch light, when he broke.

"Fuck. Please, Sharon, I need to come."

It had cost him to ask, must've grated in a way. He had earned his reward.

"Then you will. You did so well."

Wrapping her lips around his cock one last time, she didn't tease, just sucked the tender flesh while stroking up and down his length.

He came within seconds, his hands pulling at their restraints, his body shuddering, and she continued pleasuring him until he stilled.

Sitting back, she looked up at him. He was leaning against the bed poster now, his breathing labored.

Still aroused in a way that made her feverish, she pushed her own need away and got up to free him from his restraints. This had not been about her, but him.

Fetching the keys from the table, she opened the handcuffs, and he began rubbing one wrist, then the other. Sharon could see the marks that would last a day or two. Those handcuffs cushioned nothing.

Reaching up, she untied the blindfold next, letting it fall to the ground. His gaze met hers, and she was glad to see the anger from before was gone. *Good.*

He didn't give her time to gauge his emotional state and pulled her close for a kiss that took her breath and made her weak in the knees as her ignored desire flared up again full force. When he pulled away, his hands still on her waist, it took her a second to come back to herself.

"Thank you," he said. "I didn't know I needed that."

Touching his cheek, she smiled up at him. "Are you feeling better?"

"I do. Let's talk about this all later, okay?"

He took open communication between them very seriously. After a scene, even if it was a day later, he made sure to talk to her, to find out what had worked for her and what made her feel uncomfortable. It was one of the reasons she could let herself fall when being with him. It was natural they would do the same now that roles had been reversed. No matter how light the game, to talk about it was the key for the trust needed between them.

"We will. What do you want to do now? Grab some dinner on the way to your apartment?"

A slow smile appeared on his face and something in his gaze made her take a step back. He looked like a hunter, having chosen her as his prey.

"I think I will throw you on the bed and make you scream out my name." He spoke with so much arrogance that it grated her nerves.

"I've never screamed your name."

He crossed the distance between them and pulled her close.

"I know. I won't stop trying though."

As he lifted her up, she didn't feel like arguing. Her body was burning for his touch.

Chapter Nineteen

André Desoto entered Sharon's office without knocking before it was even ten o'clock on Saturday. The coffee was still dripping into its pot, and she was tired. She hadn't even booted up her computer yet.

She frowned at him. "Mr. Desoto? I didn't expect you, and I don't appreciate you coming over and barging in unannounced."

"I need to talk to you. Now."

He stopped in front of her desk, then sat on her guest chair.

Did he even hear me?

The same anger from their last meeting was present again, and his gaze wandered through her office. He had entered just a few seconds ago but the stench of sweat and alcohol had already begun to cloy the small space.

"You know, I would've come to talk to you later today," Sharon said, and the man's gaze settled on her.

"God forbid. I don't remember allowing you to come and see me whenever you feel like it."

But of course. She was sure he didn't see the irony in his statement. Getting up to fetch herself some coffee, no matter if the machine was done or not, she spoke with her back to him.

"It's not about what you want, Mr. Desoto. And it's also not up to you to decide if I come to talk to you or not. You're part of a murder investigation, whether you like it or not."

"I didn't murder anyone, and you've got no right to contact people in my environment and destroy my life."

Pouring herself some of the steaming liquid, she took in a deep breath, sighing when it didn't help with the foul odor he'd brought in. She turned back to him.

"Don't be so melodramatic. From what I'm seeing, you're better off than Warren Rawlins. What brought you here, apart from wanting to vent your anger?"

Desoto's eyes went wide, and he opened his mouth but she held up a hand to stop his outburst.

"I mean it. You've got one chance to tell me what you want, then we'll come to my questions for you. Maybe we even want to talk about the same things. But let me tell you that right now, you're our prime suspect in the murder of your former lover, and it's appearing way more likely that you did it today than it did yesterday."

"Fuck, fuck, fuck," he said, running his hand through his hair, disheveling it in the process. He looked bad, as if he had aged a few years since they'd spoken last. *Has he even slept or showered within the last day?* She waited, but nothing more was forthcoming.

"Okay, so it seems you don't want to talk," she said then reached for a thick folder. These were documents from a different case, but he didn't know that. As she had predicted, his eyes followed her movements.

He sighed, annoyed. "I don't think you're going to offer me some of that?" he asked, nodding at Sharon's coffee.

She was less than inclined to indulge him, but got up anyway. If she was too exhausted to deal with this shit, then he had to feel even worse. A couple of years ago, when she and Jenn had adjoining cubicles in the bullpen, her friend had put up a poster of a grumpy orange cat, sporting the text, "There's no life before coffee." Sharon agreed.

Handing Desoto a cup, she sat down again. "Last chance."

"Okay, okay." Desoto took a sip, wincing when it burned this tongue. His gaze met Sharon's. "I know that my good-for-nothing sister-in-law called you."

"She did what she's obligated to do by law."

"No, she's a bitch who would be glad if I were out of the picture when it comes to our future inheritance."

Sharon was not interested in their internal family struggles. "Can we focus on the case here? What did you do the two hours you disappeared the day of Warren's death?"

He had to have expected the question, yet he fidgeted on his seat, looking down at the cup in his hand.

When he hadn't answered in over a minute, Sharon leaned back and blew on her coffee before taking a cautious sip.

The slight creak of her chair made him look up at her. "I did what I did the week before and the week before that, but this time the rest of the day was spent with family. I should've known that being with them would just cause drama."

He paused, and Sharon waited. Now that he'd spared her a trip, she had all the time in the world.

"I was…with a friend during that time. I didn't see or talk to Warren at all this day."

Leaning forward, Sharon put her coffee away, then leaned on her elbows. "Mr. Desoto, I don't care what you do in your free time, and I don't judge you for as long as whatever you do is legal. What you're doing here right now is prolonging your own misery. If you didn't meet with Warren, who is this friend that you met with and where did you meet?"

Sooner or later, she'd find out the truth, but it would spare them all nerves and a lot of time if he talked to her now.

Breaking eye contact, he looked behind her, his gaze unfocused, and his voice was so quiet now, she had to strain her ears to understand him.

"Once a week I book a session at a club. It started a month or so after Warren and I broke up. I was there that Saturday, too. I had forgotten to cancel, and then I was more than ready to go after a few hours with my dear family. We all had agreed to meet Father for dinner earlier, so I had to go back, but yeah, it was good to take that break."

He looked at Sharon again, and for the first time there was a glimpse of the man behind the anger and the ambition that was born by a family's expectations. "Have you ever felt an urge, a compulsion so strong you cannot deny it, even though you know it would be better to stay away?"

Yes, she had, at least in a way. Since she had gotten to know Simon, she knew she was wired in a different way, and yes, some things would be easier if she were into something more accepted by society. But she loved Simon and cherished the special kind of intimacy with him.

"As long as we're talking about two consenting adults, nothing is out of the question," she replied.

Desoto scoffed. "I didn't know any cop could be so wide-eyed, but then what do you know about my circles?" he shot back.

Somehow, she pitied him. He was all bark with no leverage to go in for a bite.

"Nobody forces you to play by their rules. You have the education to make a name for yourself elsewhere. Not many have your freedom. But enough of that. I need the name and address of the club you attend as well as the name of your sub." She prayed it wasn't Simon's club but what were the chances?

Glaring at her, he reached inside his jacket, pulled out a business card and handed it to her. She was relieved to read it was from a club she hadn't heard of before. Not that she knew anything about the scene, apart from having been in Simon's club and attending one of Helen's parties.

"Okay, I will call them and verify your alibi. Still need the name of your sub."

"It's Roman," he spat out.

"Thank you. If that is all…"

Desoto interrupted her. "There's something else. I don't know if it's helpful or not, but I think you should know about this. After we broke up… Well, I ran into Warren one last time. It was at one of Helen King's parties, not that long before his death. When I saw him,

I wanted to leave but he intercepted me." He shook his head. "I should've left anyway. But we talked, and he suggested we *engage* one last time for old time's sake. We went to his apartment and well...had a good time." He snorted. "But when I went to leave, Warren told me that he didn't miss me anyway, that he had found somebody younger and better. He all but shoved me out and that was that. I guess you understand that I didn't feel like reaching out to him after that."

One last, tiny act of revenge from a scorned lover. It fit with her picture of Rawlins. There was the possibility that Desoto was lying, yet Sharon didn't think so. She wasn't so sure about Rawlins, though. Had there really been somebody new, or was this young lover a figment of his imagination, just like Amy had been?

There was one thing for certain. She was right back where she had begun—Helen King. Well, Desoto didn't need to know about her personal trouble with this woman, so she gave him a curt smile.

"Thank you for your openness. If your alibi checks out, you shouldn't hear from me again."

"I better not." He got up, towering over Sharon. "And if..."

Sharon got up herself. "No if, Mr. Desoto. And one tip for free. It never pays off to agitate those in charge. And like it or not, for the moment that's me."

He glared at her for a long moment, though when she refused to show a reaction, he turned on his heel and left the office, running into Jenn who was about to come in.

"Whoa, careful," Jenn said, but Desoto stormed by her without any reaction.

Jenn closed the door behind him. "Was that who I think it was?"

Sharon sat down on her chair again. "Yes, it was, and if he told me the truth, then we're back right at the beginning. Sit down, have some coffee and then you can tell me why you're here when I told you to enjoy a quiet weekend. Afterwards I'll tell you why I've got to talk to Helen King again."

Already at the coffee pot, Jenn threw her a quick look. "King? Again? Can't we just arrest her for being a major nuisance and be done with it?"

Sharon smiled tiredly, pulling her cup close, then shoved it to the side again. "I wish it were that easy."

Jenn sat on the edge of Sharon's desk. "It should be. I mean, let's be honest, she's trying to mess with your life and nobody needs that. And dear Warren. Well, it seems the world doesn't miss his charm, so we're working our butts off for what?"

Sharon touched Jenn's arm. She shared her friend's frustration. They were both exhausted. "It's our job to care, and even if Warren Rawlins was a major douchebag, there's his family out there waiting for answers. It's all anybody can do for them now."

"Yeah, yeah, I know." Getting up, Jenn walked over to her own desk. "But do you think they even want to hear the answers?"

"No, I don't think so. But it's not for us to decide. And now, what happened?"

Opening her desk drawer and getting out a bar of chocolate, Jenn began to peel off the wrapper, almost tearing it to shreds. "Nothing. Or not much."

"Argument with Brian?" Sharon ventured a guess.

Jenn stared so intently at her chocolate, Sharon wondered if there was a secret inscription she couldn't see. Her friend's shoulders heaved with an inaudible sigh.

"Yesterday, he told me that his whole family would meet for Thanksgiving dinner, and he invited me to join them." She looked up at Sharon. "I told him no. I'm a single child, I'm not good when it comes to first impressions or diplomacy. And while I love him, we've been dating for less than a few months. I'm not ready for this."

Looking at the bar of chocolate, she bit off a big chunk.

"And Brian didn't like this?"

Jenn washed the chocolate away with a big gulp of coffee. "He doesn't understand what the big deal is. He thinks I'm wonderful and that his family will love me, but it's not about that. I'm not ready."

"Did you tell him that?" Sharon asked.

"Yeah, I did. And he said he understands but then started to list all the reasons why it's not a big deal again. I was so angry that I left." She threw her half-eaten candy bar in the trash can and looked up at the ceiling. "Shouldn't it be enough when I tell him that I'm not ready? What is there to discuss?"

"Nothing." Sharon hurt for her friend and wished there was any advice that would help, but there wasn't. "To be frank, I think he doesn't even have to understand how you're feeling. He has to accept things for what they are."

Jenn faced her. "I agree. He tried calling me this morning, but I wasn't prepared to talk to him yet. I couldn't bear another discussion, and I'm not ready for an apology either if there might be one. So yeah, I thought I could hide at work and be productive at least."

Sharon gave her a small smile. "You can hide with me all you want. How about you try verifying Desoto's latest alibi? And yes, I'll tell you all about it in a second, while I decide when and where it will be best to tackle King again."

"Sounds like a plan. And, Shar? Thanks for listening."

"Not for that. And you know, why don't you text Brian and tell him you'll call him tomorrow? It's better than having him try to reach you again and again."

Jenn made a face but nodded. "Yeah, you're right, and I will. What about Desoto and his new alibi?"

Sharon took up the business card Desoto had given her and handed it to Jenn. "Well, guess who likes to use the services of a club to fulfill his needs nowadays?"

* * * *

It was almost three o'clock when Sharon and Jenn decided to call it quits for the day.

Jenn had spoken to the club's owner and had gotten the address of the employee Desoto had claimed to have been with. When Jenn had made a trip to his apartment, she had found him at home and the young man had corroborated Desoto's claim.

Sharon had spent the better part of the morning writing a report about Desoto's visit while deciding how to deal with King. She didn't think that calling the other woman or going over would give her any new information, especially in light of King's clash with Simon. Sharon didn't want to end up as a verbal punching bag once again. If a visit was necessary or she was positive it would benefit the investigation, she would deal with King, but this wasn't the case right this second.

In the end, she called Rose, inquiring about Helen's next party. Rose had no idea but called her back a few minutes later. Sharon was in luck as a party was planned for tomorrow night. This time, she didn't have an invitation, and she didn't need one. That was what her badge was good for, after all. King would be seething, which might prompt her to part with some information.

Jenn came back a short while afterward, and Sharon informed her about the plan, meager as it was. At least it made Jenn smile. After Sharon waited for her friend to finish with her own paperwork, the two of them left their office. Just outside they ran into Kelly, who had Hannigan in tow.

"Just the two people I wanted to see," Kelly announced, nodding at their office.

Sharing a gaze with Jenn, Sharon opened the door, let the two men precede them.

"What can we do for you?" Sharon asked once they all were inside, and Hannigan had occupied her visitor chair while the rest remained standing.

"Well, darling, it's what we can do for you," Hannigan snarled and Kelly's head whipped around to him.

"Address any of my officers this way again and I'll kick your ass outta here and file a complaint with your superior before you make it back to the office."

Hannigan sat up straighter in the chair. "What's wrong with you all? Instead of catching a killer, it's all about language aesthetics or what? Don't get me wrong, nobody cares about one pervert less on the streets, but how can we take care about the important cases if we're stuck with this bullshit?"

Sharon gritted her teeth and took a breath before she spoke. "I do care and so should you."

"You do? So why is this case not closed yet? But good news. You've got another week until we take this case back. And never mind, didn't you say you wanted to interview one of these homos that played hanky-panky with Rawlins? So what about him?"

As if sensing her mood, Kelly threw Sharon a warning gaze, but she chose to ignore it. "Detective Hannigan, what is your problem? Is it the fact that Warren Rawlins was homosexual or that he engaged in non-average activities?"

Hannigan snorted, got up. "Now didn't you phrase that in such a nice and polite way? Non-average activities? This guy was a fucking deviant! How deranged do you have to be to play fetch for somebody else, or whatever he did when he was wearing that collar. Not that I want to know."

"Ever heard of live and let live? No matter his proclivities, he didn't deserve to die this way."

"My, my, you've got a big heart for those miscreants, don't you?"

Kelly placed himself between Hannigan and Sharon, facing the other man. "Enough of this bullshit. I understand that Second Precinct's ass is as much in the sling as ours, but seeing that it doesn't seem you can be the least bit impartial, I'll do everything in my power so this case won't end up in your hands again."

"Oh, I see. Here it's all about political correctness. Some scum killed other scum but God forbid we say that out loud." Hannigan walked over to the door, stopping with his hand on the doorknob. "We'll see what happens next, but I can speak for my boss and myself that we won't end up looking like fools just because you can't tell your head from your ass."

He left without another word, and Sharon stared at the door even when it had fallen closed behind him, her hands balled into tight fists.

"What an asshole," Jenn said, sounding as angry as Sharon felt.

"Agreed," Kelly said. "But there's a lot of pressure from all directions to close this case. I'm trying to shield you as much as possible, but the outcries for answers are getting louder any day. We can count ourselves happy that the case hasn't garnered much attention in the press yet, but this is one tip to the bloodhounds away from exploding in our faces. Now is there anything new you can tell me?"

Turning to Kelly, Sharon was aware that her feelings were written all over her face but damned if she could change it for the moment. "André Desoto told me that he met Rawlins one more time after they split up, and Rawlins talked about a new man in his life, one Rawlins claimed he had gotten to know during one of Helen King's parties."

"So go to King and ask her about it?"

Sharon fought hysterical laughter. How to explain to her boss that King despised her for personal reasons without having to divulge those reasons? Jenn spoke before she could.

"Helen King loves mind games. Too bad that includes the police as well. We'll go to one of her parties tomorrow. Unannounced. We hope this will prompt her into cooperation."

Kelly looked doubtful. "I hope you're sure about what you're doing. The last thing we want is the commissioner riding our asses any harder. But you know her better than I do. And if that doesn't work, we can still decide to try finding somebody else who isn't Hannigan to tackle the case, even if it means telling the commissioner that we're out."

A sudden thought had Sharon's stomach churn. Nobody could know what King would tell a new investigator. She doubted her private life would remain private any longer.

Kelly gave her a long look. "Are you okay, Richards?"

She didn't even try to smile and lie. "Not yet, but I will be in a few. I know I shouldn't have let him get to me."

"He got to all of us," Jenn said.

Kelly sighed. "Your partner's right. This is not what the NYPD stands for, but sad as it is, there are still a few of us who are either relics from the dark ages or just slipped through the cracks. But I know Hannigan's superior, and no matter what Hannigan says, he will have his head."

He made his way toward the door. "If you'll excuse me now, I gotta file a complaint. And if you want my advice, go home now. The rest will wait until you speak to King."

"That was the plan, sir," Jenn said.

"Good." Kelly left, closing the door behind himself.

"Don't listen to that asshole." Jenn walked over to her, enfolding her into a hug.

It took Sharon a moment to relax, then she sighed. "Kelly is right. There aren't many of these bigots around any longer, but they can destroy your reputation in a heartbeat."

"And all of the good ones want to get rid of those morons."

"It's not that easy, and we both know it."

"Nothing worthwhile ever is," Jenn said, pulling back. "How about we leave men and secrets behind for a night and have a girls' night out?"

Sharon didn't have to think about it. "I'm in." Anything would be better than her thoughts running in endless circles. It had been too long since it just had been Jenn and her anyway.

"Awesome, let's go home, get dressed and I'll pick you up in three hours?"

"It's a plan."

Chapter Twenty

"Are you sure about this?" Jenn asked, looking from Sharon to King's house.

"No, I'm not, but I can't think of any better option."

She rolled her shoulders, suppressing a yawn. After staying out until almost three in the morning—visiting a restaurant and a couple of bars with Jenn—she'd gotten about four hours of sleep and was still tired and a little hungover at nine-thirty in the evening.

It had been good, though. When they had arrived at the restaurant, they had vowed not to talk about their boyfriends or men in general, and they hadn't. As they caught up on what was new with their families, books they had read, series they had watched, the hours had passed quickly. Twice they had to explain to some guys that they weren't interested in drinks and chatting, but the men had gotten the hint and left them alone without causing a problem. By the end of the evening, they had agreed they needed to do this more often, and Sharon hoped they would stick to it.

Now Sharon faced her friend. "As I see it, King loves to plan every step, treats people like pawns in her own personal game. She didn't plan this."

"Yeah." Jenn snorted. "If I were you, I wouldn't expect any more party invitations afterwards."

Sharon snorted. "Damn, I didn't think of that."

"See. And we're not dressed for the occasion either."

And why should they be? Both of them wore jeans and shirts, and while Jenn had chosen her trusted leather jacket, Sharon had decided on a warm coat.

She gave Jenn a wry smile. "Sorry, my leather pants are with the drycleaner. And now let's get this over with. They will stop letting people enter in a few minutes."

As they made their way over to the entrance, Sharon hoped they wouldn't have to call for back-up. She would, if it was needed, although it should be in everybody's interest to keep this as quiet as possible.

"May I?" Jenn asked, and she rang the doorbell before Sharon could.

The door opened to reveal the same guard that had opened the door for Sharon last time.

"Invitation," he demanded, looking from one to the other.

They both got out their badges and showed them to him.

"There they are," Jenn said.

Raising an eyebrow in reaction, the man didn't budge.

"What is this about?"

"We need to speak to Ms. King, and no, it can't wait," Sharon said. "Tell her that Lieutenant Richards and Lieutenant Reynolds want to talk to her. She knows who we are. And no, we won't speak with her outside.

You can either let us in, or we'll take her to the precinct with us."

Behind them a couple came up, and Sharon made sure they could see her badge before she put it away. They turned around and left.

"Now come on. Speak to your boss. It would be a pity if even more guests left because of us."

Shooting her a look full of anger, the man closed the door in their face.

"I guess now we wait," Jenn said. "You know, we should've brought a coffee. It's damned cold out here."

"I'd say next time, but I hope there won't be one."

The door opened again after less than five minutes, and the guard from before stepped aside.

"Ms. King expects you. But she lets you know that you'll have to be discreet. If you disrupt this party, she'll file a complaint with your superiors."

"Geez, for real?" Jenn scoffed. "Is this the part where we have to mention that we'll raise a stink and rat her and her parties out to the press if she doesn't cooperate? Anyway, that's not your problem, is it?" She turned to Sharon. "You know the way?"

"I'll bring you to her," the guard said.

"Thanks, we can handle ourselves," Sharon said, passing him without another glance. She and Jenn followed the hallway. They could hear the music and voices and Jenn leaned into Sharon.

"And this is the hidden, sensual underbelly of NYC?"

"Nope, this is a run-of-the-mill subculture party."

"Somebody's wearing their grouchy pants tonight, huh?"

Sharon didn't comment. They had reached the end of the hallway and they entered the main room. The party was still not in full swing, but there were a few scattered groups of people already in gear, and Sharon spotted a couple of women leaving for the more private cubicles.

People didn't pay them any mind, but why would they? They would think they were just another couple on their way to the changing rooms.

"Well, fuck," Jenn said, and following her gaze, Sharon almost froze.

King was where she had been last time, but she wasn't alone. Although she could see no more than his back, without any doubt, Simon was with her, and he had his arms around King's waist, was whispering something into her ear. No wonder King had let them in without a fight. The woman had known she'd have the upper hand. Her own hands were on Simon's back, but her eyes were fastened on Sharon.

What the hell was he doing here? And even if it was for a legit reason, he didn't need to have his hands all over her, did he?

Her stomach churning, Sharon didn't stop, didn't turn around but made her way over to the other woman. She kept her gaze on King while she spoke to Jenn.

"Make sure to get Simon away from King. If you can, make him leave. Threaten him with obstruction of justice or anything else you can think of. I want to talk to King alone."

"I'll get it done," Jenn said. Sharon was thankful there was at least one person here she could trust.

They had reached King and Simon was still talking to her when the other woman spoke. "Sharon, how nice of you to join us tonight."

Letting go of King at once, Simon whipped his head around, but Sharon ignored him. She didn't want to see the expression on his face, didn't want to hear what he had to say.

Jenn was taking his arm now, leading him away, and Sharon focused on King.

"You can cut the crap. And feel warned that I'm not up to any games tonight. So you can answer my questions, or I will make sure that everybody in this room sees my shiny badge before I'll take you with me to the precinct for further questioning. If the press gets wind of this, too, well, so be it."

King's gaze hardened, and she took a step toward Sharon so they were almost nose to nose.

"I wouldn't do that if I were you."

Sharon kept her gaze. "You don't get it, do you? I don't care for the consequences. If the commissioner makes sure I'm fired because some socialite has some dirt on him, then this isn't a job I want to have."

King laughed. "Big words. And what about your boyfriend?"

"What about him? If this was what it looked like, I'll dump him. Would I hurt, yes? But guess what? This wouldn't be my first relationship that ended, and I'd get over this one, too. And if this wasn't what it looked like, well, then I'd have a good laugh at your antics."

Enough was enough. Since this case had started, she'd been on edge because one woman hated the fact of her very existence. This whole mess shouldn't be her business in the first place, so either King delivered now, or she could discuss it with another cop.

Raising her head, Sharon spoke with care. "You have this one chance to cooperate, or this evening will be over for you and your guests."

King narrowed her eyes. "I'll make sure you regret this."

"Oh, please. I'm regretting every second I'm spending on this case. So?"

"Do we have to discuss this here?"

Sharon gave her a small smile. "Yes, we do."

Putting on a fake smile, King touched Sharon's arm, and it cost Sharon not to react.

"What do you want to know?" she asked, then looked over Sharon's shoulder and waved at somebody somewhere behind her.

"André Desoto has an alibi for the day of Rawlins' murder, but he confessed to having a hook-up with him once after their break-up. He said he met Rawlins at one of your parties. Is that correct?"

King looked at her. "How would I know?" She put on another smile, looking at somebody Sharon couldn't see.

She was almost amused at the sound of frustration in King's voice. "You don't miss much. So do you know something about this, yes, or no?"

King's gaze turned thoughtful, and when she looked at Sharon again, she spoke in a normal voice for the first time. "I wish I could give you a firm answer, but I can't. You see yourself how many people attend such a party. It's not always the same people either. I've got a mailing list of regulars who receive invitations, but I never know who'll show up or not."

Her gaze scanned the room once before settling on Sharon. "I'm tempted to say I saw Desoto talking to Rawlins, but I can't swear that it was indeed close to Rawlins' murder. He liked to come here masked up. I didn't pay them any attention either. It's not as if I had an inkling Rawlins was going to be murdered."

Fair enough. King held parties often enough that the days would blur. Something would have to stand out for her to remember the exact date.

"I understand. There's another thing Desoto mentioned, though. He said that Rawlins claimed he had a new boyfriend, somebody younger that he'd gotten to know during one of these parties. Do you have any idea who that could be?"

King took a moment to think about it. "No." She shrugged and when she locked gazes with Sharon, her arrogance was back. "You see, Warren was a nasty little man. Still, he brought money and didn't misbehave, so he was welcome. It doesn't mean I liked having him around. I saw him with men sometimes, but I couldn't have cared less."

"I see," Sharon said. Maybe it had been a long shot. At least she was sure that King hadn't tried to play her this time. "Is there anybody else you think could be more helpful?"

"Yes, there is." She smirked. "You look surprised by my answer."

"Maybe that's because you always deny knowing anything."

"Poor little Sharon. Anyway, why don't you talk to Marco? He's good with the customers, and as a bartender, he sees and hears a lot. I've seen you talk to him before, so I don't think introductions will be necessary."

Not reacting to the dig, Sharon turned on her heel. Why shouldn't she let King wonder if she'd be back for more questioning? She wasn't worth wasting Sharon's time, and it was a good tip.

Making her way over to the bar, she scanned the room but couldn't spot Jenn or Simon anywhere. Good. First the investigation, then her personal mess.

At the bar, she waited for Marco to finish with a customer, and when he turned to her, his face lit up.

"Sharon, I wasn't sure I'd see you again." He gave her a closer look. "And I see you're here on official business."

"You sound surprised. Didn't you see me talking to Helen?"

"Okay, busted. But I'm right, you're here for work."

"I am. And your boss thinks you're just the person to help me."

"Am I? I guess we'll see. But how about some water? Or something stronger this time?"

Smiling came easy around him. "Water would be great, thanks."

Marco poured her the drink, and handing it to her, he put his hands on the counter. "What can I do for you?"

Sharon took a sip, then another before speaking. "It's about Warren Rawlins again. We learned that he claimed to have been in a relationship with somebody younger right before his death, somebody he'd gotten to know here. Do you have any idea who that could be?"

Marco considered her question for a moment, then shook his head. "No, I can't recall seeing him with anybody who fits the picture. But you know what, I'll ask my brother. As he's active in the scene and works here, too, he might have noticed something I didn't. And as I told you before, Rawlins and I weren't friends."

"Your brother's not here tonight?" She hadn't paid attention to the other server. When she looked over, it was a different man than last time.

"Nope. He's not been doing well the last couple of weeks, but I'll call him tomorrow and let you know."

"Or you could give me his address and phone number, and I can do it myself." It was always better to get information from the source itself. Sometimes it wasn't just about the facts but about the tone of voice, too.

"Sure thing. Wait a moment." He reached into a nearby drawer, got out a piece of paper and a pen and scribbled down name, address and phone number. He handed the paper to Sharon. "I'm sure he'll be able to help you. He knew Warren better than I did, and not much gets past him."

As she had her wallet with her this time, she reached inside for a twenty then put it onto the counter.

Marco shoved it back. "That's not necessary."

"Please take it. I tried waitressing right after high school. I lasted two weeks as I was lousy. But if I learned one thing, it's that customer service jobs are the worst and tips are more than well deserved."

Marco pocketed the money with a nod. "Thanks. And yeah, I did a stint as a waiter, too. I wasn't cut out for that, and I'm glad for this cushy opportunity."

Sharon drained her water. "Thanks, Marco. I'll let you get back to work now."

"It's always a pleasure, and I hope to see you again."

"Somehow I don't think that Helen will be tempted to invite me anytime soon."

"What a pity."

Saying her goodbyes, Sharon took her leave, ignoring the curious glances from a few of the patrons. Jenn's and her entrance had garnered some attention but not enough that it had stopped the party. She was sure King's gaze was on her, but she didn't turn around to confirm.

She still hadn't spotted Jenn and assumed her partner was outside. Stopping in the hallway, she took a moment to compose herself. Battling wits with King had been draining, and the last thing she wanted was to go a few rounds with Simon now.

The bodyguard was glaring at her from his place at the door, so she moved again. There was nothing to be gained by lingering.

To her relief, she found Jenn right outside, and she was alone.

"There you are! How was it? Did King spill the beans?"

Sharon didn't stop and Jenn hurried after her. Sharon spoke over her shoulder. "Let's grab a coffee at the diner around the corner?"

"Sure. Are you okay?"

Sharon glanced at her partner. "What do you think? And where is he?"

Jenn snorted. "I sent him home. And before you have to ask, or even worse you want to know but are too stubborn to ask, he didn't cause any trouble, didn't try to argue, just told me to please tell you to call him soon, that he hadn't and hasn't any intention of hooking up with King again."

Sharon looked at Jenn, gave her a tired smile. "Thanks."

Her partner stopped her with a hand on her arm. "Look, Shar. I know how this looked, and I understand that you're less than happy about it. And I'll even admit that I called Simon an idiot who should've known better, but my gut tells me that this wasn't about an affair. He's pissed at King, not in love with her."

Sharon worried her bottom lip, then shook her head and snapped back to reality. "Don't you worry. I will talk to him, but I thought we had agreed that we'd handle this problem together. So even if this was not about love or lust, why didn't he tell me? And what else did he do I wasn't privy to? When it comes to King, it's personal for me now."

"I know, hon. Talk to him and kick his ass hard anyway."

Sharon was tempted to do just that, but not tonight. She was still too tired and wound up. "Come on, let's have that coffee and I'll tell you everything."

Chapter Twenty-One

The doorbell woke Sharon from a fitful slumber. Taking a brief look at her clock, she saw it was half-past-four. Groaning, she sat up and wiped her eyes. The doorbell rang again.

What the hell?

Worried, she sprang out of bed, wondering what had gone wrong that she was needed at this godforsaken time. And why hadn't they called her?

Leaving the safety chain on, she opened the door an inch. It was Simon. Worry turned to instant anger. "What the fuck are you doing here at this time of the night, morning, whatever? And didn't you tell Jenn that she should ask me to call *you* when *I* feel like it?"

Simon ran a hand through his hair, sighed. "I know. But I knew you'd get up for work soon, so I wanted to talk to you before that. I brought breakfast, too."

He held up a brown bag, and she had to swallow the urge to laugh. Breakfast? All right, then. Who cared about him being where he shouldn't have been, causing her to lose sleep before another long day when he brought breakfast? She almost snorted and considered closing the door and going back to bed.

"Please, let's talk. You can still throw me out in a few minutes."

"Yeah, I can, and I most likely will."

He nodded. "Understandable. Listen, if you want me to go, I will. I know I shouldn't have come."

Instead of answering, she closed the door and unlocked the chain. Opening the door again, she stepped aside to let him enter.

"I wish you hadn't decided to come, yes, but now that you're here, let's get this over with." She yawned. "And I'm sorry if that sounds unfeeling, but I haven't even had a coffee yet."

He gave her a long look, then walked toward her kitchenette. Putting the bag on the counter, he began preparing her coffee maker, and she let him. It was his fault she was awake in the first place. She sat down on one of her stools, put her elbows on the counter and rested her head on her hands.

As she watched him move around her kitchen as if he belonged here, her ire from last night came back full force. "What the hell were you thinking?"

He finished filling the water tank and started the machine before he turned to her.

"I was thinking that Helen is my problem and not yours. I wanted to have it out with her for once and all. I didn't know you'd be at the party."

"Well, I didn't know you'd be there either, but in my case, I was there because of work. I didn't cozy up to my ex."

No matter the reason, seeing them like that had stung. "And hadn't we agreed to deal with the problems dear Helen causes together?"

He hung his head, and she caught the smell of smoke he'd dragged in. Gosh, if she didn't break up with him now, she would either have to buy him nicotine patches or sign him up for yoga classes. This was not the way to relax. "Look at me and tell me what you thought to achieve there?"

His gaze met hers, and when he spoke, his angry voice belied the rigidity of his body. "I was pissed about the deal that almost was a bust because of her, and I was even more pissed that her behavior is causing a rift in our relationship. And I didn't want to talk about this over the phone. I wanted her to see how serious I am about this."

"And the next best option was to go to her party and get as close as possible?" Sharon drummed a nervous rhythm on the counter. Coffee couldn't be ready quick enough.

"It wasn't sexual," Simon said. "Helen might be a switch in the bedroom but she's a hundred-percent dominant in day-to-day life. She wants absolute control over everything and everyone. She likes to toy with people, wants to intimidate them. So I went to talk to her and show her that I refuse to play her games."

In a way Sharon could understand his motivation. He had wanted to butt heads with her, to show her he was at least as dominant as she, if not more.

"Do you think that if I were in an affair with Helen, she would tolerate that I'm with another woman and even worse, that she would be the other woman?"

Sharon shook her head. "No, she wouldn't. Although I rather think she would enjoy breaking us up and then dumping you like a hot potato."

Simon smirked. "I guess you're right about that."

Well, it didn't make her feel any better. "Damn, is this coffee still not ready?"

"Give it another two minutes," he said. He reached out, stopping short of touching her elbow. "I'm sorry for not talking to you beforehand, Sharon. I would have after the fact, but I know I should've talked to you before."

"Yeah, you should have. So tell me what happened before I arrived?"

Simon's hand twitched as if he wanted to touch her, yet he refrained. "I told her that if she tried one more game with either you or me, I'd make sure her reputation will suffer, and that I don't care if she returns the favor. I once had to get back up on my feet, and I can do it again."

In spite of her lingering irritation, Sharon couldn't suppress a tired smile. "So we told her the same thing."

He frowned. "You told her you want to ruin her?"

"I told her that I don't care about her antics, and that I'm willing to make sure the press knows about her involvement in all of this. Also that if I end up fired for my handling of this case, it's not a job I'd like to have, and if my relationship fails, it wasn't worth fighting for in the first place."

"Seems I went there all in vain, huh?" he said.

"Nah. I don't think having to hear it twice hurt her." While the coffee still wasn't finished, its scent began to permeate the air, reviving her spirits enough she was more awake now.

Now what was she to do with the man in her kitchen? Her gut told her things had been what he'd said—that he hadn't wanted to hurt their relationship, although he had gone and talked to King without her knowledge.

Heck, she didn't need to know what he was doing all the time, and didn't want to. They were still separate people with their own jobs, their own friends. He was her first partner in years who didn't try monopolizing her time, who didn't seem to think his career was more important than hers. In addition, there was the fact she was in love with him. He had gotten to know her at her snippiest and still wanted her. With him, she could be herself while enjoying his company.

"Just talk to me the next time," she said, covering his waiting hand with one of her own.

A flicker of relief passed over his face, and she gave him a small smile.

He nodded once. "I will."

"You better. I wouldn't let you in another time. Never mind. Right now I'm too tired to even consider kicking your ass."

"Let me help you to some coffee and how about some breakfast?"

Withdrawing his hand, he began filling her cup, while she reached for the breakfast bag, finding two fresh bagels and two croissants inside.

"Which one would you like?"

"A bagel, please." He put her cup in front of her and handed her two plates before preparing coffee for himself.

Sharon chose a bagel, too, and Simon nodded at the paper bag. "Why don't you take the rest to the office with you? I'm sure Jenn wouldn't say no."

"Good idea." She lifted the bagel to take a bite but stopped midway. "Simon, would it be possible to keep your distance from Helen until this case is closed? Or at least until I'm finished with it? I've got another lead, but even if it doesn't pan out, Second Precinct is raising a stink and trying to take over the case again."

She let the bagel sink back onto her plate. "I know that you need closure, or rather that you want to define your boundaries when it comes to her, and I understand, I do, but sometimes this feels as if I'm trying to lead two battles at the same time."

He had taken a sip of his coffee and put his cup on the counter now. "I promise. I don't have any intention of talking to Helen for the time being anyway. Believe it or not, before this case had come up, we hadn't spoken in close to two months and even then it was a brief conversation"

"Thanks." It didn't sit quite right with her to ask this of him, but all she wanted was a week to wrap this case up, to concentrate on work without having to wonder what kind of unwanted surprise would jump at her next.

Taking a bite of her bagel, she could taste its freshness. Still, food was far from her mind right now. Swallowing, she looked down at her cup for a moment, then back at Simon.

"You know, when I got to know Helen, almost the first thing she did was to tell me about your past, how you lost your job, your fiancée and that you invested your money so you could open your club a year later. She wanted me to know that she knows you way better than I do, and that I'm not what a man like you needs."

Simon narrowed his eyes, and he put down his own breakfast.

"She didn't have any right to insinuate something like that. Yes, that is my past, but guess what? It's over. Knowing who I was back then doesn't mean she knows who I am now and what I want from life or what I'm looking for in a partner."

His anger was palpable, and this time she reached out for him and linked her fingers with his.

"You're right, and yet... I never asked many questions, almost as...." She sighed. It was never easy to look at one's shortcomings, but how could she better herself if she ignored them? "I wanted and want to be with you, but I also tried to ignore the fact that you're much different than my past partners, that I am different with you. It was almost as if I didn't learn more about it, about you, then I could still pretend I'm normal. And dammit, I am normal and nothing about what we share is wrong."

Squeezing her hand, he said in a quiet voice, "At some point you have to decide what you want. I told you before, people are less likely to investigate your private life than you think and nobody is forcing you to volunteer any salacious information. But you can't be with me while trying to hide it, too. It's not fair to me, and it's not fair to yourself."

He had spoken in a kind tone, yet his words burned, tears beginning to prick at her eyes. Wonderful. No, she would not cry now. "I know. Believe me, I know. And I want to be with you."

"Good. Then don't be too hard on yourself. You're always your worst enemy, Sharon."

She nodded, then took a big sip of her coffee, picked up her bagel again. "So tell me, how was your life before me? I know you've got your own private rooms at the club. Did you use them for private games only or did you use them for business? And how often did you play the Dom for a customer?"

Simon's eyes glinted with amusement. "You sound like a cop during an interview, do you know that?"

"Sorry." He wasn't the first partner to tell her. Somewhere along the way she must have lost her ability for simple conversation.

"Don't be. Anyway, I used my room for both, and it wasn't sexual as often as you might think. Anyway, at the beginning, I had regulars who booked sessions with me, but later on, I offered those for beginners who wanted to test the waters and that was it. I've got great employees, and I trust them all, but..." He shrugged and trailed off.

"But you like to be in control of things and being the one to initiate them, you could be sure it happened the way you would have wanted it to." She wasn't so different when it came to her cases.

"Exactly."

Pulling at her bagel, crumbling some of the dough between her fingertips, Sharon wasn't sure how to phrase her next question. Maybe there wasn't a good way. "Do you plan to take a more active role in the club again at some point?" she asked, keeping her voice as neutral as she could.

His answer was direct. "No. At least not for as long as we're in a relationship. At the end of the day, this is just a job, too, but it relies on trust and intimacy between two parties. We both know that BDSM doesn't have to be sexual, but it's always intimate. It just wouldn't feel right to me. I want what we have, and it's more than enough."

Relief washed over her. While it was his decision, she wouldn't be able to deal with knowing he'd been intimate in whatever way with another woman. "I want what we have, too," she said, and they shared a smile.

Looking at her watch, she saw it was after five by now. She sighed. "I should get ready for work soon."

"You should ask for a pay raise, you know."

"Wrong job for that." The dark circles underneath his eyes gave her pause. "Did you even sleep last night?"

She could read the answer on his face, and shook her head. "Even you need sleep."

"I do. But I felt bad about last night. Before us, I hadn't been in a relationship for quite some time, and the thought I could endanger what we have because of a personal feud kept me awake."

Sharon took a last sip of coffee, then got up. "I don't know if you have any plans this morning, but if not, my bed should still be warm. Feel free to catch up on sleep."

Nothing about her living space was a fraction as luxurious as his was, but he'd never minded. As he ran his hand over his face now, yawning, she could see how tired he was.

"Thank you. I think I'd like that," he said after a minute, and she walked around the corner, kissing him.

"Good. And how about we see each other tonight? I've got no idea how late I'll be, but how about dinner and a quiet evening? I'm beat."

His gaze turned tender. "Then we'll have a nice stew, a glass of wine and play it by the ear."

"Sounds good. Is it the evening yet?"

"Almost."

Giving him a last brief kiss, she left for her bathroom. When she had showered, she found him in her bedroom, already under her covers, and it was more than tempting to slip in with him, for an hour or two.

"You shouldn't look so…inviting," she groused.

"Don't you think it's rather the bed than me?"

"It's both." Turning her back to him, she chose her clothes for the day and was out of the house twenty minutes later. She hoped Marco's brother would be able to provide the break they needed.

Chapter Twenty-Two

When Sharon called Stephen Traeger at eight a.m., nobody picked up. Sharon had spent most of the morning preparing her testimony for a different case and had hoped she could set up a meeting with him now. Debating her options, she decided not to call again later but to go to his apartment herself. If he wasn't home, she would call Marco and ask if he knew where else his brother could be. It wasn't as if she had something better to do and being out and about should help with the lingering tiredness. Leaving a note for Jenn, she grabbed her coat and left.

Stephen lived in Melrose and most of the buildings on his block were on the older side, some of them in dire need of repairs. Days like this one she was thankful for her small but clean Queens apartment. It would never compare to Simon's but was so much nicer than a lot of places in the city. The building Steven lived in had twenty units, and his was on the third floor. The stairwell smelled musty and somebody had been cooking fish.

When Sharon entered his hallway, one of the units had their TV blaring and she couldn't hear if there was any movement in Stephen's apartment after she'd knocked. After waiting for half a minute, she raised her hand to knock again, when Stephen opened the door.

Having gotten a brief glance at him just once, she was still shocked at his haggard appearance. He looked like he hadn't showered in days and smelled that way, too.

"Yes?" he said. His voice was rough as if he hadn't used it in a while.

"Mr. Traeger? I'm Sharon Richards with the NYPD. I tried calling you earlier, but you didn't pick up. I've got some questions regarding Warren Rawlins, who was a regular guest at Helen King's parties. Your brother thought you might be of help to me."

"Why would he say that?" He shook his head. "I know nothing about that murder. If you'll excuse me now."

He tried to close the door, but Sharon spoke before he could.

"Please, Mr. Traeger, could we talk inside your apartment for a few minutes? The other option is you come to the precinct later today."

Tapping a nervous rhythm with his foot, he took a long moment to answer, and Sharon wondered if he was under the influence of drugs. He looked feverish, and his eyes were unable to focus.

"Come in," he said then went back into his apartment, leaving it to Sharon to open the door farther and follow him in.

A short, dark hallway led into a small one-bedroom apartment. It was cluttered and messy. Dishes were piling up in the kitchenette's sink and clothes were strewn about most of the floor.

Stephen sat down on his couch and buried his head in his hands. He didn't offer Sharon a seat, but she wouldn't have wanted one anyway.

"I'm here because I want to know if you noticed something about Warren Rawlins' behavior the last times he attended these parties. Ms. King says you're very attentive."

Looking up at her, Stephen shook his head. "No, I noticed nothing, and why would I have?"

"Well, your brother said that Rawlins liked to get his drinks from you instead of him."

"What? Yeah, I guess." His hands were shaking, and he put them under his knees.

"Mr. Traeger, can I get you a cup of water? Or is there anything else I can do for you?"

He looked at her for a moment, then his gaze became unfocused once more. "No. I'm fine. I think I got the flu or something like that, so you might not want to stay for too long."

It wasn't the flu, and they both knew it. This was not a drug raid, though. "If you answer my questions, I'll be out of your hair in a minute."

"I can't tell you anything. Rawlins wasn't a pleasant guy. People didn't like to be around him for long. For a sub, he had the worst attitude."

Sharon bit back the comment that identifying as a submissive was one part of one's life, one aspect of one's personality, nothing else. Being a part of the scene, he should know that himself.

"There's word around that Rawlins hooked up with a younger guy. Did you notice anything about this?"

For a second Stephen stilled, his gaze meeting hers. "No. That's the first time I've heard that."

He was lying to her. Why though, she couldn't say.

"Are you sure? There are a lot of people who would like closure in this case. Any information you might possess could be valuable. So if you can think of anything at all, please tell me."

"But I don't know shit." His hands shot out from underneath his knee, balled into fists. He took a ragged breath. "I'm sorry. It's just that I'm not feeling well. I swear I don't have any information that might help you. And if I can think of anything after all, leave me your number, and I'll call you."

Sharon gave him a small smile. "That would be nice, Mr. Traeger. I'll leave you a business card." Getting one out of her wallet, she put it on the small dirty table in front of him. "I hope you'll feel better soon."

After leaving the apartment, Sharon was glad when she was back on the street and could take in a deep breath of what passed as fresh air here. Stephen Traeger knew the man they were looking for, Sharon was sure of it. What was his reason for hiding it from her? And what about his general behavior? Did Marco have any idea about the bad shape his brother was in?

After she made her way back to the office, Sharon looked on her desk for Marco's number, then called him even before she had gotten out of her coat.

He answered the phone after a few seconds. "This better be good."

He yawned. No wonder. Who knew when he'd gotten home this morning? Too bad murder investigations couldn't take individual sleeping cycles into consideration.

"Hey, Marco. It's Sharon from the NYPD. Sorry to wake you. How long did you have to work?"

"Sharon, hi," he said, and he didn't sound annoyed by the untimely call. "I left around four, and I guess it was six before I was asleep. But what can I do for you? Did you speak to Stephen?"

If he had no idea of his brother's condition, he'd be in for a shock. This was the part of her job she hated the most. Her visits or calls sometimes destroyed the lives of people who had no idea that she would pull out the rug from under their feet.

"Yes, I did, and he says he knows nothing that could be helpful to the investigation. But I wanted to ask if you have any idea what your brother is suffering from?"

"Why?" Worry crept into his voice, making Sharon want to sigh. "He's got a cold as far as I know."

Sharon suppressed a sigh. "You know, I don't think it's a cold. I hate to ask, but do you think your brother could be into drugs?"

Marco was silent for so long, she wondered if he would answer at all.

"Fuck. He was. In the past. But it was almost ten years ago. He hung with the wrong crowd and got into heroin, but he was over it. I can't believe it. Or I don't want to believe it."

Sharon wrapped a finger around a hair strand and began to pull. "I can't be sure, Marco, but yes, my impression was that he's under the influence of drugs."

Marco growled. "You know, I was worried about him. It wasn't like him not to show up for work twice in a row, not to answer my calls. But then he picked up and said he was feeling under the weather, and I believed him. I wanted to."

"You couldn't have known. This is not your fault. You know, his apartment is a mess, too. Is this a habit of his or…"

"Nope. He used to be neat," Marco said in a clipped tone, void of any emotion. "Anything else I should know?"

"Not that I can think of. But do you have the faintest idea what could have prompted your brother to relapse?"

"He broke it off with his boyfriend not that long ago, but he said it was a mutual decision and that he was okay with it."

"Again, you couldn't have known. Say, do you know his boyfriend?"

"Nope. I suggested we could meet at a bar or at the park a few times, but Stephen said his boyfriend wasn't ready yet. I figured he might not be out of the closet and that it wasn't my place to pry or to put up any pressure." He sighed. "I wish I had been there for Stephen when he needed me. How do you handle the line between giving people the privacy they deserve and the help they need?"

It was an age-old question that would never have a definite answer.

"You can only try and trust your gut. And sometimes you'll make what later feels like a wrong decision. And there's no guarantee that an intervention would've changed a thing. Marco, is there anything I can do for you? We've got flyers about some good rehab programs here."

"Yeah, that would be great. Damn, this is going to destroy my mom."

"I'm sorry." If she could, she'd take her words back, but the truth would've come out sooner or later anyway.

"This is not your fault," Marco said in a flat voice.

"Hang on tight. I'll scan the flyers and send them to you in an email if that's okay with you."

"Yeah, thanks." He gave her his email address and they ended the phone call soon after.

What a way to start the week.

When Jenn came in after a while, Sharon was still staring into space.

"Are you okay?"

Telling her partner about her visit at Stephen's and her subsequent call to Marco, she began to doodle on the paper in front of her. "Something's way off here, and I can't help but wonder if Stephen knows who we are looking for."

"You think this might be the boyfriend Stephen had broken up with and the situation sent Stephen into relapse."

Sharon looked up. "Something like this, yeah."

"Sounds about right if you ask me. So how about you do what you promised to do and send Marco the flyers, and I'll try to find out more about Stephen Traeger and his elusive boyfriend." Jenn snorted. "This feels like chasing a string of boyfriends, doesn't it?"

"It does. Speaking of boyfriends, how is yours doing? Did you talk to him?"

Jenn averted her gaze for long enough that it was clear this was still a sensitive topic.

"I did. And he still thinks I'm making too much of a big deal out of nothing." She slapped the desk with her hand. "I didn't, Shar. I've got a right to my own feelings."

"Yes, you do." Sharon had just met Brian a few times, and he had made a nice impression on her. He'd seemed kind and patient. As a pastor he should be. Although how he dealt with his flock didn't have to be the same way he dealt with personal matters. He was a people person, Jenn was not and he should see and accept her for who she was. "So?"

"So, I told him I'd need a few days and that no matter what he thinks and says, there's no way in hell

I'm going to change my opinion. He didn't like it, but tough luck."

"For what it's worth, and I know it's nothing, you did the right thing."

Jenn gave her a small smile. "I know. But why does doing the right thing feel so shitty?"

Sharon made a face. "I wish I knew. You know what? Let's get some more work done, then we'll head out for lunch."

"Yeah, sure."

Maybe there was nothing that she could do to make the situation better, but she could be there for her friend.

Chapter Twenty-Three

Standing in front of Simon's open door, Sharon frowned as the person opposite her was not the one she'd expected to see. The family resemblance was uncanny, yet she was taken by surprise.

"You've got to be Andrew, and I'm sorry, but I must've forgotten that you would arrive today."

Simon's brother gave her a warm smile. He was a bit taller than Simon, and his hair was dark blond, although he had the same dark eyes as his brother.

"You couldn't have known. I'm a couple of days early and asked Simon if he'd like to meet anyway. He suggested dinner at his apartment, so here I am."

He held out his hand, and Sharon took it. Andrew had a firm handshake, and his smile never wavered.

"Now come on in. Simon's in the kitchen."

"Not cooking, I hope," Sharon said, wanting to bite her tongue the next moment.

Andrew laughed. "No, I'm the one cooking, but I made him sous-chef, so to say. He's slicing some vegetables."

He let Sharon enter, and together they made their way to the kitchen where Simon stood with the sleeves of his shirt rolled up. He looked up from his task, frowning, and Sharon almost felt bad for the poor vegetables.

"Hey, you don't mind that I invited Andrew for dinner, do you? I tried calling you at the office, but Jenn said you had just left. I guess I should've tried your cell phone next."

She shook her head. "No worries, I don't mind. Didn't you promise me that your brother is the one who has all the dirt on you?"

She exchanged a look with Andrew, who grinned at her. "That I do. So how about I start with the fish and you help Simon with the vegetables? Then you can decide if you'd rather hear the story of Simon's disastrous first date with the girl he had a crush on in high school or the day our mother found a *Playboy* magazine in his room."

Simon stopped his work and glared at his brother. "It was Dad's. And you were just pissed at me—again—and hid it under my pillow."

"Yes, you're right. But hey, that's what happens when you forget to knock," Andrew shot back. He looked at Sharon who was getting out of her coat. "You have to know, the week before that...incident, Simon barged into my room, and while nothing wild was going on in there, I was with a boy I had a big crush on, and I was working up my courage to kiss him. Let's say the urge was gone after dearest brother almost gave me a heart attack."

"I didn't know," Simon shot back.

"And you should've knocked anyway."

Amused by their argument, Sharon put her coat away. She remembered similar arguments with her brother James. Siblings—they were heaven and hell.

Washing her hands, she joined the two brothers in the kitchen.

Andrew handed her a cutting board and a knife, then a cucumber as well as some tomatoes. "For the salad."

Sharon glanced at Simon who still didn't look convinced that this was what he wanted to do. "You think we'll survive such a healthy meal?" she teased him.

He gave her a wry smile. "I think one healthy meal won't kill us."

"Excuse me, but what do you guys usually eat?" Andrew asked.

"Takeout," Sharon and Simon answered at the same time.

"But we try to keep that healthy, at least," Sharon said.

"And we buy pre-made salads on a regular basis. So don't you worry, we're not trying to kill ourselves."

Andrew rolled his eyes. "Yeah, but nothing beats a self-made meal. I'll be here for a couple days longer, so let's see if I can teach you one or two simple recipes." He shook his head. "And you call yourself adults."

Their banter continued while they worked, and half an hour later they sat down with salmon, a sauce with vegetables, rice and a side salad. Sharon had to admit preparing the meal hadn't been all that hard, and it tasted nice. Too bad that she could never say how long her days would run. Starting to cook at nine or ten in the evening was too exhausting to contemplate.

"So when's Garrett's appointment at the clinic?" Simon asked, and Andrew looked from him to Sharon.

"He told you that my partner tested HIV positive earlier this year?"

Sharon put her fork down. "Yes, he did. And how are you doing, if I may ask?"

Andrew's smile was gentle, and he looked at Simon. "His appointment's next week." He turned back to Sharon. "We're doing okay now. It was a terrible shock for Garrett and me. For a few weeks, we cursed destiny, then we became angry. By now we've both accepted that we can't change what happened, but that it's up to us how we deal with it. Medicine's advanced so much these last decades that they say it's possible to live an almost normal life and to have a normal life expectancy."

"You will," Simon said with conviction and the two brothers looked at each other for a long moment.

Andrew looked away first. "So, yes, we're doing okay now. Thanks for asking."

"I'm glad to hear that. By the way, Simon let me have some of your cookies. They were amazing,"

"Thank you. Simon, did you even tell Sharon that I'm a chef by trade?"

Simon shook his head. "No, and now she'll be way less impressed by your skills."

"Of course, I'm still impressed. So now I know a real chef. Where do you work and what kind of cuisine do you specialize in?"

For the rest of dinner, they talked about his job, then a bit about Sharon's. When Andrew got up to fetch them dessert, Sharon looked over at Simon. "Your brother is wonderful."

"Yes, he is. We had our differences growing up, but I don't know any siblings that don't. You know, he was still young when he became interested in cooking and on days when Mom came home late from work, Andrew often made sure that my sister and I had something to eat, and that there were leftovers for Dad when he came home from night shift."

Reaching over the table, Sharon took Simon's hand. Tonight, he was less guarded than usual, and she loved the glimpses she got into his past. Getting to know Andrew and seeing their bond first-hand, she understood even better why the news about Garrett's HIV infection had rattled him so much.

Back then, she'd been angry and hurt when he'd left the city without much of an explanation and hadn't checked in with her for several days. Although once back in New York, she was his first stop—he had come to her for comfort. It humbled her that he had trusted her that much.

"There must be a ton of good memories."

"There are. It's just a pity that you won't get to meet my parents. You would've liked them, and they would've loved you."

Andrew came back with a tray of cheese. "You two look cozy. Good." He sat again. "It makes me miss Garrett." He faced Sharon. "He sends his regards, by the way. He hopes for the chance to get to know you soon."

Sharon would like that very much and hoped she'd get the chance. Right now, Simon and she were going strong, but things could change in a heartbeat. A few days ago Jenn would've sworn every oath she was happy, too.

"That would be great. Please give him my regards back." She looked at both brothers in turn. "Now I know that your family consists of a businessman and an excellent chef. What career path did your sister decide on?"

"Interior design," Andrew said, and he made a face.

"I figure your sister's taste in interior design differs from yours?"

It was Simon who answered. "You know, although we're not that close, I love my sister. She's a wonderful person, full of energy and plans, but yes, her taste is rather eclectic. She was here not more than twice, once when I'd just gotten the apartment and asked her about her opinion regarding design. She told me to paint at least one wall orange as it was all the hype, or so she said."

Sharon had to bite back a laugh. "You didn't follow her suggestion? What a pity? Orange is such a lively color. And wouldn't it be something for the club, too?"

Andrew didn't have any qualms and laughed, while Simon just sighed.

"Laugh all you want," Simon said and looked at Andrew. "Have you already forgotten the time she tried to convince Garret and you that you needed those tie-dye armchairs?"

"How could I? They were something to behold. Now Sharon, if you ever need any designing advice, I'd be glad to give you Lauren's contact details."

Sharon snorted. "I think I'll pass, but thank you so much."

Simon picked up a piece of cheese and offered it to her. She opened her mouth so he could put the morsel of food on her tongue. She gave his fingertip a quick lick, loving the way his pupils dilated. The cheese all but melted on her tongue, and she almost moaned.

She never mourned she hadn't chosen a more lucrative career, but tasting this expensive cheese, she had to admit there were advantages of not having to pay attention to the budget.

"You know, I wouldn't be so quick to dismiss Lauren's advice," Andrew said. "She's successful from what I heard."

Sharon leaned back in her seat. "That might be. But I don't care if I fit in with the trendy crowd. I can live with what I have well enough." She meant it. She had always lived this way. Although if that were true, why couldn't she stand by Simon without a second thought? Her heart began beating faster.

"Everything okay?" Andrew asked.

"Yes, everything is perfect," she said, forcing herself to smile. And it was right now, so she better enjoy these moments for as long as they lasted.

* * * *

Lying in bed a few hours later, Sharon turned to Simon. "This was a great evening."

"It was. Evenings like these make me regret that we live so far from each other."

"How about you try to visit him more often?" She snuggled closer to him, relishing the way his body heat warmed her. If never getting up again was an option, she'd be tempted to choose it.

"Yeah, I should. Have you been to San Francisco before?"

"No, I haven't. I've never even made it to the West Coast. Shocking, I know."

His bedside lamp was bathing the room in a gentle light, and she could see his smile. "The most shocking thing I've heard in a while."

She snorted. "Uh-huh."

"So what do you say we go down and visit those two whenever you can take off some time? I'm sure you'll love Frisco."

Not having expected the offer to tag along, she liked the idea.

"With all the overtime Jenn and I are compiling during this case, it shouldn't be too hard to convince Kelly to grant me some leave. I've also got some vacation days left."

Simon rubbed her hip. "Then let's do it. Family is important and time for us is important. You'll like Garrett. He's an architect. He's done some impressive work in the Bay area. He's quieter than Andrew, but he'd do everything for the people he considers family."

"Then I can't wait to meet him. And it should be warmer and sunnier than here, too." For a moment, she allowed herself to dream of the vacation, of being away from it all. As much as she loved her job, the last weeks had drained her.

"How's the case going anyway?" he asked.

And as quickly as her daydreaming had begun, it was over. Not that she could blame him. This unholy affair had affected him as much as it had her, if not more. "We've got another lead. Let's hope it won't prove to be another dead end. One of the bartenders Helen employs is behaving shady, and it seems he's back on drugs after being clean for years. He, too, broke up with a boyfriend not that long ago, and we want to find out if this ex-boyfriend might've been Rawlins' younger new boyfriend."

Simon sighed. "Stephen's on drugs? I don't know him well, but he seemed like a good guy. Always calm, always charming."

"Yeah. I visited him today, and he was twitchy as hell. Marco—his brother—told me about his history with drugs."

Simon had begun trailing a finger up and down her arm, and a small shiver ran down her back. She locked gazes with Simon, and seeing the carnal hunger in his eyes, she bit her bottom lip. What was it with him that he could make her want him with just a touch, just a look?

"What do you think you're doing?" she asked.

"Seducing you, I hope?"

"Your brother's in the spare bedroom," she reminded him.

"Walls are thick in here—I made sure of it, and even if he hears something—I'm sure he'll understand."

"I don't know."

"It's not like you to be shy."

He lifted her hand to his mouth, letting his tongue run over the inside of her wrist, and she admitted defeat, not that she minded losing in this case. She loved his touch, to caress him in return.

Some nights he was her Master, and others an equal partner who made her tremble underneath his touch. Being with him felt right no matter what.

"Once this investigation is over, let's celebrate in the dungeon," she suggested, and the look in his eyes got darker.

"If that's what you want?"

"It's what I need, and don't tell me you don't need it either."

He rolled her on her back and kneeled between her parted legs, reaching for the T-shirt of his she'd donned earlier.

"I do. So yeah, let's celebrate soon."

Leaning down, he nibbled at her throat, and she slung her arms around him, scratching his naked back.

It was time to close this case and celebrate the future. Their future.

Chapter Twenty-Four

The call came when Sharon was about to leave her office for a status meeting with Kelly. Seeing it was an external number, she picked up the phone, sitting down on the edge of her desk.

"Sharon Richards, NYPD."

"Sharon, I need you over here at once."

It was King. The poster child of composure sounded rattled.

"You do?" It might be petty, but Sharon was wary this was just another game.

"Yes. I've locked myself into my apartment. Stephen Traeger's in my house. He's got a gun and seems out of it."

Sharon could hear a loud banging in the background. "Is that Stephen?"

"Yes, he wants me to talk to him."

Stephen was likely on drugs and having an episode. Time was of the essence now. "I'll be on my way. Don't talk to him, hide somewhere if you can, just in case he busts through the door. I'll make sure other units are alerted as well."

"I will. Please hurry."

Helen hung up, and Sharon told Jenn, who had already sprung up and donned her jacket, that they had to leave right away. Calling for back-up first, Sharon contacted Kelly next so he knew where they were going.

At the car, she threw the keys to Jenn. "You drive."

New York traffic unnerved her on a good day and today they needed to be as quick as possible. Having grown up in the city, Jenn was a pro at navigating the crowded streets, finding the fastest ways.

Sharon had just buckled up when Jenn revved up the engine. Racing along the streets with sirens blaring and cars trying to get out of their way, they made good time.

Sharon was relieved when they got the message that the first unit had arrived at the location, but wished they were already there. While it was always bad to run headfirst into a critical situation, it was all but unbearable having to listen to what was unfolding without being able to do a thing.

"The subject's pointing a gun to his head, saying he's going to shoot himself if we don't leave him alone."

Sharon shared a desperate look with Jenn, whose knuckles turned white around the steering wheel.

"Tell him you can't leave but won't come any closer. We'll be there in about ten minutes. Tell him that Detective Richards is on her way to talk to him. He knows who I am."

"Yes, Detective."

Reaching for her cell phone next, Sharon hoped she wasn't wrong with her time estimate and called King back. She answered at once.

"He's not shouting any longer," the other woman greeted her. "The police are here, and I think he's trying to kill himself."

"That's what they told me, yes. I'll be there in a few minutes, give or take. Are you all right?"

"Yes, I am. What's going on with him?" King said, calmer again. There was no bite to her voice this time.

"I'm sure he's on drugs, although I've got no idea why he came to you. But we're going to figure it out."

Ending the call, she leaned her head back against the headrest and took a deep breath. This was the second time in her career she was about to deal with somebody suicidal. What if she said or did the wrong thing and he killed himself? What if they didn't arrive in time?"

"It's going to be okay, Shar," Jenn said.

"We will see."

"No. It has to be okay, so it will be. If we don't believe in ourselves, how's he supposed to do it?"

Knowing Jenn was right, Sharon still found it hard to ignore the feeling of impending failure.

"Last time I was in such a situation, the guy jumped off the bridge not even a minute after my partner and I arrived."

"I know. But this time you know this guy, have a connection to him." When they took a right, the next street was emptier, so Jenn sped the car up.

"There just doesn't seem to be a reason for his actions," Sharon said. "Why go to Helen King and threaten her? Is it because she's the center of this investigation? Does he blame her for his boyfriend leaving him?" There was something she wasn't getting yet, a piece of the puzzle that was missing.

"That's what we're going to figure out," Jenn replied, braking hard when a car ahead of them did the same. "You know what would suck though?"

"More than this? No. What?"

"Mandatory therapy if things go south. You'd think growing up with shrinks would give me a get-out-of-jail-free card but no such luck."

"Don't remind me." It was good that therapy was a must in such cases, good that it was offered in the first place. Although, it was its own form of torture as they were expected to talk about something they might not want to even think about, at least not with the person assigned to needle them. "Let's resolve this whole thing without any incident so the paperwork will do."

Jenn threw her a brief look, a quick smile. "See, that's what I'm talking about."

Double-parking the car right in front of the house a few minutes later, Jenn sprang out of the vehicle, followed by Sharon. Three other units were already there. Meeting up with two officers in front of the house, Sharon addressed the oldest one, a man she guessed to be in his late fifties. "How's the situation, Detective?"

"Quiet. The last thing we heard is that the guy is sitting on the stairs, holding a gun to his head, muttering to himself."

Sharon looked at Jenn. "We'll go in together, but I'll talk to him alone."

"Okay, but put on a vest before that."

Sharon wanted to argue. She didn't want to lose more time. Instead, she turned back to the car, got a vest out of the trunk then put it on. There was more than one officer who was still alive because they'd taken the precaution of safety gear, and she knew one who had died from a shot to the chest. Taking the second vest, she closed the trunk and threw it to Jenn in passing.

"Just in case Stephen tries to make a run for it and gets trigger-happy."

"Sure."

Telling the uniforms to stay alert, she walked inside the house and was met with more officers on each level, the last on level three.

"Good luck," the officer, who was around her age, said to her. "The guy's fucking twitchy. He repeated that he needs to talk to Helen several times and also that he will make things right. No idea what he meant."

"Thanks. Let's try to get him out of here alive, okay?"

The officer nodded and Sharon took the last set of steps, stopping when she could almost see Stephen. He still sat on the last step and was rocking back and forth, the pistol now in his lap, although he raised it back to his temple as soon as he spotted her.

"Stop. If you come any closer, I'm going to shoot myself."

Stephen's eyes were unfocused, and he was sweating. His hand was shaky, and Sharon worried he could shoot himself by accident.

Standing still, she spoke as quietly as she could. "It's okay, Stephen. I will stay right here, I promise. Do you remember me? Sharon Richards from the NYPD? I just want to talk to you."

It had been years since her training in suicide assessment and intervention, and looking at Stephen now, she wasn't sure she could do it. But there was no time to wait for anybody with more experience.

Stephen gave her a short glance, then looked away again. "I don't want to talk to you. I want to talk to Helen. Now."

"I understand, but you can't talk to Helen as long as you've got this pistol. Give it to me, and I'm sure she'll talk to you."

For a second, Stephen gave her a clear look. "No." He laughed, the sound manic. "You think I'm stupid, don't you? And I'll tell you what. I want Helen to die. She deserves to die." He let the weapon sink for a moment, then put it up again.

"I don't think you mean this, Stephen. Nobody has to die."

What had happened that had brought this young man here? He'd been in a bad shape yesterday, but now he was out of control.

"Yes. She has to die. You've got no idea what she did."

Sharon nodded. "You're right. I don't. Why don't you tell me what she did so I know how I can help you best?"

Stephen laughed again, this time pointing the gun at Sharon for a moment. "I could shoot you, too, you know. But I don't think I want that. Not yet anyway."

He didn't sound threatening but more like somebody talking to himself. Still, Sharon didn't want to risk agitating him further.

"Stephen, please, talk to me. I'm here because of you and not because of Helen. I'm worried about you. I got to know your brother Marco and he's a wonderful man. He loves you, and he wouldn't want to see you like this. So please, talk to me, and we'll figure something out."

When she mentioned his brother, he stilled, his eyes darting to her and keeping contact. "Don't tell Marco anything about this. Anything, you hear me?"

There was no way for her to sweep this under the rug. They both knew it. There was no sense in arguing with him, so she didn't, lifting a hand. "I won't if you don't want me to. But you don't want him to worry about you, do you?"

"Marco's the best. The best, you hear me? He's got nothing to do with this. Nothing at all. You know, for the longest time, I thought I was the idiot, but then I realized this wasn't my fault. This is all the fault of this bitch up there."

"What was her fault, Stephen?"

The young man took a shaky breath. "It's her fault I'm a murderer."

For a moment she didn't understand, then the sudden realization made her breath catch. Stephen had never had an anonymous boyfriend he had separated from and Warren Rawlins' lover hadn't been unknown.

"You killed Warren, didn't you?" she said in a soft tone, not wanting to spook him.

Stephen had begun to cry, and he growled out in anguish. "I didn't mean to. And fuck, I should've killed Helen and not him."

"What happened, Stephen? What made you so angry?"

Stephen didn't react for a while, then he let the gun sink into his lap once more, and he took a shaky breath. "He wasn't like people thought he was."

"Who was not? Warren?"

"Yeah." Stephen looked up at her. "If you didn't know him, you'd think he was a jerk. He insulted people, made nasty jokes, but he could be so very different. I know he cared for Desoto, was hurt when that jerk ended the relationship because he was afraid people might find out he was gay."

Sharon had to treat Stephen with care. "Wasn't Warren afraid of the same?"

"Yes. No. It was different with him. Warren had told everybody he had a girlfriend, but he'd realized he couldn't do this any longer, that he wanted his family to get to know his boyfriend. He told Desoto, and the dirtbag ended the relationship."

Sharon wasn't convinced this was the truth. Desoto hadn't mentioned any of this, and Rawlins' family had never spoken of any plans to meet the mysterious girlfriend. She thought it had to have been a story Rawlins had told Stephen to get his pity. This man had been a user who hadn't given a fuck what others were thinking about him.

The sad truth was that, apart from his family, his murderer was the one person who was sad he had died.

"I see. And what happened next?"

"Well, Warren came to some of the parties, but he didn't hook up with anybody. We started to talk, and I could see behind the façade. I know how it feels when the whole world misunderstands you, shuns you."

"You're talking about the time you were taking drugs?"

He nodded, then lifted the gun halfway for a moment before letting it sink again.

"At one point my whole family turned their back to me."

Because there was just so much one could do for a person who was in the claws of their addiction. If the addict didn't want to get out of their situation themselves, there was nothing anybody could do.

"So the two of you were kindred spirits?"

"Yeah, we were. And one night we were talking, and he said that he shouldn't come to these parties any longer, that there weren't any good Doms at any of them, and I suggested we meet up, that I could show him a good time." When he locked gazes with Sharon, she got a short glance at a different man, one who was still in control. That had to have been the man Warren got to meet, a man who was just good enough to provide relief.

"And it was good, wasn't it?" Sharon said in a gentle tone.

"It was perfect. When he was in his role, he was perfect. He took everything, the pain, the insults. Whatever I gave him, he wanted more."

"And the two of you had a good time? And you fell in love with him?"

Rawlins had been the submissive, but he still had been the one in control. He had seen a weakness in Stephen and used it.

"Yeah. He wanted me. He loved me. It was good. I could be myself with him, and yes, he was older than I am, but still, I thought we could have a future together."

Shaking his head, Stephen let it hang and when he looked back at Sharon, his gaze was full of anger. "It could've been good. It could've been it. You know, IT. And then Helen destroyed it all."

Agitated as he was, Sharon spoke even slower and quieter, hoping that nobody would interrupt them now. With mood swings like this, things could go south any second.

"What did Helen do?"

"It's what she didn't do. She knew Warren and Desoto had broken up, and she still allowed both back. And one night, Desoto was there again, attending one of the parties after weeks of being absent. I saw him talking to Warren, but I was busy, and when I had a minute and tried to find Warren, he was gone. I asked some other customer I knew, and he said the two of them had left together."

It had to have hurt. Had it dawned on Stephen then that he was nothing more than a replacement?

"I understand. But why did you go and kill Warren days later? If you were angry with Helen, why didn't you speak to her?"

"I should have. Yes, I should have. And I should've killed her, too. But I tried to call Warren a few times that night. He never answered. And when I went to speak to him the next day, he said it was over between us."

"That must have been hard."

"It was!" Stephen shouted. "And you know what? After he ended our relationship, he turned his back on me and blocked me. It was as if I hadn't existed at all."

Stephen had been the means to an end. Desoto ending the relationship on his terms must have enraged Rawlins, maybe even hurt him, and when he saw an opportunity to take revenge on Desoto, he took it and discarded his new lover almost right after that.

"The kicker was when Warren came to another party and ignored me as if I didn't exist. The bastard."

A few nights before his death, right.

"What did you do?"

"Warren left early, and when I took my break, I made it a longer one. I went to Warren's apartment and we argued. I tried to make Warren see sense, but he didn't want to hear a thing about it."

That was what the neighbor must've heard. The puzzle pieces began to fall into place, but the picture wasn't a pretty one.

"But the two of you met once more at his apartment?"

Stephen nodded, gave her a nasty smile, full of hate. "Yeah. See, at the end of the day Warren was pissed that Desoto didn't want him. So Warren called me, wanted to meet with me, and of course I went." He looked down at the pistol for a long moment before he continued. "When I arrived, we had some cocaine, and then he said that we used to have a good time and that he'd like to get back to it. I told him I loved him, that he hurt me, and..."

"And?" Sharon prompted when nothing else was forthcoming.

"He said that nobody had spoken about love. Ever. That I was just good at scratching his itch."

"That made you angry?"

"Of course it did. We were in the kitchen, and... Well, I grabbed a knife and told him that he wouldn't make a fool out of me again. Never again." Stephen laughed and the tears were back. "You know, he begged then. Told me he didn't mean it this way, he told me he loved me. And I told him to undress. He did in his bedroom, and we went into the living room. When he was naked, I put the collar on him. I then told him it would be okay for as long as he told me the truth. Then I asked him if he loved me."

"What did he say?" Sharon's legs began to tremble from trying to stand still, yet she didn't dare move.

"What he said? That, no, he didn't love me, but he loved to play with me."

For Rawlins, honesty had been the wrong choice, although Sharon didn't think that lying would've made a difference.

Stephen shuddered, and this time when she met his gaze, he looked miserable. His hand began shaking harder, too. Whatever drugs he'd taken were beginning to wear off.

"You don't have to ask. Yes, I killed him. I stabbed him. Again and again. When I saw he was dead, I panicked for a moment, then I realized that this all wouldn't have happened if it wasn't for Helen. I still had her card, and after wiping it, I let it fall into the pool of blood. I took the rag, tried to wipe everything I'd touched. It took hours. I undressed myself, got some of his clothes since mine were bloody and then I took everything with me when I left."

He stopped, then got up. "And now I need to talk to this bitch. Thanks to her I lost everything."

"No, Stephen. Don't do this. You're not like this, and shedding more blood won't get Warren back. And think of Marco, please. He wouldn't want you to hurt anybody else."

She made a cautious step into his direction, praying it wasn't the wrong move. "Please. Nobody can change the past, nobody can revive Warren, but you can get better. You have to let me help you, let your brother help you."

Stephen sneered, looked at the closed door of Helen's apartment for a second then back at her, lifting the gun to his temple once more.

"Nobody can help me."

Oh, please, he couldn't shoot himself now.

"Don't give up, Stephen. Please. Years ago, you got clean again and you can manage it once more. You still have so much more of your life ahead of you."

"In prison. Right. Great."

"And you might get out again. It's not too late to try and turn things around. Please."

There were no guarantees he'd ever get out of prison, but it could happen. While she was sure that not many people mourned Warren Rawlins, a lot of them would mourn Stephen Traeger.

"For Marco," she tried again.

Long seconds ticked by and finally, he put down the gun and let it fall to the ground with a loud clunk. Despite her heart racing a mile a minute and a bout of lightheadedness, Sharon closed the distance between them and put some cuffs around Stephen's hands. He had gone limp in the span of a minute.

Shouting downstairs that things were secure, she waited for an officer to take Stephen then called Helen on her phone.

"Yes?"

"Stephen's with an officer now and will be taken to the precinct. You can get out now. I'll wait for you to let me in." Sharon ended the call before King could decide she wouldn't want to see her now.

It didn't take long before the door to King's apartment was unlocked. King took a step back to let her enter. Sharon took a good look—King was pale and her hands were shaking.

It was no wonder. Having Stephen threatening her, ranting in front of her door, must've been scary. Once she got off her own adrenaline high, Sharon wouldn't fare any better.

King turned her back to Sharon, and following King into her kitchen, Sharon waited while the other woman filled water into an old-fashioned kettle she then put onto her stove. When she was done, she faced Sharon, offered her a seat at a sturdy but small teak table. Sharon took one of the four chairs and King sat down opposite of her.

"Thank you for all the help today. I guess you saved my life." King looked over Sharon's shoulder, taking a deep breath. She shook her head, then locked gazes with Sharon.

"Why? Why did he want to hurt me? What happened?"

For once it was an honest question, not another game, and it was Sharon's first true glance at a woman who knew how to appear larger than life.

"Stephen was Warren Rawlins' boyfriend. He killed Rawlins and is convinced if it weren't for you, he wouldn't have lost it all. After their break-up, Desoto and Rawlins met again at one of your parties, so it's your fault that Warren decided he wanted his ex-lover back."

There was true shock in Helen's eyes. "Stephen killed Warren Rawlins? I can't believe it. I always thought he was one of the good ones, not another arrogant dirtbag like the man he killed."

Sharon raised her eyebrow at the unexpected outburst. It wasn't that she disagreed, but the exclamation was far from how King typically presented herself.

She explained the situation to King in detail, and the other woman did her the courtesy of not interrupting. King got up at some point to fix their tea, coming back with a small tray, and this time Sharon accepted the offered beverage.

"So Warren used Stephen and got murdered for it, and now Stephen's life is ruined," King said, lifting her cup, then putting it down again. "There's no excuse for murder, I know, but I don't feel bad for Warren. I do feel bad for Stephen." She spoke in a quiet voice, and her lips were a thin line.

"Me, too. But Stephen had a choice and he made the wrong one."

King focused on her, her eyes cold. "It's so easy for you, isn't it? It's all black and white."

Tired, Sharon snapped back. "No, nothing about this is easy. From what I gathered, there were no redeeming qualities in Warren Rawlins. And here's Stephen, a young man who once overcame addiction, falling right back in when Rawlins made him think he wanted a relationship. But believe it or not, Stephen had a choice, too. He knew what he was doing when he grabbed that knife and killed Rawlins. If it were okay to murder every asshole on this planet, overpopulation wouldn't be a problem any longer."

Sharon took a deep breath and reached for her tea, surprised when King remained silent. Taking a sip, she wished it were coffee but was glad for the warmth. "Anyway, we'll need you to come in for a formal statement tomorrow and then you won't have to deal with me any longer."

King leaned back, then shook her head. "You're still in Simon's life, so you're still in mine."

Sharon couldn't suppress a snort. "We both know that Simon's not interested in engaging with you at the moment."

King smiled, and it was the arrogant upward tilt of her lips that Sharon hadn't missed. "He might be a bit grumpy now, but give it a week or two and things will go back to normal."

"You keep telling yourself that." She got up, wanting to leave, though then she looked at King again. "Can you be honest for once?"

King frowned. "What makes you think I'm not?"

Sharon sighed. "Because you're a manipulator, just like Rawlins was, although I don't think you'd go as far as he did. That said, can you please tell me what I ever did to you? If it's not wanting to get back with Simon, what is it then?"

King's gaze hardened but Sharon refused to look away. "I don't like people messing with my plans. And whether you wanted to or not, you did."

"What plans?"

King tilted her head and was silent for so long Sharon gave up hope she would get an answer, though when she wanted to turn around, King spoke.

"Simon's a friend, a good friend, but also a cunning businessman. I had plans to buy a property with him, a location with a dungeon in the basement, some privacy suites and a place for parties in the penthouse. I wanted it to be a spot for the rich, the famous. Whether you believe it or not, there are more affluent people with a taste for a bit of spice in their life than you might think, people who can afford the prices I have in mind."

Sharon shrugged. "And? What was stopping you? Did you even talk to Simon about this? What the hell does this all have to do with me?"

King got up as well, stepped closer to Sharon until they could almost touch each other. "I didn't get to talk to him about it. He all but vanished from the scene from one day to the next. I had to hear from others that there was a murder at his club, and later I heard from the same people that it seemed like he got himself a girlfriend."

King was glaring, ice-cold anger radiating off her. Sharon had enough and instead of stepping back, she took a step toward King, so they were almost nose to nose. "So whenever you hook up with somebody, or whenever you enter a relationship with somebody, you go and consult with Simon? I don't think so. No, you just had expectations and plans and Simon defied them by living his own life. It's all about control with you, isn't it? But the people in your life aren't puppets and they make their own decisions, whether you like it or not."

King held her gaze, though she took a step back and looked Sharon over from head to toe, making it clear that Sharon was failing her inspection.

"Simon and I were a good team before you came along. And God, you're not an asset to the scene. You live in constant fear somebody could find out you are with Simon, that you dabble in BDSM. This is a way of life and not some kind of dress you put on when you find it in your closet and decide it fits your day."

Sharon scoffed. "Oh, I didn't know you're one to let everybody know what kind of games you like to play in the sanctity of your own four walls. What about Desoto and Rawlins? They didn't share their proclivities with the rest of the world. And what about the commissioner who dragged me into your mess? I'm sure he doesn't want anybody to speculate if he likes to be whipped or led around on a leash."

King shook her head. "It's one thing to out yourself to your environment but a different thing whether you're honest about your relationship. Tell me, how many people apart from your cop friend even know that you're dating a former suspect? A sex club owner?"

"I've always been a private person. I've never made a show out of my relationships." Although King was right. With previous relationships, she had mentioned her boyfriends at least in passing.

When it came to Simon, she had been avoiding discussing her private life at work, and it was wrong. She could do better and make him a part of all her life without mentioning their inclinations.

King studied her for a long moment, and Sharon almost flinched under the scrutiny. It must have been close to a minute before King spoke again. "One day you'll have to decide between your relationship and your job, and I know it's not Simon who'll be the winner."

Could there be any truth to her statement?

For now she had a good, solid relationship, and it was up to her what she made out of it. "You can think whatever you want, but one word of advice—if you don't want to lose Simon as a friend, you should stop meddling in his business and his love life. He won't stand for it. That said, I'll leave you to it. Work isn't finished yet."

She turned her back to King, and the other woman called after her before she even made the first step.

"Wait."

Facing her again, Sharon crossed her arms. "What?"

"I don't like you, and I don't see that changing, but I'm appreciative of what you did today and these last weeks. Thank you."

"You're welcome." Not wanting to prolong their conversation, Sharon left.

She hoped with the end of the investigation King would disappear from her life as well, but King was right—she wouldn't. There might be a dent in Simon's and King's friendship, but this wouldn't be the end of it. King wasn't one to let go and what she had done wasn't enough for Simon to hold a grudge forever.

She ran into Jenn halfway down the steps. Her friend took a look at her and frowned. "Geez, girl, you look as if somebody drowned your dog and not like somebody who just saved the day."

Heading downstairs, the two of them made their way out of the building. "The case might be solved, but it leaves a bitter taste in my mouth and well, King knows how to sour any given day."

Jenn sighed. "I wish I could say I don't understand how somebody can piss you off within a few minutes, but I had the bad fortune to meet her myself. Anyway, you're shaking, let's get you something warm to drink."

Jenn was right. Sharon hadn't noticed, but her hands and legs were trembling as the adrenaline left her system. Once outside, she answered the questions of the uniforms still around, then Jenn was back with a coffee. It was anybody's guess where she had gotten it.

Getting into the car, she looked up at the loft and thought the curtains were moving on the level of King's apartment.

A case might have been solved, a fight won, but the war was far from over. She leaned her head back and closed her eyes.

Chapter Twenty-Five

It was almost midnight and Jenn had been gone for hours. Sharon had stayed as she wanted to finish the paperwork. It had been a long afternoon that had started with updating Kelly who promised to inform Second Precinct the case was solved. Afterward, Sharon and Jenn had begun to interview Stephen, who didn't want a lawyer and admitted to having killed Rawlins. They still stopped halfway through as Stephen had been sweaty and shaky, his withdrawal symptoms getting worse with the minute. They sent for a doctor, then postponed the rest to tomorrow.

What had gotten to her the most was calling Marco, who had started crying when Sharon had told him his brother was a murderer.

While she had never had to walk in his shoes, she had seen it often enough. Disbelief was followed by anger, then shame. Somebody close had committed a heinous crime, and they hadn't had any idea, hadn't done nothing to stop this.

Sharon wasn't sure anything could have been done. Rawlins had spotted Stephen's weakness, had used him as he saw fit, not realizing Stephen was unstable. Rawlins had paid the price for playing with fire.

Her cell phone rang and, too tired to look at who was calling, she accepted the call.

"Sharon Richards."

"Hey, it's me." *Simon.* With a start, she sat upright, cursing herself for not calling him hours ago as she'd wanted to. Did he sound annoyed? She wasn't sure.

"You heard the case was closed?" she asked in lieu of a greeting.

How much of a splash had today's arrest made in the scene, in the news? There had been reports in the paper right after Rawlins had been killed, the gruesome nature of the case being something deemed newsworthy, but they had managed to keep quiet about the fact he'd been found naked apart from wearing a dog collar.

"Yeah, I did."

So yes, he was annoyed, which she knew by the lack of emotion in his voice.

"Who told you?"

"Is it important?"

"No, but I wanted to know if the press is all over it yet."

He sighed audible. "Dammit, Sharon. To be frank, I don't care about the news. I care about the fact that you went to talk to a guy who had a psychotic break and who was armed with a gun. I care about the fact you could've ended up hurt."

It lay on the tip of her tongue to tell him she was not, and if he was so well informed, he would know that himself. She swallowed the thought. What sense was there in arguing? He was right, anyway. If things had been reversed, she would've wanted to hear it from him, too.

"I'm sorry. I swear I wanted to call you once I was back at the precinct, but I was at once busy with work and then I wanted to get the paperwork done. I'm sick of this case, Simon. It was ugly, still is. As always, there are only losers and I hated how it affected us. I want this to be over."

"I understand, I do. Still, it would've taken you less than a minute to let me know you're okay."

Tears of exhaustion began pricking at her eyes and she had to swallow hard. "Yes, you're right. I'm sorry. I am."

"I know," he said, and his voice softened. "Anyway, it's late. Let work be work for a few hours."

Maybe half an hour longer and she'd be done. She looked at her computer, considering. No, he was right. This could and would wait.

"I'll pack my stuff now and head home. You feel like talking again later? Don't worry if not."

He snorted. "I'm waiting in a cab in front of the precinct and was ready to throw you over my shoulder had you refused to leave."

She didn't know if to laugh or cry. Shaking her head, she saved the open document and logged off. "You think I'd have let you?"

"I might not be a trained officer, but if you're as exhausted as you sound, I'm sure I'd have stood a chance."

"Fair enough. Anyway, give me five, okay?"

They ended the call, and after packing her bag, Sharon made her way out of the building, nodding at a few officers from the night shift. Nobody batted an eye at her being around so late. This was the job and regular hours seldom applied.

Outside, she shivered as soon as the cold wind hit her, although it might as well be the day that she had had. Spotting the cab, she made her way toward it, and Simon got out, opening the door for her.

Their gazes met and from the way he frowned, she guessed she looked like hell. Once she had gotten inside, Simon climbed in through the other door, then gave the driver the address of his apartment.

He turned toward her, and she spoke before he could. "I'm glad to see you."

This had been neither her first gruesome case nor the first that had made her leave that late, but before him, she hadn't had anybody waiting up for her. Either she'd been single or her boyfriends hadn't cared.

He touched her cheek, and his fingers were warm against her skin. "I'm glad to see you, too."

For a long moment, neither of them spoke. With a tired smile, Sharon gave in to the impulse to sidle closer to him. When he put his arm around her, she rested her head against his shoulder.

"It was Stephen. Marco's brother. You know, the bartender from Helen's parties."

"I know. She told me."

Sitting up again, she looked at him. "She? Helen? She called you?" Couldn't this woman give it a rest and leave them alone, even if just for a day?

Simon's lips curled into a smile as if he sensed her inner turmoil. "She tried. I didn't pick up. She then sent me a text, told me it's over, that it was Stephen who killed Rawlins and that he tried getting to her. She also told me you saved the day, although I'm not sure she's happy about it."

Sharon snorted. "She's not."

"No surprise there. But all I did was thank her for the info. I am not inclined to deal with her right now. Afterwards, I waited for your call."

Her bad conscience came back in full force. "I'm…" she began, and he interrupted her.

"Don't. I understand why you forgot, and I'm sure you understand that I was a little worried."

Sharon took a shuddering breath as her feelings threatened to overwhelm her once more. Taking his hands into hers, she squeezed them. "I'll do better next time, although I hope there'll never be such a next time. I hated every moment of this miserable case."

She looked at Simon, and it wasn't hard to see that he was as tired as she felt.

"You look beat. How about the cab takes you home? I'll go on to my apartment and you can sleep in."

"No." He shook his head. "Once you're done with the paperwork, we'll both take a day off and relax."

"This will be another few days. We've got to finish interviewing Stephen, have to dot the I's and cross the T's and then there's a stack of other cases waiting."

Simon's eyes narrowed. "Yeah, and that's why I said we take one day. The NYPD will survive without you for a day."

It would. She was one cop of many. Nobody would die because she took a day off. Nobody was irreplaceable, and while she would always strive to do a good job, there was no need to overestimate herself.

"Agreed." She stroked his knuckles, smiling to herself. She could get used to having somebody to come home to after the draining cases. Leaning back in her seat, she closed her eyes. Just for a minute. "Any plans for that day?" she asked, a yawn slipping out.

"Yeah."

She startled when he leaned in so he could whisper in her ear. "That day I'll take you to the club, down to the dungeons, then I'll take my time with you." He bit her earlobe, and Sharon couldn't suppress a shudder.

"Too bad it's still going to be a few days," Sharon said, her voice not more than a hoarse whisper. While part of her was way too tired, another part of her was still strung tight from the stress of the day.

"Well, we'll be home soon," he replied, grazing the shell of her ear with the tip of his tongue.

Wild desire flooded her body, pooling at the apex of her thighs. If it weren't for them being in a semi-public space, she'd have turned around to straddle him and taken what her body craved.

"Hold the thought, will you?" she said and was disappointed when he complied.

Sitting back, he answered her with a simple and quiet, "Of course."

When she met his gaze, she thought his look would seem impenetrable to most, but she recognized the trace of smugness that had the corners of his lips curl upward.

"I'll make you pay," she said, raising an eyebrow.

"Oh no, you won't," he replied. The edge in his voice told her he had a different kind of satisfaction in mind. "It'll be my game, my rules. So, what do you say?"

After this day, sleep should be foremost on her mind, yet it wasn't. The stress of the last weeks demanded a release, and he offered the best. "I say let's give it your best shot."

His eyes darkened, and as if he couldn't stop touching her, he lifted her chin.

"Tonight you'll be mine, and I'll enjoy every minute of it."

Even knowing they weren't far, she couldn't arrive home soon enough.

* * * *

Closing the door behind him, Simon spoke before she had the chance to get out of her shoes or unbutton her coat.

"Wait here," he said, and there was no inflection to his voice. Tonight's game had already started, and she knew better than to argue. He must have seen the questions in her eyes, as his gaze softened.

"I want to prepare some things. If this is not what you need or want tonight, then..."

"It is. It's what I need and want right now." She smiled before continuing. "Master."

He narrowed his eyes, then he transformed from her worried partner to the man in charge of her body and her mind, at least for the night.

"As I said, you wait here. And don't move."

In contrast to her, he got out of his coat, then he put it away, along with his shoes. Afterward, he turned his back to her, and she watched him enter his bedroom. He closed the door behind him. She could hear no more than faint noises.

All alone, she got bored after less than a minute, and the tiredness that had been forgotten came back, making her yawn once again. Maybe she should've chosen sleep after all. Her back began to hurt, and she soon was too warm in a coat meant for the freezing temperatures outside.

She was thankful he returned not that long after. Without speaking a word, he made his way over to her, unbuttoning her coat. Taking it, he put it next to his before he stepped back.

"Shoes next. Then I want you to go into the bedroom and get out of your pants and socks."

Just her pants and socks? This was new.

"What…?" She spoke before she had thought about it.

"I don't want you to speak. Just do as I say."

Nodding her okay, Sharon got out of her shoes, put them beside his before she passed him then made her way into his bedroom, trying to puzzle out what he had in mind. She stopped once inside, looking around. The lighting was dim. One bedside lamp had been switched on and there was a single chair standing in front of the bed. Where had he gotten it from? What was its purpose?

Looking over her shoulder, she found he had followed her, was not more than a step behind her. His gaze gave nothing away, and there'd be punishment for speaking out of turn.

If she wanted to know what he had planned, she had to follow his directions. Something akin to relief flooded her nervous system when realization hit that she wouldn't have to make any more decisions today, that she could give in, sink into whatever sensations he'd bestow on her.

He hadn't told her where to place her clothes, and as she wanted to see how he'd react, she walked over to the chair where she got out of her pants and socks, then put both on the chair.

"I see I wasn't clear enough," Simon said. She could swear there was a trace of amusement in his voice.

Instead of giving her another command, he came over and took her clothes, which he then put in the hamper that stood in one corner of his bedroom. Facing her, he scanned the length of her body.

She had to look ridiculous, in her old shirt and a pair of black cotton panties. He had to know she'd feel self-conscious and must have wanted it this way. He nodded once and came back to her, stepping in close enough she could feel the heat of his body.

"Look at me."

To do so, she had to crane her neck. The impulse to touch him was hard to ignore…although he hadn't forbidden her to do so. Seldom able to be fully compliant, she touched his chest.

"No. No touching either. It seems I'm lacking when it comes to clear communication today."

He tangled a hand in her hair, then pulled at the strand in his grip, making her head crane back even more so that it bordered on uncomfortable.

"Here's the plan for tonight. I want you to lie on the bed, on your stomach, and I will restrain your hands and your feet. Then I'll test the new cane I bought as I think it will distract you in quite a nice manner. Afterwards, I'll untie you, take a seat and watch how you'll make yourself come. Do you agree to my plan? You may speak."

Did she? They had used the restraints attached to the corners of his bed more than once before, and she liked being helpless under his ministrations. They had never used a cane. She had seen them at the club but he hadn't suggested one before and she hadn't asked to try either.

She had read it could be a too intense sensation if not done right. Simon was a pro though, and he would know what her body could take and what it couldn't. BDSM was always a question of trust, and she trusted him.

If it got too much, she could stop this any moment. She nodded.

"Yes, I agree, Master."

"Good." He took a step back. "Then get on the bed now."

It lay on the tip of her tongue to ask if she shouldn't get out of the rest of the clothes, after all, but if he had wanted it, he'd have said so. Crossing the room, she stopped in front of the bed. Sitting, she positioned herself so she came to lie face down in the middle of the bed, her arms stretched out in front of her.

Simon was with her a few seconds later, securing first her wrists, then her ankles to the bed with soft, padded handcuffs and ankle cuffs that were attached to the bed via nylon straps. It was possible to move in them, although just a little.

"Are you comfortable?" Simon asked when he was done.

"Yes, I am, Master."

"Good. Then relax while you can."

His words, spoken without any kind of malice, made her breathing speed up. These moments where anticipation and trepidation met were part of the beginning of detaching from a reality she'd rather not engage with for the moment.

She startled when his hands came to rest on her ass. He hooked his finger under the edge of her panties.

"I don't think you'll need them again tonight."

He began pulling them down a little at a time until her behind was exposed.

"I like the sight," he said, running a finger over the soft mound, making her shiver in reaction. She moaned and he halted his movement.

"Sharon, look at me."

Opening eyes that had fallen closed, she turned her neck farther so she could meet his gaze.

"You trust me, right?"

"Yes, Master."

There was a reason for this question, and she didn't have to wait long to find out. Reaching into the back pocket of his pants, he got out an army knife. Her eyes widened when he released the blade.

He wouldn't cut her, would he? She would put a fast stop to everything if he tried.

"Don't worry," he said. Reaching for her panties again, he cut the seam on one side before she understood what was happening. Cutting through the other side, he pulled the panties out from underneath her and put them to the side before snapping the knife closed again.

"Better," he remarked, then he ran the palms of his hands over her round flesh and began a gentle massage that warmed her skin. He stopped far too soon for her liking, then got up from the bed.

"Nice as this feels, it wasn't the plan."

He crossed the room, then opened the sliding door of his closet.

"There it is. "

He closed the door, then walked back to her and around the bed before kneeling down in front of her, showing her the cane he'd gotten out of the closet.

"This is a rattan cane. One-quarter inch. This one won't leave deep bruises. That is not what we want for your first time with caning."

Telling her what he was about to do and what he was using was just as much to inform her as to build up the anticipation.

"If it becomes too much, use your safe word."

He got up. From her position on the bed, she couldn't see his face but she could see how he held the cane in one hand while he stroked along the length of it with the other one.

He remained standing where he was. A long minute passed while she tried to control her breathing, to prepare herself for the impact.

He moved his arm and before her mind had the chance to grasp what was happening, the cane came down on her bottom. Her breath caught, and a searing sensation shook her body, her arms and legs pulling at their restraints. The harsh sting brought tears to her eyes, and it took a few seconds until the pain morphed into warmth. It took this one stroke for her to understand that this was a more intense sensation than the paddle or the flogger, and it was right for tonight.

There wouldn't be room left for thoughts of the tragedy that had left her stressed and worrying for weeks.

The sting had just dissipated when another one followed, this time landing on her other buttock. She took in a sharp breath, a moan slipping out. Again, he left her body the time it needed to absorb the impact, so she was almost looking forward to the next blow when it came.

She stopped counting after a few minutes, her mind retreating into its subspace, calming down. She was still pulling at the restraints, every hit was met with a moan when the pain hit her, yet it was what she needed tonight. After a while, she was in an almost dreamlike state.

A fingernail stroking over the spot he'd just hit made her hiss and the pain receded while unexpected pleasure made her bite down her bottom lip.

He did this a few times more, amplifying her arousal.

She almost spoke in protest when he stepped back.

"This is enough for tonight."

No, it was not. She wanted more. Although when Simon ran his hand over her backside, she groaned. There was a limit to what her skin could endure.

"You will think about me when you sit down at work tomorrow."

He sat down in front of her again, stroking her cheek with the pad of his finger. She wasn't surprised to see it was wet.

"Are you okay?"

"Yes, I am, Master."

"Good. I'll get some salve to put onto it before we continue."

"Why now?" Under normal circumstances he treated her after they were done with a scene. She had spoken without his consent. She was expecting him to tell her what her punishment would be now, but he just gave her a slight smile.

"There are some welts that'll feel a lot better tomorrow if we see about them now. And if you speak again, then I'll have you pleasure yourself in front of me and stop you right before you come."

He would, and if he did, she wouldn't stop crying. Tonight, she needed this release, so she better not slip again.

"Do you understand?"

"Loud and clear, Master," she replied, her voice rough from the tears.

"Good, then wait here."

He left and while she waited for him to come back, it was hard to ignore the burn of her abused skin. It was on fire. She took in a shivering breath.

She was thankful it wasn't long before he sat beside her.

"I love the look of my marks on you," he remarked, running the tips of his fingers over them once again. Pain battled arousal, and she bit her lip to remain silent.

"This will feel cold and sting for a moment," he said. She could feel the trickle of some fluid on her buttocks. Hissing, she cursed, making him chuckle.

"It won't feel this way for long." With care, he applied the balm. True to his word, the sting lessened, her discomfort abating.

She was caught up in the sensations when he moved and placed a kiss right below her neck and over her sweater. Light as the touch was, it ignited her nerve endings in the most pleasurable way. There were still needs that hadn't been met and that her body wouldn't let her forget.

His hand gliding under her sweater made her shudder. Starting at her shoulders, he mapped out her back, his touch light but assured. Not speaking, he took his time. It was torture of a different kind as she wanted to touch him, too.

He stopped right when he reached her behind, though then he bit one cheek. She moaned, her hands pulling at the restraints while her hips ground into the mattress, looking for friction that wasn't there.

She almost asked him to take her, but he wouldn't. He'd deny her release after all. Sighing, she willed her body to relax.

"Good girl," he complimented her, making her hate him just a little for enjoying her predicament.

"You know, I thought I'd untie you, let you undress and proceed, but now I'm not so sure."

He didn't elaborate but started with releasing her hands before untying her ankles. Once free, she rolled on her back, catching her breath when her ass made contact with the mattress. Yes, she would feel this tomorrow for sure.

Simon offered her his hand and helped her upright. Without giving her time to think, he reached for her sweater, and she lifted her arms. Helping her out of her bra next, he let it glide to the floor before cupping her cheek, meeting her gaze.

When she had first met him, she'd considered him arrogant, cold, and while he was some of the former, there was nothing cold about him. He didn't carry his heart on his sleeve, but she had learned to read him. What had been his first impression of her? She would have to ask him one day.

Letting go of her, he got up from the bed.

"Lie on your back again. As I said, I've changed my plans, and I'll tie your ankles again."

She'd be spread-eagled right in front of him, bared to his sight. Things like that had been uncomfortable at the beginning of their relationship and although she couldn't say she had gotten used to it, the idea didn't make her hesitate any longer.

Lying down, she spread her legs so he just had to attach the soft cloth around her ankles. She expected him to get up next, but instead he ran his fingertips from her ankles all the way up to the inside of her thighs, stopping at her hip bones. This wasn't fair. He had made sure she was already keyed up to dangerous levels before she even started caressing herself.

This was and would always be a worse kind of torture than any kind of toy could provide. Leaning in, he kissed the top of her mound, his lips lingering for a long moment before he stood then walked to the chair in the middle of the room.

"How are you feeling?" he asked her, sitting down.

She laughed. He knew very well how she felt. "I'm doing splendidly… Master."

"Don't be cheeky, Sharon. You're going to prolong your own misery. So do you want to try again?"

Did she? Well, she better answer him to his satisfaction. For as long as they were in the scene, he was calling the shots.

"I'm doing okay but I'm way too aroused, and I want to come."

"See, this wasn't so hard. Now be a good girl, give me a good show, and I'll consider letting you come. You may feel free to start any moment now."

Closing her eyes, she focused on her breathing for a minute. She could do this. It wasn't the first time.

Opening her eyes again, she raised her hands to her breasts, stroking them, the palms of her hands brushing against nipples already hard. Flicking them with the pads of her thumbs, she tried concentrating on everything else but the pulse of desire shooting through her body right to her core.

Pressing her behind farther into the mattress, she concentrated on the discomfort instead of the arousal that was caused by her own actions. Continuing pleasuring one breast, she glided her other hand down her body, not hesitating before slipping between her spread legs. She moaned, chiding her body for wanting to speed things up, for demanding more from her when more would be her undoing.

Slipping one finger inside of her wet core, she ground the palm of her hand against her pleasure point, her breath catching as white-hot desire caught her in a tight grip.

No, she couldn't do it. Either she stopped now, or she would come. And then? He wouldn't let her be. No, he'd punish her before bringing her right back to the edge, refusing to let her go over it.

Tears of frustration pooled at the corner of her eyes, and she let them fall. If she tried fighting her feelings, she'd be lost.

Taking a few deep breaths, she moved again, adding a second finger to the first sliding in and out of her core. Running her other hand all over her chest, she tried distracting herself, to think of anything else but her body's need for release. Her mind didn't play along, refusing to be anywhere but this moment, where her whole being was centered about her need to let go. So she added a third finger, fucking herself faster, knowing she shouldn't and doing it anyway, never mind the consequences. Sliding down a mattress a little, so she could put up her feet, she began arching her hips into the touch of her own hand.

"Stop." Simon's voice, harsh and cold, made her freeze.

He rose, walking toward her, and she tried to focus on his face, although it was hard to ignore the erection straining against the fabric of his pants. Her sex clenched at the thought of him inside her, of moving with him toward a climax that would leave the two of them short of breath. The idea alone was almost enough for her to tip over the edge, and it wouldn't take much more than another thrust, a flick of her hand, and it would be over.

"You are close, aren't you?"

"Yes, Master," she ground out between gritted teeth.

"You want to come, don't you?"

He was toying with her like a cat with a mouse, and in these moments she was annoyed with him, although she never forgot she had given him the power over her body and reactions. It was up to her to stop it anytime.

"Yes, I do, Master."

He crouched down in front of the bed, one hand tangling in her hair in a way that was borderline painful, the other resting over her throat yet not applying pressure. Could he feel her erratic pulse? He had to.

"You were amazing. You always are."

Leaning over her, he met her mouth with his in a searing kiss. Parting her lips for him, she relished his tongue slipping inside her mouth, mapping it, playing with her own, and she moaned into the kiss.

When he stopped a few moments later, she groaned in frustration. Looking at him, she found him smiling at her.

"I've decided that I won't let you come."

It took her a second to understand his words, and when they did, the sudden onslaught of frustration made her hand curl into fists as she bit back a string of curses.

He had the audacity to chuckle. Bastard.

"Don't despair. You see, I've decided to *make* you come."

Bastard indeed. She would make him pay—but she was in no position to do it and needed what he had just promised her.

He rose, and watching him getting undressed, Sharon couldn't wait for him to finish. God, he looked good. She didn't think the view of him would ever get old to her.

"Just one rule," he said, getting on the bed. "No touching."

What the hell? No. She wanted to hold him close, to rake her nails over his back, to feel the play of his muscles then glide lower to his ass.

"A bit more obedience would suit you," he said, settling between her legs. She wouldn't even be able to wrap them around him, thanks to the restraints. If he moved a little now, he'd be able to slide right into her, but of course, he didn't.

Instead, he took first one of her arms, then the other, positioning both of them over her head.

"I think you deserve a little treat for being good so far," he said, his gaze meeting hers. "You may come as often as you can."

His words took a second to register, but he didn't wait longer, just slid into her with one long thrust. Her breath caught, and her climax hit her at once, her body having been too close to the brink.

Waves of intense sensation crested over her while her eyes fell shut. Simon didn't stop, just continued fucking her in a hard and fast rhythm. After this day, he too, had reached the end of the rope. She was more than fine with that. She wanted him to take her as hard as he could. As he moved inside her, filling her, one climax seemed to morph into another.

She was not coherent enough to stay still while he used her in the most delicious way. When her body calmed down, she came back to herself just in time to feel him tense, groaning as his own release overtook him.

Watching him bite down his lip, his body still rocking, Sharon had to smile. He, too, trusted her with his body, allowed himself to be vulnerable in these moments.

Lowering himself on his arms, he kissed her once more, softly this time, and it was a playful back and forth. Withdrawing, he looked at her, his eyes warm now.

"The game's over."

"Good," she said, then snorted. "Does that mean you can untie me, so I can wrap myself around you?"

"Hold the thought," Simon replied, brushing a sweaty strand of hair from her face. "Let's clean up first and have another look at those bruises. I want to check your wrists and ankles, too. And yeah, then we can sleep."

She sighed. There'd be not much of the night left, although given the choice she would've changed nothing. "I don't want to move again. Ever."

He kissed the top of her nose. "Finish the case and we'll take a little break."

"Yes, Sir," she said, playing with strands of his short hair.

"So I've been demoted, huh?" He chuckled, and she laughed, too.

She was still exhausted to her very bones, but the tension and frustration was gone for the moment.

"Just for the night. Anyway, thanks for sticking with me through this case and well, everything else."

His expression became serious. "I love you, and I do what I can to support you, to be there when you need me. At least I'll try, even when I mess up sometimes."

"Yes, you do. Support me, that is. And I love you, too." She had thought she had loved before, but it had never been to this extent. She had never trusted her partner this much.

She pulled his head closer for a tender kiss that lasted for a long time. Faint desire began to simmer inside her, although she had no intention of doing anything about it. It was Simon who pulled away.

"Let's check you out now."

He sat up, offering her his hand, then pulling her upright. She winced when more of her weight rested on her behind.

"About time," he stated. Together they walked toward his bathroom. She stopped him in the doorway, smiling when he frowned.

"I don't want our relationship to suffer because one of us thinks they have to make a secret out of it, okay? Or rather, because I want to make a secret out of it. For me, my private life will always be private, but I won't try to hide it anymore."

His gaze bore into hers as if probing her seriousness. "Are you sure you're ready for this?"

She laughed. "No, I'm not, but we won't know it unless we try it. This relationship deserves it. You do."

"I'm glad to hear it." He kissed her again, the brush of his lips against hers light and tender.

She would lie if she said this didn't scare her, though since when were good things ever easy? This relationship could still fail, but at least she'd have tried. Ending the kiss, she walked past him, then looked over her shoulder.

"Come on then, before it's time to get up."

The next morning would come soon enough.

Chapter Twenty-Six

"Are you sure?" Simon asked her, holding the door of her apartment open for her.

"Yes, I am." At least as sure as she'd ever be. Giving him a last once-over, Sharon had to say he looked more than a little attractive in a simple pair of black jeans and a white T-shirt. He would fit right in with the crowd that would meet at Van Cortland Park for a barbecue.

Leave it to a bunch of cops and their loved ones to meet in the middle of autumn on a chilly Sunday for such an outdoor gathering. Well, it had been a tradition for as long as Sharon had been with the precinct, and she'd gone every year—except one when she'd just gotten a case.

While most of the others took their families or partners, Sharon had brought a boyfriend once and never again. Not that most of her boyfriends had been people to write home about. Simon was, and he deserved to be a full part of her life.

After finishing the Rawlins case, she'd vowed to herself to do better and today was the chance to put her money where her mouth was.

"You look as if you're going to be dragged to an execution," Simon remarked. "Look, if you'd rather…"

She interrupted him. "No, first of all, I promised Jenn we'd be there. She's still down after breaking up with Brian and I hate to see her this way. And I don't want to hide such an important part of my life any longer."

He stepped closer to her, his hands resting on her hips. "But you don't like this."

If she backed out now, he'd understand. Still, he had been patient long enough. He was her boyfriend and partner, not a dirty secret.

"Look, I've never quite liked sharing my private life and that hasn't changed, but this is my problem. Also, a wise man once told me that nobody is going to ask what kind of games I like to play in my free time. I think he was right. And I know a few female officers who will be green in the face when I bring you."

"So you think I'm wise and attractive?" he asked with a light smile. She reached around, pinching his ass.

"You're not an ugly old toad, okay? Although you've got enough ego for the two of us. Anyway, let's go before I can reconsider."

Taking his hand, Sharon pulled Simon along. While nobody knew what tomorrow would bring, it was about time she stopped trying to hide this part of her life. It was one of the best.

Want to see more like this?
Here's a taster for you to enjoy!

Pocket Full of Posies

L.A. Kennedy

Excerpt

Saturday, December 7, 2013
Vancouver, Canada
Received and printed by The Vancouver Sun

Letters from a deranged mind,

Why did you not print my last letter? I found it to be elegant and honest. Was I too fucking candid? Perhaps in the way that I described how I wanted to fuck the dead man but fiddled with myself instead? I think that shows control when I could have killed his entire useless family. Did I offend your sensible fucking morals? I doubt that, given you are a newspaper and reporters lack those just like a dog lacks wings. It's what gives you the guts to photograph dead babies for ratings. I suppose you have limited options in life. You either become a journalist or you become a lawyer – then the one percent become me.

I will kill someone in your name. I will whisper your name in their ear as I carve the flesh from their twitching body. Are you happy now? Are you fucking listening now? Or do I need to sling them up in a schoolyard to let the little kiddies see what real art looks like? Not the worthless crap that the old cunts past retirement try to jam down their throats. The teachers of today are breeding the useless minds of tomorrow.

Humanity is fucked, but I've got your back. Give me a few more weeks, and I'll weed them out.

Let's review the rules, shall we? When I speak, you fucking listen. When you ignore me, I will express myself through the flopped carcasses that I'll line your dirty fucking streets with. I'll nail them to your front fucking door. Do you think your bastard children would like that? Shall I give them a little lesson in etiquette, since you clearly have no idea what that is?

I am your wickedest nightmare. I am the incubus of your sanity and safety, because I know it isn't your own pain you dread the most. It is the pain of your loved ones you fear more than anything I could possibly do to you. But isn't that the crux of love? I don't feel love. I don't drink from the pool of poison, but understanding it makes my art grander. It makes those moments all the more memorable. It gives me inspiration. The brilliance is that I won't have to guess who you love. You will show me willingly without noticing I am even watching you. But I'm always watching you. You're a pawn to me, each one of you. Your worst nightmare is my most cherished dream. I savored the moments where I knew I had taken your loved ones and twisted them into the grandest of memories. Their last breaths, the very last seconds, the moments their lights go out are orgasms for my soul. Yes, I still have one of those. Can you say the same? For most of you, you're shells of what humanity was meant to be.

Vancouver is strange, but so am I and so are you. I've seen worse – worse places and worse people than you or me. I saw the inner cockles of the cesspools we call home. It makes one feel dirty just stepping off the plane, like the disgust is seeping into your pores and coating your veins with the tears of every whore who drinks down dirty men for blow. I've met folks who make you want to remove a layer of skin from just one touch. It's not just this handsome city. It's in every corner of this world. The evil you all try to ignore is like that bat-shit crazy grandmother you only bring out for Christmas – ignored until the reading of her will.

Our cities hold parts they wish to hide from the rest of the sophisticated world, spewing out of the crack-infested alleys like crawling cockroaches and beggars, cities built on broken dreams like the jagged-toothed grin of an old junkie, tucked behind the shops in places you see on commercials, holding the colorless, forbidding, grim, faded graffiti and dirty needles that will kill faster than the shit it once held.

The women pursue fresh cock in their meager outfits and boots so high they rub on their dirty cunts while they search for a new, diseased lap to spread their legs for. Their drugged-out bodies are as thin as dashes, their cheekbones jutting out through their colorless skin. They already look dead. They make my stomach roll and pinch at my sanity. The carefully constructed façade is more fragile than the glass that is blown for the tourists. Little glass balls bring the foolish downtown for the beggars and dealers to mug. The circle of life is a dirty fucker. It brought me here after all, didn't it? Maybe you can thank your God for that or Mother Nature – or whatever fucking lies you tell yourself. Add it to the other bullshit like "Daddy loves me. He isn't hurting me. He loves me."

What's oddest about Vancouver, different from other places, is the blunt truth thrust in your face the moment you step outside. There's no bullshit. Its welcome sign should read 'This is us. Don't like it? Get the fuck out.' I can respect that. But respect don't pay the bills, and it won't keep me from turning your gutters red or stringing intestines from your charming little Christmas trees. I say it would add a festive flare to the excitement of the season, but that's just me. I've waited and watched and noticed how the holidays remove basic manners and human dignity. It's made my shopping all the easier.

It is insanity out there, and it's killing you all – granted, slower than I would. We rip babies from vaginas, some to kill and some to sell for money. We devised a system that doesn't rely on mercy or true freedom or love, and you say I'm mad? I'm crazy? You created me. Mankind has built a living and breathing creature that starves children to their deaths, and I get more coverage than babies dying. We produce disease but can't afford to cure it, yet you pump money into my capture? People kill people in the name of a God because he differs from someone else's God, and you will kill me because I believe in no God? If there ever was one, he left long ago. Search around you. The only omnipotent person here is your dealer, your whore and your cell phone company, yet you look at me as though I'm evil. I'm no different from those you pay to run our countries into the fucking ground, only I don't bomb nations or kill children. Who am I kidding? If I had a bomb, I'd undoubtedly use it.

Tomorrow I will show you all what ignoring me does. I haven't yet decided if I will take the husband or the wife. Maybe I'll take both? 'Tis the season for giving, after all. The husband is a fraud and a prevaricator. His spouse is an ignorant, cock-sucking moaner. Her weeping in her car is enough to make me want to plow her into oncoming traffic – not out of hate but out of clemency. Putting that bitch out of her wretched misery would be a kindness to us all, like seeing a mangled cat on the freeway and running it over again.

The trepidation is killing me. Decisions, decisions, decisions. Do I go left or right? Do I kill for mercy or for rage? We shall see. What I know for certain is that if you keep ignoring me, you will find me on your fucking doorstep, giving candy to your spoiled-rotten children.

The newest will make a divine display of the grotesque humanity the world wades through every day. A perfect specimen, either one I select. I will wrap my hands around their snappy little throat and take away what they don't deserve – life. I will wait in their house built of cards on a foundation of lies and bring it crumbling down around them.

Until we meet.

Your friend always, TNK, The Nursery Killer.

* * * *

Brock

"Hale, briefing in five." A voice pulled my attention from the article in the paper.

A budding serial killer had written to *The Vancouver Sun* and its headlines had gone worldwide. The press had coined him The Nursery Killer, TNK, glamorizing the sick fuck. Ratings meant everything nowadays. There wasn't a single officer in Canada who wasn't gunning for TNK, and every state was on the alert for the possibility of the killer jumping borders. TNK taunted them, warning them for months leading up to the murders and relishing in the fact that they hadn't caught up with him yet. The bastard was about to kill again and there wasn't a fucking thing anyone could do about it. Vancouver was on the verge of mass panic. It was a fear so great that the FBI was called in for help. TNK wasn't the first killer who had caused cities to damn near board up their windows, and he wouldn't be the last.

I pushed the printout from the newspaper to the side, downed a few antacids, grabbed my folder and headed for the door. I'd be offering up some additions to a makeshift profile on TNK, a desperate attempt at understanding the fuck who was running the streets of Vancouver. I slipped into the conference room and stood at the back. The meeting was already in full swing. I knew the drill—shut up until asked to speak. Enough years with the FBI and I could gauge the pressure by just how many people were in attendance. Forty suits with one name and one focus—TNK.

In all my years, I hadn't ever seen horror like the carnage left behind by TNK. And I had witnessed enough shit to pour my ass into two divorces, a case of

Scotch and enough hookers to keep a bottle of penicillin on standby. TNK was different. There was something about the killings that was more personal than anything I had ever seen. Days and weeks had gone into the planning of the most gruesome deaths I'd had the misfortune of seeing in all my days. At any moment, the phones would be ringing with another scene. It wasn't a matter of *if* it would happen, only *when* it would happen.

With one nod, I stood at the front and did my song and dance. I had analyzed every letter and had come up with a few details no one else had thought of. I wished I could have taken credit for it, but it had been an academy class that connected the dots. Kiss-asses, the lot of them. TNK might not even be Canadian. We could be looking for a tourist or a border jumper. Everything about the letters had suggested TNK was American. And if that were true, the FBI would be balls deep in someone else's pond, trying to clean up their little slice of home. Usually, with the prospect of jumping borders, I was pounding Advil, trying to ward off the pending headache it would bring me. Not this time. This time they wanted the FBI there, and I was thankful I wouldn't have to go. I had too many open cases on the burner, and for once, I was grateful for that.

I closed up shop and headed home. By home, I meant the pub on the corner. There's no place like home. Arnold's Pub was as close as it was going to get. My apartment was empty, not of possessions though. My newest ex had been fair in the division of assets, but it was bare of everything that gave it a sense of home. It reminded me of what I'd lost to climb the ladder in a job that damn near killed me each day. Every case took a piece of my soul with it. Each day I walked through the front doors and faced pure evil and a small slice of my sanity was left behind at the crime scene.

The glamorous life of an agent felt like a slow drag behind a pickup truck to the loony bin if I didn't eat my gun first.

About the Author

Sira Banks is an European author who is utterly in love with reading and even more so with writing. Always daydreaming, she began writing short stories as a young adult as the characters occupying her mind didn't stop poking her until their stories were told.

Participating in NaNoWriMo one year, she started her first novel, and after a lot of hair-pulling, too much coffee and chocolate, she finished it some time later. Finding out that writing longer stories is addictive, she's not quite sure she could quit it now.

She likes strong female characters with flaws who are not afraid to tackle their problems head on and male characters who are actually willing to listen and communicate.

When she's not writing, she works as desk jokey and manages her small family, consisting of a preteen daughter and a cat aspiring to become the world's most efficient hunter.

Sira loves to hear from readers. You can find her contact information, website details and author profile page at https://www.totallybound.com

TOTALLY
BOUND
Home of Erotic Romance

www.ingramcontent.com/pod-product-compliance
Lightning Source LLC
LaVergne TN
LVHW091024080826
845145LV00002B/345

* 9 7 8 1 8 0 2 5 0 9 4 7 2 *